Praise for the Da
DONN

5! Top Pick! "An absolute
to end, it's an incredible ride." —*Night Owl Romance*

5 Hearts! "I definitely recommend *Dangerous Highlander*, even to skeptics of paranormal romance—you just may fall in love with the MacLeods."
—*The Romance Reader*

5 Angels! Recommended Read! "*Forbidden Highlander* blew me away." —*Fallen Angel Reviews*

5 Tombstones! "Another fantastic series that melds the paranormal with the historical life of the Scottish highlander in this arousing and exciting adventure. The men of MacLeod Castle are a delicious combination of devoted brother, loyal highlander, Lord and demonic God [who] ooze sex appeal and inspire some very erotic daydreams as they face their faults and accept their fate." —*Bitten By Books*

4 Stars! "Grant creates a vivid picture of Britain centuries after the Celts and Druids tried to expel the Romans, deftly merging magic and history. The result is a wonderfully dark, delightfully well-written tale. Readers will eagerly await the next Dark Sword book."
—*Romantic Times BOOKreviews*

"Totally captivating and entertaining . . . Cursed by dark magic, the immortal MacLeod brothers are a force to be reckoned with." —*Fresh Fiction*

ST. MARTIN'S PAPERBACKS TITLES BY
DONNA GRANT

Dangerous Highlander

Forbidden Highlander

Wicked Highlander

Untamed Highlander

Shadow Highlander

Darkest Highlander

DARKEST HIGHLANDER

DONNA GRANT

St. Martin's Paperbacks

DARKEST HIGHLANDER

For information address St. Martin's Press, 175 Fifth Avenue, New York, NY 10010.

ISBN: 978-0-312-53349-6

Printed in the United States of America

St. Martin's Paperbacks edition / February 2012

St. Martin's Paperbacks are published by St. Martin's Press, 175 Fifth Avenue, New York, NY 10010.

10 9 8 7 6 5 4 3 2 1

For Steve.

I love you.

ACKNOWLEDGMENTS

Thank you to my wonderful editor, Monique Patterson, for simply everything. I'm blessed beyond words to be able to work with you. I love your ideas. You help me become a better writer, and for that, I'll never be able to thank you enough.

To Holly Blanck—you rock! To Jessica Preeg—for being so ready and willing to help me. And to everyone else at St. Martin's who helped get this book ready.

To my amazing, brilliant agent, Amy Moore-Benson.

A special note to Leagh Christensen and Melissa Bradley. I'd be lost without the both of you. I cannot express how much I appreciate you both.

To my street team, Donna's Dolls. What can I say? I've got the greatest readers ever! Y'all are the absolute best! ::smooches::

Steve, my wonderful, marvelous husband. I love you. Thank you for your support, battle scene concepts, and just for being you. I found my real-life hero.

To my kiddos, who are the best support team a mom could ever ask for. I'm so proud of both of you!

To my parents and brother—thank you!

ONE

It was the growl, the low, menacing rumble that implied doom for her.

Sonya sucked in a ragged breath and lifted her head from the damp ground of the forest floor. Her spirit was broken, her body fading rapidly.

She raged with fever, a fever she couldn't heal. Just as she couldn't heal the cut that sliced open her palm. At one time, the barest of thoughts would have propelled her magic to take care of such injuries.

But that magic had failed her.

Nay, you failed.

Sonya squeezed her eyes closed to shut out the loud and persistent voice in her head. She was nothing without her magic. How could she help the others at MacLeod Castle? How could she look each of them in the eye day after day, knowing her magic was gone?

Vanished. Disappeared. Lost.

Everything she was, everything she had been, was no longer there. Her life had been defined as a Druid. Without magic she could no longer call herself a Druid.

And that tormented her far worse than her sliced palm.

Another growl, this one closer, more looming. She tried to gain her feet, but she was weak from lack of food.

Sonya had been dodging the wolf for days. Or was it weeks? She had lost track of time after her flight from MacLeod Castle. She no longer knew where she was, and even if she wanted to return to the castle, she couldn't get there.

If you want to live, get up. Run!

Sonya wasn't ready to die. She didn't give up easily.

Liar. You never try for the things you want. Like Broc.

A tear slipped down Sonya's cheek at the thought of Broc. Each time she closed her eyes, she could see the Warrior kneeling in the midst of the bloody battle at the castle, holding Anice in his arms as he bellowed for Sonya to heal her sister.

A sister who had known him. Broc, the one man Sonya had wanted for herself. The one thing she hadn't had the courage to make her feelings known about.

Sonya shoved aside thoughts of Broc as she grabbed hold of the nearest tree with her good hand and pulled herself to her feet. She leaned against the trunk and glanced around the forest for the wolf.

Nowhere did she see the creature, but she knew he was near. The black beast was large and ravenous. It would take just one bite from its huge teeth to end her life.

Sonya cradled her wounded hand against her chest and wondered how much longer she could evade the wolf. It was a cunning animal.

The trees swayed above Sonya, reminding her of the magic that used to allow her to commune with them. How she missed their knowledge, their words. Their magic. Being among the trees had always soothed her, but no longer. Not since her own magic had abandoned her.

Sonya knew she had to move if she wanted a chance at survival. Remaining meant certain death. After a deep breath, she stepped away from the tree and turned, only to freeze in place as the wolf stood in front of her.

It growled again, lifting its lips to show large fangs that dripped with saliva. The animal crouched with its ears back against its head, its muscles tensed, ready to spring at her.

Time slowed to a standstill. With her heart pounding slow and hard, Sonya knew she had only once chance to get away. She lifted her skirts and ran to her left.

Her feet slipped on the dried leaves and pine nettles coating the forest floor, but she kept moving. Behind her, she could hear the wolf as it crashed through the trees, chasing her.

And rapidly gaining ground.

With hair tangling about her sweat-soaked face, Sonya glanced back and saw the wolf almost upon her. A scream lodged in her throat, but before the sound could be released, the ground fell from beneath her.

Suddenly the earth rose up to meet her face. Sonya grunted as her head slammed into the ground and she began to roll. She tried without success to grab hold of anything that would slow her descent. The sky fused with the ground to become a whirl of colors that spun around her as she continued her brutal tumble.

When she finally came to a grinding halt, it was with her body wrapped around the trunk of a young elm. The breath left her lungs in a whoosh, her body wracked with blinding pain. She tried to stay calm and suck in air, but the more she tried to breathe, the more her body refused to obey such a simple request.

When breath finally filled her lungs, Sonya drew it in deep and winced at the agony that exploded through her. She opened her eyes, but her world had yet to stop spinning.

And then she heard the familiar growl. Much closer than ever before.

Broc clenched his hands, urgency and fear filling his stomach as he flew across the sky in his search for Sonya. Not even concern about discovery by mortals could keep him to the thick rain clouds above him.

He knew in his gut Sonya was in trouble. Her leaving the castle was so unlike anything she would do, but then again, he had yelled at her, blamed her for Anice's death.

Broc regretted his words more than Sonya could possibly know. He'd been angry at himself—was still outraged—for failing to keep Anice safe, as he had promised the girls when he found them as babies.

It proved to him yet again that anyone who got close to him died. His grandmother had called it a curse. And it had followed him into his immortality.

For a while he had thought the curse was gone, but then Anice died. But he wouldn't allow anything to happen to Sonya. Even if it took him leaving her life forever, he'd do it just to keep her safe. And alive.

He flew faster, his wings beating loudly in his ears. As a Warrior, a Highlander with a primeval god bound inside him, he had special abilities. Each god had a power, and his was the capability to find anyone, anywhere.

It was just one of the reasons he had gone in search of Sonya. Even if his god hadn't given him the power to find her, he'd still have looked for her. Because he had been connected to her since the moment he lifted her in his arms so many years ago.

Broc was close to her. He could feel it.

A smile pulled at his lips, but it died almost immediately as lightning lit the sky and it began to rain.

"Shite," he murmured and tucked his wings to fly above the canopy of trees.

Broc's claws scraped the leaves atop an ancient oak as the rain dripped down his face and into his eyes. He adjusted the satchel strap that lay on his back between his wings and over one shoulder.

The strap chafed against his wings, but inside he carried food, coin, and clothing for both him and Sonya. The pain was a minor inconvenience as long as he found her.

Inside Broc, Poraxus, the god of manipulation, roared with anticipation. It was a signal they were very close to Sonya. Every time Broc hunted someone, he could feel them when he neared. Their heartbeat, the flow of blood in their veins. Their life essence.

It was no different now. Except this was Sonya. He had saved her as an infant, watched over her as she grew. He would not fail her now.

Broc clutched his chest as he felt fear spike through Sonya. The closer he came to his target, the more he felt it. If the terror now coursing through him was any indication, he was too late.

Just thinking she might be in danger sent rage flowing through his veins. His god roared again—this time for blood. And vengeance.

Broc reined in his god. Sonya might need him, and he couldn't allow himself to reach the edge and his god to gain any control. The more he fought against Poraxus, the more his god struggled to take over.

It was because his god knew how much Sonya meant to him. Even if Broc refused to admit it to himself.

Broc peered through the dense canopy of trees to try to see her, but it was near impossible, even with his superior sight. Broc then maneuvered between two trees. He hated flying in forests. He wasn't able to spread his wings as he needed to in order to fly or glide.

So he rode the air currents with his wings stretched as far as he could get them. Several times the wings scraped against a tree and its branches, tearing the leathery wings. Thanks to his immortality, he began to heal almost immediately.

And then he saw her.

Not even the rain could hamper his enhanced vision. Broc tucked his wings and dove for Sonya, who lay unmoving on the ground, curled around a tree.

Dread spurred Broc to her side. He knew she wasn't dead. He could still feel Sonya's heartbeat, though now that he had found her, it was fading from his senses.

His gaze scanned the area for whatever caused her fear and spotted the lone wolf approaching. Broc spread his wings and landed on his feet between Sonya and the wolf.

The wolf snarled, its anger palpable. Broc peeled back his lips to show his own set of fangs and growled. He didn't want to kill the wolf, but he would if it continued to threaten Sonya.

After several tense moments, the wolf sensed it was beaten and reluctantly backed away. Broc stayed where he was, listening long after the wolf was out of sight to make sure the creature didn't circle around to attack again.

Once Broc was certain the wolf had departed, he turned to Sonya. He was so unprepared for what he saw that, for a moment, he couldn't move. For one heartbeat, then two, he could only stare at the woman who was the one thing he wanted above all else.

Sonya's vibrant red hair, which was always secured in a single thick plait, was now wild and free in a tangle of curls about her. Her dark green gown was coated in dirt and drenched from the rain. One sleeve was torn at the shoulder, and she had another tear at her hem.

But what made Broc's stomach plummet to his feet was the wound he saw on her palm. She had wrapped a portion of her chemise around it, but the thin material had already fallen away, leaving the ragged injury exposed.

Broc fell to his knees beside her. He was afraid to touch her, but he needed to feel her at the same time. He spread a wing to shield her from the rain and leaned close. Only then did he realize she was unconscious.

Careful that his claws didn't cut her delicate skin, he gently caressed a finger from her temple down her cheek to her jaw. He longed to have her open her eyes so he could look into their amber depths.

Her skin was smooth and luminous. She had a high forehead where finely arched eyebrows, the same vivid red as her hair, curved above her eyes. Her nose was aristocratic and her chin stubborn. Her lips, however, were those of a siren—wide and full.

And tempting as sin.

Tenderly, Broc lifted her hand in his to inspect the wound. The cut went from her index finger across her palm to end at her wrist. The slice was deep, and the skin around the wound was blackening.

The dark yellow pus that oozed from the gash propelled Broc. He gathered Sonya in his arms and spread his wings, ready to jump into the air and fly to MacLeod Castle.

It was the lightning bolts that forked across the sky in a vivid and dramatic display of power that halted him. If he flew, there was a chance he could be hit by the lightning. Though it would pain him, he would survive.

Sonya wouldn't be so lucky.

He couldn't put her in that kind of danger. Reluctantly, Broc set her down long enough to remove the satchel and search through it for a cloak.

Once he found one and had secured it around Sonya, Broc tamped down his god. He watched the indigo skin of his Warrior form, along with his claws, fade from sight. Nothing showed of his wings or his fangs. When he wasn't in his Warrior form, no one could tell him apart from a mortal man.

It was a small blessing having an ancient god inside him. And it had all begun with the invasion of Rome on Britain's shores. The Celts had battled the Romans for years before going to the Druids for help.

The *mies*, Druids with pure magic, could offer only guidance. However, the *droughs*, Druids with their black magic, had an answer—call up primeval gods from Hell to inhabit the strongest warriors.

And it worked. The men became Warriors and soon drove Rome from Britain. Yet, their need for blood and death didn't end, and soon they were killing any who crossed their paths.

It took both the *mies* and the *droughs* combining their magic to end the Warriors. No matter how hard they tried, they couldn't make the gods return to Hell. Instead, they bound them inside the men.

But the gods took their revenge by passing through the bloodline to the next strongest warrior of that family. They were unable to get free until a *drough*, Deirdre, found an ancient scroll that told her how to unbind the gods.

Ever since, Deirdre had been relentless in finding the gods and unbinding them. Broc was one of several at MacLeod Castle intent on putting an end to Deirdre for good.

Broc jerked on a tunic before he slung the strap of the satchel over his head. Once more he took Sonya into his arms and stood. There was a village several leagues away. There he could get Sonya out of the weather and tend to her hand.

Then he would beg her forgiveness for driving her away and hopefully convince her to return to MacLeod Castle. Everyone needed her there. No one more so than him.

He cradled her gently, but securely, against his chest, shielding her face from as much of the rain as he could. He rested his chin on her forehead and felt her skin blazing with fever.

Broc looked down into her oval face, a face that had haunted his dreams and every waking moment of his life since she had come into womanhood and he had been tempted beyond his control.

"Live, Sonya. I refuse to let you die."

Why hadn't she healed herself, as he knew she could? She was a Druid with powerful healing magic. The Druids at MacLeod Castle had put an incredible amount of strain on Sonya for her healing, but as a *mie* nothing should have restricted that magic.

Even Quinn MacLeod, another Warrior, once had need of Sonya's healing because of Deirdre's magic.

Broc growled just thinking about his enemy. All *droughs* gave their blood and their lives to Satan in exchange for black magic, but Deirdre had gone beyond that. She worked in league with the Devil. Deirdre had lived nearly a thousand years, and during that time she had destroyed many lives.

Broc cursed Deirdre with every step he took, but he cursed himself even more. From the day he had delivered Sonya and Anice to the Druids, he had sworn to protect them.

He had failed Anice, and if he didn't get Sonya to cover quickly, he would fail her as well.

The thunder had become almost a constant boom, it sounded so close together. The storm was right over them, as was evident by the lightning striking closer and the wind howling around them.

One lightning bolt landed on a tree just in front of them and caused the pine to burst into flames and split in half. Broc turned away before being crushed as part of the tree fell and landed in front of him.

He lifted his face to the sky and roared his anger. His rage fed his god, and it was all Broc could do to keep him tamped down. It had taken too many of his two hundred and seventy-five years learning to restrain Poraxus for Broc to lose control now.

But when it came to Sonya, his emotions always ran high.

Broc had to get out of the storm. He took a deep breath and leapt the burning tree. He held Sonya tight and ran, using the incredible speed his god gave him.

He didn't slow until he spotted the village.

TWO

Broc strode to the inn and shouldered open the door. The force of the wind caused it to bang against the wall and had every head turning his way.

The few patrons scattered about the dining room watched him with mild curiosity, but the short, plump woman behind the counter let out a squeak before she ran to the door and closed it.

"A wicked storm we're havin'," she said, eyeing him.

"I need a chamber."

The woman set a hand on her hip and twisted her lips. "Is your . . . wife . . . ill?"

"My wife fell from her horse. The storm spooked them."

Broc didn't want to dwell on how right it felt calling Sonya his. The curse, or whatever it was that caused people around him to die, would prevent there ever being a future between them.

"Ah, these storms can be vicious," the woman said. "Ye lost both the horses?"

Broc gave a single nod. "I'd like to get my wife out of these wet clothes and a warm meal in our bellies."

"That I can do for ye. Ye have coin?"

"I do."

The woman rolled her eyes. "I'll be seein' it before ye get the room."

Broc glared at the innkeeper. The lines that bracketed her face told a story her lips never would. She had seen hard times and lived through them. Now she ran the inn with an iron fist.

"Follow me to the chamber and you'll have your coin," Broc said.

The woman drummed her pudgy fingers on the counter. "All right. But I warn ye, if ye try anythin', Colin'll be waitin' for ye."

Broc glanced over his shoulder to find a burly man standing partially hidden by the shadows in a corner. Broc didn't spare Colin another look as he followed the innkeeper up the stairs.

She stopped at the last door on the right. "I assumed ye'd want some privacy."

"You assumed correctly."

Her dark eyes narrowed. "Ye're nobility, aren't ye?"

"Nay."

"Nay reason to lie to me," she said as she opened the door and walked into the chamber. "I not be carin' what you are."

But Broc knew she would care if she realized what kind of monster she had allowed into her inn.

Broc strode into the room and to the bed. Gently, he laid Sonya down and reached for the bag of coins in the satchel. He gave her more than needed.

"I'll have the food sent up directly," the innkeeper murmured as she tucked the coins between her enormous breasts. She smiled, showing a missing tooth on the left side of her mouth. "Anythin' else, milord?"

Broc looked at Sonya's hand. "Bandages."

When the door shut behind the woman, Broc began to build a fire. Once that was done, he went to Sonya and inspected the wound.

He was going to have to open the wound again so

the infection could be drained. He was thankful she was unconscious so he wouldn't cause her more pain.

Broc lengthened one claw and quickly cut open her injury. Sonya moaned and tried to turn away. Broc held her arm still and turned her hand so the pus could drain.

A knock sounded a moment before the door opened and the innkeeper walked in with a tray of food. She set it on the table near the hearth and dusted off her hands.

"Ye need to get yer wife out of those wet clothes."

Broc swallowed, his gaze landing on the swell of Sonya's breast. "Aye."

"I'll help."

"Thank you," Broc said as he rose to his feet. "What is your name?"

The woman smiled. "Jean."

Broc let her take charge in removing Sonya's gown. The material ripped easily beneath Broc's hands no matter how careful he was.

"Yer wife took quite a tumble."

"Sonya is strong. She'll heal."

Jean's brows rose at his words. "No' by the look of her wound. It looks to be infected."

"It is."

"Lift your woman's shoulders," Jean directed as she pulled Sonya's gown and chemise over her head.

Broc tried not to stare at Sonya's alluring body. Many nights he had dreamed of holding her in his arms, of drinking in the sight of her naked flesh, of the feel of her warm skin against his. He dreamed of hearing her sighs of pleasure as he sank into her body.

All the blood rushed to his cock while his gaze feasted on her full breasts and pink nipples pebbled against the cool air. Nestled between her legs was a triangle of red curls just begging for his touch. It was more difficult than

Broc realized to release Sonya as he laid her against the linens.

Jean tossed the clothes to the floor, where they made a squishy thud before she spread out the cloak to dry. "Eat, milord. I'll remove her shoes and stockings."

When Broc hesitated, Jean shooed him away with her hands. "I'll take care of yer Sonya, milord. Eat while ye can."

My Sonya.

Broc quite liked the sound of that.

With nothing else to do, Broc sat. He was hungry, but he could go days without food if he needed to. The god inside him protected him in more ways than one.

The smell of the food drew him, however. He ate some bread as he watched Jean. Then he tried the meat while she cleaned Sonya's wound.

Soon he was devouring everything on the trencher, glancing up every now and again to see Jean's progress. She was gentle with Sonya, and a sight better than Broc's own large hands would have been.

By the time Broc was done with the meal, Jean had finished tending Sonya.

"I've put some salve on the wound to help draw out the infection," Jean said. "Her fever worries me. I've some herbs that can help. They need to be mixed with water and forced down her."

"I'll do it." Anything as long as it made Sonya better.

"I'll bring it to you, then." Jean nodded approvingly as she gathered the now empty trencher and goblet and started toward the door.

Broc rose and followed her. He raked a hand down his face and let out a long sigh once Jean had left. Unable to stay away from Sonya, he strode to the bed and inspected her hand.

Jean had done a fine job of cleaning and bandaging

the wound. Broc just hoped it was enough. He thought of Phelan, another Warrior who had escaped Deirdre's prison. Phelan's power was in his blood. His blood could heal anything.

Broc would do whatever it took, even returning to Cairn Toul Mountain and Deirdre, if he could get some of Phelan's blood for Sonya.

He was tempted to search for Phelan, but he didn't want to leave Sonya, not when she was ill. She had always been so vivacious, so full of life. Seeing her lying still, her skin pallid and her glorious red locks dulled, made Broc feel as if someone had ripped out his heart.

What had Sonya been thinking in leaving MacLeod Castle? She had been protected there. She had been part of a family. It was a mixed family of immortal Warriors and Druids, but it was the only family Broc had.

He stayed there because it took more than sickness and a sword wound to kill Warriors. And there had been Sonya with her healing magic for the Druids.

Broc had thought the curse wouldn't be able to touch those around him. But the reality was that it could—and it did. Anice was gone forever. He had vowed to keep her safe, but he'd been unable to fulfill that promise.

Did he dare try to honor it with Sonya?

As much as he knew he should return to MacLeod Castle and allow Fallon to retrieve Sonya, he couldn't. Not yet. He needed time with Sonya. Time and memories which would sustain him in the decades to come.

He leaned against the wall to let his gaze feast upon Sonya's beauty. So many years he had spied on Deirdre, carrying out her orders when he had no choice, and saving everyone he could. There had been times he had almost lost himself in that evil mountain of hers.

Each time he got close to giving in, he would visit Sonya. She never knew of it. He would hide, content to just watch her as he did now. Her mere presence eased him. Appeased his rage and quickened his blood.

How many times had he told himself he could never have her? How many times had he tried to keep his distance from her?

And then she had traveled to MacLeod Castle.

It had been a shock when he learned she was there. Seeing her every day, hearing her voice, touching her, was both a gift and a bane.

To have her so near, but to never *have* her.

It was worse than the years he had been locked in Deirdre's prison and tortured daily. It was worse than being taken from his family and being able to do nothing as his god was unbound within him.

For so many decades Broc had kept to himself at Cairn Toul because of the curse and because he trusted no one. Then he had betrayed Deirdre and helped the other Warriors kill her. Except her black magic had prevented her death.

Broc had returned with the Warriors to MacLeod Castle. It hadn't been easy at first to be among those he now called brothers. To give his trust and know they would watch his back when he hadn't trusted anyone in centuries was . . . difficult.

Yet, now he would like nothing better than to have his friend Ramsey with him. Ramsey was a quiet man and like a brother. They had bonded in Deirdre's mountain. During those awful years Ramsey was the only one Broc had trusted, the only one Broc had listened to. And the only one he had dared let close.

When the time had come to escape, Broc knew someone had to stay behind and spy on Deirdre, to gain as much information as they could. He had volunteered.

Ramsey hadn't wanted to leave him, but Broc hadn't given his friend a choice. It had been one of the hardest things Broc had ever done. He knew he had taken a huge risk in thinking he could maintain his charade with Deirdre.

His ruse had been rewarding, however. He had nearly lost his soul in the evil pit of Cairn Toul, but he had discovered crucial information about the MacLeods as well as how to help them.

Each Druid, if he or she had enough magic, was able to use that magic in a special form. For Deirdre, she could move stones. Inside Cairn Toul, she had made herself a fortress complete with layers of dungeons deep inside the earth.

Evil bred and grew stronger each day in that mountain. It now spread over Scotland like a plague.

Broc turned his thoughts away from Deirdre. It would only lead to anger, and he needed to concentrate on Sonya. He swallowed and tried to look away from her bare shoulders, but he wasn't strong enough.

When it came to Sonya, the control he was known for vanished.

THREE

Cairn Toul Mountain

Deirdre stared at the parchments open before her. The writings were faded, the paper crumbling before her eyes. If she didn't do something quickly, whatever information the parchments held would be lost to her.

She leaned over the scrolls as her magic built inside her. Deirdre pushed her magic out of her mouth as she blew on the scrolls.

The writing glittered as her magic came in contact with it, darkening the words so she could read them. Almost instantly, the scrolls burst into flames.

It was a counter to *drough* magic, but she had been given enough time to see what the scrolls hid. There was an ancient burial mound that held an artifact.

Deirdre hadn't been able to determine what the artifact was, but she knew where to look: Glencoe. However, she had also seen where no *drough* or any evil could enter the mound.

She left the scrolls to burn as thoughts tumbled through her mind. There had to be someone who could enter the tomb. A *mie*, perhaps? Or even a mortal. Deirdre would have to use them in order to gain the artifact.

Deirdre knelt in the middle of her chamber and called forth the evil, the darkness that made her magic so powerful. Once she could feel it rushing over her skin, she began the singsong chant she hoped would be able to help her find who could enter the tomb.

The spell had never worked in helping her locate Druids before, but perhaps this time was different.

A wall of flame erupted before her, reaching the vast stones above her and scorching them before the blaze subsided. Inside their red-orange depths she saw a face and heard a name.

Broc.

Deirdre threw back her head and laughed. Who would have guessed it would be a Warrior who could enter the tomb? And Broc at that. She wanted revenge on him for betraying her. Nevertheless, she would have him open the tomb. And he *would* do her bidding in the end.

With a smile and excitement coursing through her, she rose and called to her wyrran. First, they had to find Broc.

Sonya missed the cocoon of warmth that had surrounded her. Strong, muscular arms had held her, carried her. Protected her. Of that she knew.

Before the blackness had taken her, she could have sworn she saw indigo wings fly over her before something landed between her and the wolf.

Could she miss Broc so desperately her fevered brain imagined him saving her? It didn't matter. The wolf might not have killed her, but the infection running through her body would.

Each time she would begin to wake, Sonya grasped the darkness and refused to let go. She didn't want to open her eyes and see where fate had delivered her. The blessed darkness took her away from the pain of the humiliation and fear of her magic abandoning her.

No longer could she call herself a Druid. What good

would she do anyone at MacLeod Castle, now that she couldn't heal?

Broc.

Sonya cried out and tried to turn away. Someone held her shoulders with large hands. A voice tried to reach her through the fog of unconsciousness, but she refused to listen. Nothing they said could help her now.

She wanted to curl in a ball. The pain in her heart too much to bear.

But oh, to see Broc's face, his soft brown eyes, and his long fair hair that brought out the bronze of his skin. To feel the ripple of his muscles as she held his shoulders when he lifted her in his arms and flew her to the trees.

Sonya had never felt such exhilaration as when she soared through the air with Broc. His mighty wings had taken her so high into the sky, so high she felt she could almost touch the clouds.

Not once had she been afraid. Not as long as Broc held her. With him, she had always felt safe, always knew he would protect her.

Sonya was pulled from her thoughts when her wound began to ache. It was a healing ache, though. As if someone put some herbs into the cut.

She forgot all about the injury as her shoulders were lifted and she was once more against the warmth of a rock-hard chest. Sonya allowed herself to imagine it was Broc, allowed herself to fantasize that he would want to hold her.

"Drink for me."

She frowned. It had sounded suspiciously like Broc's voice. Was it her imagination? Or had he found her?

Something was placed against her lips. As parched as her throat was, she was unprepared when the liquid filled her mouth, choking her.

Sonya coughed and felt the liquid run down her chin. She could wake, could force open her eyes and see who held her. But did she have the courage? If it was Broc, he would have been sent by the others. Everyone would want to know why she left.

How could she tell them about her magic when she couldn't bear to think of herself as anything other than a Druid?

"Sonya, please. Drink for me."

This time, she knew. The voice was Broc's. She could hear the concern, the worry in his tone. As with anything to do with Broc, she was powerless to refuse him.

It took several attempts, but Sonya forced open her eyes. Her breath caught in her lungs when she gazed up at Broc. His brown eyes watched her carefully. His brow was furrowed, his wide lips held in a tight line.

She had been surrounded by Warriors at MacLeod Castle. All of them handsome men in their own right. But Broc had been the one who captured her attention. The only one she sought out.

"Sonya?"

She wanted to reach up and stroke the strong line of his jaw. She gazed at the heavy growth of whiskers, but she didn't mind it. It accentuated the hollow of his cheeks and the dangerous ruggedness of his angular face.

His hair was damp. Long strands of blond hair fell over his forehead and into his thick black eyelashes, but he didn't seem to notice or care. His eyes continued to search hers, as if he waited for her to say something, anything.

But the words stuck in her throat. It wasn't just finding him holding her sister's body, although that was part of it. It was the knowledge that the very person she was would be gone forever.

"I need you to drink," he said.

Once more Sonya felt something against her mouth. This time she parted her lips and allowed Broc to tip a portion of the water onto her tongue.

She swallowed the cool water and let it fill her. There was a harsh aftertaste.

Broc tipped the wooden cup once more. "It's herbs that will help you. You must drink it all."

Sonya didn't have the strength to fight him as he poured more of the water into her mouth. It felt so right, so good to be held in his arms. She wanted to run her fingers through his hair, to feel the wind ripple around her while his leathery wings propelled them through the sky. She wanted to see his eyes alight with wonder as she allowed him to hear the trees speaking to her.

But all of that would never be again.

"Why did you leave?" Broc whispered.

She wanted to answer him, to tell him everything. Anger and resentment and fear mixed inside her, swelling her emotions until her eyes clouded with tears.

Though she tried to keep her eyes open, whatever had been in the water was pulling her back into unconsciousness. The quiet darkness awaited her, and she needed it.

Just before she gave in completely, she could have sworn she heard Broc ask, "Why did you leave me?"

Broc watched as Sonya slipped back into oblivion. It was the only reason he asked her why she had left him.

The question had come from nowhere. One moment he was watching the herbs begin to take effect, and the next, the words fell from his mouth.

When she had opened her eyes and he'd stared into her amber depths, there had been so many things he wanted to say to her. The pain in her eyes bothered him, but not half as much as the panic he saw.

Just what had happened to her? More importantly, why wasn't she using her magic?

Broc set aside the empty cup and removed his arm from around her slim shoulders. He wrung out the strip of linen Jean had left in the bowl of water and bathed Sonya's face.

He was used to fighting, used to releasing his god and killing anything that got in his way. He couldn't battle what made Sonya ill, couldn't fight whatever had sent her running from MacLeod Castle.

And he'd never felt so inadequate in his life.

It reminded him of when Hayden had said much the same thing while he had watched his woman, Isla, fight an illness. Broc hadn't understood then, but he did now. Now that it was Sonya lying in the bed, her life hanging in the balance.

With each beat of her heart, Broc knew fate was against her. Sonya had to want to live, had to fight the infection if she was to survive.

Hour after hour he wiped the sweat from her face and neck. Time and again he would hold her down as she thrashed on the bed, screaming Anice's name, then mumbling incoherent words.

He never left her side, never took his eyes off her. With the first streaks of light over the horizon, Sonya's fever finally broke. Broc had never been so relieved. He waited impatiently for Sonya to open her eyes again, to do something, anything.

Instead, she didn't move. Didn't utter a sound.

Broc, an immortal nearly three centuries old with a primeval god inside him, was powerless. Ineffective. Useless.

If he thought it would help, he would get down on his knees and pray to the God of the Christians, but

Broc had learned many years ago that if there was a God, he had long since abandoned them.

Broc rose and walked to the window that overlooked the village. People went about their daily lives never knowing of the evil Druid intent on ruling the world. They didn't know Deirdre hunted other Druids to kill them and steal their power. They didn't know of the vile wyrran, creatures Deirdre had created to aid her.

They didn't know of the Warriors.

If Deirdre had her way, all too soon the world as everyone knew it would change. Broc and the others had halted Deirdre for a while, but he knew her well enough to know that her retribution would be swift and vicious.

Where she would strike was the question. Already she had sent the MacClure clan to attack MacLeod Castle. The mortals hadn't stood a chance against the Warriors. Many men had died needless deaths.

But Broc knew it was just the beginning for Deirdre. She had once wanted the MacLeods allied with her. Now she would want their deaths along with any Warrior who had sided with them.

With Sonya away from the castle and its protection, Broc feared Deirdre would discover her and seek to have Sonya for her own.

His betrayal of Deirdre would not be forgotten either. If Deirdre found out his affection for Sonya she would use it against him, forcing Broc to her will. And he would do it.

He'd do anything for Sonya.

Broc braced his hands on the sides of the window and blew out a deep breath. The storm had passed during the night. As soon as Sonya woke, he would fly them to MacLeod Castle. They could not stay out in the open. Not with Deirdre seeking revenge.

Whether Sonya wanted to or not, she was returning to MacLeod Castle.

He knew the moment Sonya opened her eyes. Broc looked over his shoulder to find her watching him. He walked to her wondering where to begin, how to begin. But as usual Sonya did things her own way.

"Where are we?" she asked.

"A village not far from where I found you. I would have taken you back to the castle last night, but there was a storm."

Her tongue peeked out to lick her lips as she looked away from him. "I've no wish to return to MacLeod Castle."

Broc had suspected as much. He could argue with her all day about the need for her to return with him, but he had already decided her safety was worth her hatred. Yet, he still wanted to know why she had run.

"Did someone harm you?" he asked.

"Nay."

"Then tell me why you left."

Her eyes closed on a weary sigh. "You shouldn't have come for me, Broc. I don't belong at the castle anymore."

"Why?" he demanded, and took another step toward the bed. "I want to know why."

Her eyes snapped open, but instead of the anger he expected, there was only sorrow. "My magic is gone."

Broc blinked, taken aback by her words. How could she think her magic was gone when he could still sense it, still feel the sensual tingle it caused whenever he was near her? It wrapped around him, enveloping him in everything that was Sonya. "You're mistaken."

"I'm not. What other explanation is there for this?" she asked, and held up her injured hand. "This should have been healed. I should never have gotten ill, but I did."

"Sonya . . ."

"Stop," she said wearily and briefly closed her eyes. "I know my magic is gone. I tried to heal Reaghan and couldn't. I was barely able to heal little Braden during the attack. I've always known this would happen."

Broc wanted to reassure her, to tell her she was wrong, but he couldn't find the words. Despite the magic he felt, Sonya was sure it had left her. He had no proof it was still inside her, and if she no longer felt it, then he would have to try to help her find it again.

"You must be hungry. I'll acquire you some food and order a bath."

He walked to the door and grabbed the handle, then paused. He lifted his gaze to Sonya, wishing there was a way he could restore the confident, smiling Druid he had known. It was enough, though, that she was alive.

Broc pulled open the door and stepped into the hallway. Soon they would return to MacLeod Castle. Surely there one of the other Druids could help Sonya find her magic once more.

Magic or not, it didn't change his feelings for her. Or the all-consuming desire to take her in his arms as a lover and kiss her.

Hold her. Feel her.

It was the one thing he wanted above all else.

The few times he had held her while he flew her to the forest so she could speak to the trees had been wonderful. And complete torture.

Her body fit perfectly against him. The way her breasts pressed against him, how her hands slid into his hair, and the way she would look at him so trustingly with her amber eyes.

He cherished each of those memories. They helped him get through the long, lonely nights.

But Broc was getting just what he had always

wanted—time alone with Sonya. Maybe he wouldn't return them quite so quickly to MacLeod Castle.

Then he recalled the deaths associated with him before he was made immortal. And the one after.

If he stayed near Sonya, he risked her life. But how could he stay away? He was drawn to her like the tides to the moon.

She was his breath, his heart.

She was . . . everything.

FOUR

Malcolm Monroe stood silently as he stared at the road before him. It was well worn by carts and horses and people making their way between the mountains.

It was also the path home.

Malcolm blew out a breath and wondered why he didn't feel so sad that he could never return to his clan. It wasn't just because his arm was ruined and useless. He could still use his left arm to lift a sword, not that it would make a difference to his clan.

A laird had to be fit. He had to be whole. And Malcolm most certainly wasn't whole anymore. Thanks to Deirdre.

It wasn't just his arm or the vicious scars on his face and chest. How could he return to a world where there was no magic or Warriors? How could he return to his home and forget his cousin was the lone female Warrior and could turn invisible? How could he return to his clan and forget he had seen Druids and watched them do unimaginable, beautiful magic?

The simple answer was that he couldn't.

Nor could he stay at MacLeod Castle. He needed to make a life for himself. Somewhere. He just wasn't sure where or how just yet.

Malcolm was sure it would come to him soon enough.

Until then, he would wander the majestic mountains of Scotland's Highlands and let the land soak into his soul.

He would be alone, but it was for the best. He held too much darkness and resentment inside him to be good company for anyone—even the moody Warriors at the castle.

Malcolm turned away from the road and looked at the mountain on his left. There were many villages and clans hidden in the mountains. Maybe it was time he found them.

He adjusted the sporran around his waist, which held his few coins. His sword now rested on his right hip to make it easier to grab with his left hand. Much in his life had changed, and he was trying to adjust to all of it.

Larena, his dear cousin, worried too much. She was married now and needed all her concentration on defeating Deirdre. Larena couldn't do that as long as he was at MacLeod Castle reminding her that he was mortal. He couldn't fight with the Warriors, nor would be go with the women to hide.

So he had left.

Malcolm knew he should have said farewell, but everyone would have only tried to convince him to stay. He had given his departure a lot of thought, and it was the only way. For him, it was the only answer that made sense.

He tried to flex his ruined hand, but as usual only got a small twitch of his fingers. He could lift his right arm, but not without tremendous pain that only grew worse each day.

Deirdre's Warriors who had attacked him had certainly done their job. If only Broc hadn't stopped them, Malcolm would be dead instead of living as half a man.

As a Highlander, half a man wasn't acceptable. Still, it wasn't as if Malcolm had given up on living. He planned to continue on, just not alongside immortal Warriors and magical Druids where he was only in the way.

Malcolm inhaled deeply and started up the incline of the mountain. What lay on the other side he didn't know. It was something unknown, and for now, that kept him going, kept his mind from the fact that he could use only one arm.

For now, it was enough.

With her belly full of tasty broth, Sonya let her mind drift as she soaked in the hot water of her bath. Her injured hand rested on the rim of the wooden tub, her head against the back.

The water was doing wonders to ease the aches of her body. Too bad it couldn't heal her wounded heart as effortlessly.

Sonya sat up and reached for the soap. It was going to be difficult to wash with just one hand, but she would make do. Broc would leave her alone for only so long.

She bathed her body easily enough, but it was her hair which took the most time to lather and rinse. Sonya was exhausted by the time her hair was clean once more.

The water was now tepid, and if not for the fire, she would be thoroughly chilled. She reached for the drying cloth and tried to stand. Her injured arm slipped on the side and plunged into the water.

"Damn," she mumbled as she looked at the now soaked bandages.

With the drying cloth once more in her hand and again on her feet, Sonya began to dry herself. Water dripped from the ends of her hair and onto the backs of her legs, sending chills racing over her skin.

She hadn't realized that she had become so weak that something as simple as giving herself a bath could tire her to the point that she was about to collapse.

The end of the drying cloth fell into the water. Sonya hastily jerked it out and realized she needed to get out of the tub in order to finish. It was such a simple task, stepping out of the wooden tub. Yet, it seemed an impossible feat.

Already her legs shook from the few moments she'd been standing. She was filled with anger at her magic leaving her, putting her in this position.

The Druids who had hidden her and Anice had cautioned them not to take their magic for granted. Sonya hadn't bothered to listen to them. After all, once a Druid was born, the magic would always be with them.

What a fool she had been.

Her eyes brimmed with tears, but she refused to let them fall. She could get out of the tub without falling. She *would* get out without falling.

Sonya took a deep breath and lifted one foot over the rim of the tub. She placed it on the floor, her legs shaking, but she continued to stand.

After a moment's hesitation, Sonya lifted the second leg. Her foot hit the side of the tub and she overbalanced trying to keep upright. She began to fall backward when strong arms enveloped her.

"Sonya?"

She let out a breath when she heard Broc's voice. His deep, sensual, all-too-beautiful voice in her ear. "I fell."

"I saw that."

Was it her imagination or did his voice shake? And that's when she realized she was naked except for the drying cloth she held against her front.

Broc's warm breath fanned her neck, his breaths coming harsh and shallow. She stayed as she was, afraid to move and afraid not to. She hated how she liked being in his arms. She hated that he felt nothing for her while her body went into a whirlwind of longing and desire anytime he was near.

His hand shifted slightly. Sonya sucked in a mouthful of air, her blood heating with the feel of his fingers beneath her breast. Her head was against his chest, the cloth of his breeches rubbing against her bare legs and bottom.

Chills of a different kind raced over her body then. How she had longed to be in Broc's arms in such a fashion. To see his eyes filled with desire for her. To know his kiss, his touch. His body.

"You're shaking," he murmured.

Sonya's mouth was dry, her heart drumming in her ears. She closed her eyes and let herself feel the hard sinew of his chest behind her, the strong arms around her. "I'm chilled."

That's all it took to put him in motion. One moment she was leaning against him, and the next she had a blanket around her shoulders as he took her cloth and dried off her legs.

"Better?" he asked as he stood in front of her.

She nodded, afraid to look into his eyes lest he see the desire his small touch had brought her.

The bed seemed a league away, and she would have to walk around Broc to get to the chairs, neither of which she could do on the strength rapidly leaving her body. So Sonya lowered herself as gracefully as she could before the fire.

"Cara packed this for you."

Sonya looked up to find Broc holding her comb. The mention of Cara, who was like a sister, made Sonya's heart ache. Every woman at the castle, Druid or not, was like a sister to her. Each had been more of a sister than Anice.

Anice had always been concerned with wherever her mind had taken her from day to day. Some days she was coherent. Other days, not at all. Because of Anice's affliction, they had never been close.

The women at MacLeod Castle—Cara, Larena, Marcail, Isla, and Reaghan—were her true sisters in every sense of the word. And she had left without a word to them.

"Thank you," she said, and took her favorite comb. She began to try and brush through the vast tangles, but it would take hours, and Sonya simply didn't have the strength.

She set the comb aside and stared into the orange flames of the fire. It was Broc's gentle touch on her injured hand which drew her gaze.

"You weren't supposed to get the bandages wet," he said with a small grin. "Jean will no' be happy."

Sonya watched as he tenderly unwrapped her bandages before tossing them into the fire. There was a hiss before the flames engulfed the material. A moment later, fresh bandages covered her wound.

"My hand slipped while I tried to stand," she explained.

"I knew I should have stayed to help you. You're still weak from lack of food and the fever."

Sonya nodded, knowing he was right. She deserved the irritation she heard in his voice. She had been reckless, something she had never been in her life. Even now, she couldn't explain why she had left the castle.

Her world had tilted, the anchor that kept her doing as she must snapping when she had seen Broc holding Anice. The savage grief etched on his face would forever be in her memory. Just thinking of it made her turn away from him.

"There's another gown and underclothes for you in my satchel," Broc said.

Sonya heard movement but didn't turn to see what he was doing. Then she felt a soft tug on her hair as a comb was pulled through the strands.

"Everyone is worried about you," he continued. "We searched everywhere before I left to find you."

Sonya knew he wanted some sort of explanation. He deserved one, as did everyone at the castle. She just didn't know if she could give it to him yet.

"I wasn't sure what to pack for you. Cara, Isla, and Larena took care of most of it. If you doona have what you need, I've coin."

Each time he came to a lump of knotted hair, he would take his time and slowly work it free. Not once did he pull her hair. The slow, even strokes began to lull her, as did the warmth of the fire and blanket around her.

"Anice is buried in the forest behind the convent ruins."

Sonya blinked to hide the rush of tears. "I didn't look for her after the battle. I assumed she was safe in the castle. I should have looked for her."

"Too many Druids lost their lives that day. I'm sorry I wasna able to save them all."

"You did what you could. We all did."

He blew out a breath as his fingers moved her wet hair away from her ear. "You weren't the only one to run away."

"Malcolm." It wasn't much of a guess. Sonya had feared he would leave one day. It made sense that he would do it while everyone was occupied with the battle.

"Aye."

Sonya tugged at the end of the blanket. "He didn't

think he could help in the battle, and he didn't want to hide with the women."

"Larena wants me to look for him once I return with you."

Sonya turned to look at him over her shoulder. "Malcolm left because he no longer wants to remain at MacLeod Castle. You cannot force him to return."

"Him? Nay. You? That's a different matter entirely. You are a Druid, and if Deirdre learns you are no' protected at the castle anymore, she will come for you."

She was unable to continue to look into Broc's brown eyes. They were such a deep, rich brown that hid so many secrets. She had once thought she might be able to get him to share some of those secrets.

But everything she had thought she knew of Broc was wrong.

Sonya turned back to the fire and licked her lips. "I warned Larena that Malcolm might leave. She thought for sure he would stay."

"Did Malcolm ever mention where he might go?"

"He didn't say much of anything to anyone. Deirdre's attack scarred more than just his body. His soul is shattered."

"Aye," Broc said softly. "I know."

She had forgotten that Broc was the one who found Malcolm as well as the one who fought off the Warriors to save him. "You risked much in helping him."

"Nothing more than anyone else fighting against Deirdre. I only wish I could have gotten to Malcolm sooner."

It was something in his voice, some dark emotion, that made Sonya turn to him. "What did you see?"

Broc wouldn't look into her face. "You doona realize what it was like living in Deirdre's mountain. She wanted the Warriors to be animals, to act like animals. That's what I found when I saw the Warriors attacking Malcolm. They were about to rip him apart. It sickened me."

"But you saved him. You brought him to the castle so he could be healed."

Broc's eyes lifted to hers. "I brought him to you. The only one I knew could help him."

FIVE

It had been a long time since Broc had felt so at ease. He didn't want the moment to end. Sitting with Sonya in front of the fire while he combed her hair seemed so ordinary, yet it touched a part of him he feared was long since dead.

Broc tucked a strand of red hair behind her ear and shifted so he could inhale her scent of lavender. It had always intoxicated him, always made him yearn to be near her.

Her scent filled his body and made him burn. His fingers tightened their hold on the comb as he fought against dragging her against him, of laying claim to her tempting lips.

He mentally shook himself as he thought of where they were. And why.

"Sonya, why did you leave?"

She glanced down, hiding her amber eyes from him. "Sometimes the course we take seems the right one."

"You still feel as though you are on the right path?"

Her slim shoulders lifted in a shrug. "I don't know much of anything anymore."

He knew she had left because of Anice. Because he had known Anice. It was time Sonya knew the truth, the whole, ugly mess of it.

"Do you know Ramsey and I were caught by Deirdre

about the same time? His god was released first, but I soon followed."

"I'd heard something like that," Sonya answered before shifting to turn toward him.

"In Cairn Toul, you trust no one. You never know who is working with Deirdre and who is no'. Yet, somehow Ramsey and I befriended each other. In the depths of that vile mountain was forged a friendship deeper than blood."

Sonya's brow furrowed as she leaned toward him. "What happened?"

"Freedom. Ramsey had a chance at escape, and I urged him to it. Someone had to stay behind and spy on Deirdre."

"Why you?"

Broc smiled wryly. "Ramsey is . . . special. Deirdre couldna learn everything there was to know of him."

"Isn't that true of everyone?"

"Aye, I suppose."

"So you stayed behind," she urged him to continue.

Broc thought back to that day so long ago. How freedom had been so close he could almost touch it. He had nearly given in and left with Ramsey, almost forgot everything but his own wants and needs.

"We had discussed escaping for so long. Ramsey wanted me to go and him to stay as a spy."

Sonya's head cocked to the side as she studied him. "You didn't let him. You willingly stayed? Why?"

"For Ramsey. For the other Warriors. For Druids and every innocent life Deirdre would snuff out without a second's thought."

Broc took a deep breath and readied himself for Sonya's reaction—whatever it might be.

"I soon became someone Deirdre wanted near her at all times. I overheard things, learned of her intentions.

I never hesitated to do the deeds, however dirty, that she sent me on."

Sonya's lips pressed into a frown. "You killed people."

"And captured Druids."

Her eyes widened. "But you said you stayed behind for Druids."

"I stayed behind to learn all I could and relate it to Ramsey. Deirdre didna trust me for many years, and in all that time I never saw Ramsey. But I continued to listen, to watch and learn. I gathered the information I hoped would end Deirdre."

"Did it?"

"In a way. You see, one day I was sent to destroy a village of Druids. I was to capture all of them and return them to Deirdre. There were twenty wyrran with me, and soon things got out of control. Fires were started, and a few Druids were killed by the wyrran in their attempts to capture the Druids."

Sonya turned away. "I don't want to hear any more."

"You have to," Broc said. "As I walked down the middle of the small village, I heard a child crying. I doona know what drew me to the child, but I went. I found her sitting beside a cradle that held a baby. The cottage was burning down around them, but the child wouldna leave her sister."

Broc paused and wound a curl of Sonya's red hair around his finger. "I knew if the wyrran found the girls they would be brought to Deirdre. They would be raised by her and her evil, but in the end she would kill them and drain them of their magic."

"What did you do with them?"

"I gathered them in my arms and flew away. I hid them with an elderly couple while I went back to the village and finished the job Deirdre had sent me to do. Then I began my search for a group of Druids who could raise the girls. It took me weeks, but in the end I finally found them."

Broc stopped, unsure if he could go on, but he had begun the tale. He had to finish it.

"I left the girls with the Druids and returned as often as I could to check on them. I watched the youngest take her first steps. I watched the oldest the first time she did magic. They were happy, content. But most importantly, they were safe from Deirdre."

"Those girls were me and Anice?"

"Aye."

"So much makes sense now," Sonya said softly. "All those times Anice would run off into the woods as if she were looking for someone. Then the time she mentioned your name. All that time I thought Anice's mind wasn't there."

"It wasna." Broc hadn't wanted to tell her, but Sonya needed to know just how sick Anice had been. "The Druids knew it no' long after I brought you to them. They said something wasna quite right with your sister."

Sonya raised her brow as she turned to look at him. "Did they know what you were?"

"They suspected. They never asked. I never told."

"But you met my sister in the woods, didn't you?"

Broc rubbed his jaw, hating himself for what he had done. "Anice caught me watching you one day. I kept to myself in Cairn Toul, never speaking to anyone unless I had to. Anice was so happy, so alive that I couldna help but talk to her."

"You did more than that."

Broc searched Sonya's amber gaze but found no compassion. Not that he expected any. "To my shame, aye. I knew as soon as it happened it was a mistake. I told Anice I couldna see her again, but she somehow knew when I would come. She was always there. I'd like to say I was strong enough to turn her away, but I'm just a man."

Sonya rose to her feet. When she swayed, Broc hastened to aid her, but she jerked away from him. "You let Anice believe there was a future with you."

"Nay, I didna." Broc stood quickly. The flush on Sonya's face had nothing to do with the fire and everything to do with her anger. "It had been years since I touched Anice. I would talk to her, warn her about things if I could. I never led her to believe there was any sort of future with me."

"Why didn't you tell me sooner? Why didn't you tell me you knew Anice? And why didn't you talk to me as you did Anice?"

He felt as if each word were a stab in his heart. The anguish twisting her face, the shaking of her voice. All of it told him how much he had hurt her.

"I'm sorry, Sonya. I never wanted her to know me. I feared Deirdre might someday learn what I had done and come to take both of you. The moment I took you from your village I sealed your doom."

"Because you saved us?"

Broc fisted his hands as he felt his claws begin to lengthen. "Because I cared. Deirdre will use it against me. It's what she has always done."

"You mean she would have."

"I mean she will. It's inevitable. It's why I've tried to keep you at MacLeod Castle. It's why I worked so hard to get Anice and the Druids to the castle before it was too late. Deirdre cannot hurt Anice now, but she can get to you."

For the first time since he began his tale he saw Sonya's anger waver. She now understood the precarious position he was in.

What she didn't know, and what he hoped to keep

from her, was his attraction to her. He feared that if he gave in to the desire to touch her, to kiss her, to claim her that if Deirdre ever took Sonya, Broc would be torn apart.

So Broc kept silent. Selfishly silent.

"What aren't you telling me, Broc?"

He turned away and faced the wall. It wasn't just his attraction he wanted kept from her. It was the curse. He was unable to look at her as his desire, his longing threatened to overwhelm him. "That is everything."

"So you watched me through the years?"

"Aye."

"Had Anice not died, you wouldn't have told me all of this, would you?"

Broc shook his head.

"You cared for her very much."

"Of course I did. I saved both of you. You were my responsibility. I vowed to do everything and anything to keep both of you out of Deirdre's path."

Sonya moved to stand in front of him, the blanket wrapped tightly around her while her red hair curled about her face and shoulders. "I saw your face. I saw how devastated you were when you held Anice's dead body. I heard the words you yelled at me."

"Words spoken out of grief. I know you cannot bring anyone back from the dead. I had no right to speak to you as I did, and I ask your forgiveness."

Some of the fire left her gaze. "You have it."

Broc gave a slight bow of his head. "As for the rest, as I've told you, I cared for Anice as if she had been my family. Though neither of you heard my vow to keep you safe, it was spoken. I neglected to protect her."

The words were truer than Broc had ever realized. He carried a heavy burden now. The soul of Anice. He just hoped Sonya could forgive him eventually.

"Do not blame yourself," Sonya said. "You didn't kill my sister."

He saw the same guilt he carried in Sonya's eyes. If she wouldn't allow him to carry it, he wouldn't allow her. "And neither did you."

The smile Sonya sent him didn't reach her eyes. "Ah, but, Broc, I begged her to come to the castle. Had I heard the trees sooner, we would have been able to get them to the castle."

"Aye," he said, and took her arm to guide her to the bed. The dark circles under her eyes and the way her body weaved where she stood told him she had used all of her strength. "But things didna go as they should have. We were attacked, and we all did the best we could."

Sonya sat on the bed and turned her face up to his. For the barest of moments he saw the trust she had once given him, trust that would never be his again.

"Anice was a gentle soul," Broc said. "Deirdre will no' be able to harm her now."

"Aye, at least Anice is safe."

Broc gently pushed Sonya to the side and lifted her feet onto the bed. He ignored the bare flesh of her calf when her blanket fell open.

He pushed aside the rush of desire that filled him from the swell of her breast as she snuggled into the bed. He ached for her touch, his soul empty and depleted.

"You will make me return to MacLeod Castle, won't you?"

Broc adjusted the extra blanket around her and straightened. "Aye. Even if I hadna given you my vow, I would return you. For the sake of every living creature, Deirdre cannot be allowed to gain more Druid magic. Especially no' yours."

Sonya snorted. "That will be difficult since I have no magic."

"You keep saying that, yet I feel it. It's as strong as it's always been."

Her eyes snapped to his. "Don't lie to me, Broc."

"I'm no'. Your magic is still with you."

"Then why can't I heal myself?"

He ran a hand through his hair and sighed. "That I doona have an answer for. Rest. We will talk more in the morning after you've had a good night's sleep."

Broc didn't wait for her to respond but went to stand by the window. He stood to the side so no one would be able to see him from below. He couldn't shake the feeling that Deirdre was about to find them.

It was that instinct which kept Broc by Sonya's side instead of flying to MacLeod Castle. He couldn't chance anything happening to Sonya.

How Deirdre would know Sonya had left or where he had found her, Broc couldn't guess. She had her evil ways he had never understood.

Then he remembered. The peregrine falcon.

Logan, another Warrior, was sure the falcon was a spy for Deirdre. They had all felt the magic around the bird, but Logan most of all. If it was Deirdre using the falcon, then Broc had little time to get Sonya back to MacLeod Castle.

SIX

Broc tried to focus on anything but Sonya. But he couldn't get the feel of her against him out of his mind. The press of her wet, naked flesh sent need shooting straight to his cock.

Breathing became impossible. His blood burned. Blazed. Singed.

All for Sonya.

The weight of her breasts had touched the back of his hand, reminding him how near he'd been, how easy it would have been to turn his hand and cup the plump mounds, to feel her nipples harden in his palms.

The longing, the yearning had been so intense, so compelling that for a moment Broc had nearly covered Sonya's breasts with his hands.

There had only been the thin drying cloth between his hands and her skin. Even as he ached to touch Sonya, he knew he couldn't. To surrender to his hunger was to give Deirdre something else to use against him, and Broc couldn't allow that. For Sonya's sake, he wouldn't do that to her.

So he had reluctantly and resentfully released Sonya to move beside the window. He pretended he couldn't hear every soft breath that left her body, pretended he didn't crave her warm skin against his.

Pretended she wasn't the only thing that could alleviate his loneliness.

Broc didn't know how long he stared out the window watching for signs of anything out of the ordinary. So far there was nothing, but how long could they go before trouble found them?

Before Deirdre found them?

Not long at all, Broc surmised. The sooner he got Sonya out of the sleepy little village, the sooner they could be traveling back to MacLeod Castle and the safety it would give her.

You cannot force her to go.

As much as Broc hated to admit it, he couldn't. Sonya and Anice had been the only reasons which kept him from giving in to the evil that surrounded him while spying on Deirdre. He couldn't stand to have Sonya's hatred, and that's exactly what would happen if he forced her to return.

But what was he supposed to do? Sonya was stubborn. Once she had her mind set, he wouldn't be able to sway her.

He glanced over his shoulder and sucked in a breath when his gaze landed on the bare expanse of Sonya's back. She had rolled onto her other side and the blanket had fallen from her grasp.

Unable to keep away, Broc walked as silently as a ghost to the bed. Sonya's mass of glorious red curls were laid out behind her on the pillow as if straining to reach him.

He loved to see her hair unbound. It was such a rare occasion, and he found himself reaching to touch a silken strand.

Broc lifted a long lock to twirl about his fingers before he let it drop back into place. Ever since Sonya had come into womanhood, he'd been unable to deny the pull of her stunning body, her tantalizing mouth.

Slowly, hesitantly, Broc let the pads of his fingers graze down her spine until he reached the blanket, which rested precariously on the enticing swell of her hip.

It would take the smallest of tugs to remove it. Then he would be able to let his eyes feast on her creamy skin, her long, lean legs.

Broc closed his eyes and turned away. What kind of man took advantage of a woman who trusted him?

But you aren't a man.

Nay, he was a Warrior. Immortal. Powerful. He would endure alone while he watched Sonya age and die. Had the *droughs* known the cruelty they inflicted on the first Warriors? Had they even stopped to wonder what would happen if the gods were unbound again?

Did no one question how a Warrior would feel as those he cared most about died while he carried on century after century?

The silence that filled the small chamber was all the answer Broc needed. No one had cared. No one had given a second thought to the Warriors. They had been a means to an end with the Roman invasion.

That he understood. But now—now the enemy wasn't Rome but a *drough* bent on total domination. For the better part of two hundred and seventy-five years Broc had either been Deirdre's prisoner or her minion.

It wasn't until he had found Sonya and her sister that he had thought about the mortals and the life he had been taken from.

Things had grown more complicated when he'd helped the MacLeods free Quinn and return to MacLeod Castle. Every day Broc saw the love between Lucan and Cara,

Fallon and Larena, Quinn and Marcail, Hayden and Isla, and now Galen and Reaghan.

The only Warrior who didn't have to worry about his wife aging and dying was Fallon, but that was only because Larena was a Warrior herself. The only female Warrior.

How Lucan, Quinn, Hayden, and Galen coped with the knowledge that one day their wives—the women who had captured their hearts—would be gone, Broc didn't know.

He couldn't fathom it. And didn't want to try.

It was his need for Sonya, the ache in his chest to have her near that reminded him of his curse. A curse that had begun when he was just a lad. Any female not related to him by family had died by either sickness or some freak accident.

His grandmother had told him it was something he had done in another life that he was paying for now. All Broc knew was that he would spend his life alone instead of risking a woman's life.

Broc looked at Sonya resting so peacefully. If there ever was a woman who he could imagine having by his side to share his days—and his nights—it was Sonya.

Beautiful, beguiling Sonya.

The one woman he couldn't allow himself to have.

Deirdre drummed her long fingernails on the stone table as she sat and contemplated the last few months. The stones, her stones, gave her the comfort and solace she needed. She had stayed in her mountain too long, however. Soon she would have to leave Cairn Toul.

For the first time in over two hundred years she was going to venture into the world. She had her revenge to dole out, and what better way than to see her enemies suffering before her very eyes.

Oh, she could use her black magic, but it was time Scotland knew who she was. And just what power she held. For too long she had allowed the insignificant humans to continue their existence without knowing of her.

That was all about to change.

Soon word would spread from Scotland to England and then into France and across the rest of Europe. She had spent too long trying to bring the MacLeods into her fold when she should have dominated Britain.

It would have only been a matter of time before she had found the MacLeods and forced them to align with her. But she had been blinded with her need for Quinn, a need that had nearly cost her everything.

The child of the prophecy would have to wait. She had to build up her army once more. Many of her Warriors had died, but the gods inside them weren't gone—they merely found the next man in the bloodline.

All Deirdre had to do was find the strongest fighter, the bravest warrior of those clans and she could once more have her Warriors.

It would take time, but after living a thousand years, what was another few? While her wyrran searched for the Druids who continued to hide, Deirdre would seek out the clans for her next Warriors while taking vengeance on the MacLeods and anyone loyal to them.

It was going to be glorious and bloody. Once the MacLeods were imprisoned and the Druids dead, she was going to tear down MacLeod Castle stone by stone. There would be nothing left standing to give anyone hope.

And when she was finished with the MacLeods, everyone would realize there was no use fighting her.

She would win, and if it meant killing the Warriors and starting again, she would do it.

"Mistress."

Deirdre stiffened and looked at Dunmore over her shoulder. He was the only mortal in her mountain, the only mortal she had allowed to be close. He had been useful, and her promise of immortality and wealth had kept him loyal.

But Dunmore was aging. Already his dark hair was streaked with gray. There were lines around his eyes, and he wasn't as strong as he used to be. If things weren't so chaotic, Deirdre would kill him. But, unfortunately, she still needed Dunmore. For a bit longer.

"I've returned with Druids," he said and lowered his gaze to the floor.

With the tiniest of thoughts, Deirdre's white hair, which hung to the floor, twitched. It was a weapon she used to defeat many men. Her hair could flay the skin off a person or choke the life out of anyone.

"How many?" Deirdre asked as she rose and turned to face Dunmore. She ran her hands over his wide shoulders. There was still muscle there, still strength.

"Fourteen, mistress."

Deirdre was impressed. She, of course, wouldn't tell Dunmore that, however. "So few?"

"They are the Druids who lived on Loch Awe. The ones who ran from MacLeod Castle," he said and turned his head to watch her as she continued to walk around him.

Deirdre stopped in front of him and raised a brow. "The artifact? Tell me you brought Reaghan with the others."

"I wish I could, mistress. I saw the artifact, but one of the MacClures delivered a mortal wound to her."

Deirdre hissed as anger surged within her. The need to hit something, to see blood pool at her feet surged through her. "What happened?"

"The spear severed her spine."

"There is a healer at MacLeod Castle."

Dunmore swallowed and lowered his gaze. "I doona believe they reached her in time."

Deirdre brushed past Dunmore and stalked out of her chamber. She could hear the terrified screams of the Druids as her wyrran put them in the dungeons. That fear was just what she needed to calm the rage burning inside her at the loss of Reaghan. "Bring a Druid to the ritual chamber. Now."

She didn't wait to see if the wyrran who always followed her obeyed. She knew they would. She had created them, and they were loyal only to her.

Deirdre strode into the chamber and looked at the two empty spots that had once held Druids prisoner. Her magic had created the black flames which kept Lavena alive for hundreds of years. It had also given Isla's sister more power to her magic in which to aid Deirdre.

The other spot had contained Marcail in the blue flames. Those flames would have killed Marcail—should have killed Marcail. But the MacLeods and the other Warriors had freed her, and somehow managed to keep her alive.

Deirdre didn't know who the *mie* at MacLeod Castle was with such magic. But she was going to find out.

Deirdre heard the soft whimper of the Druid being hauled down the corridor to her. She turned and looked at the large stone table in the center of the ritual chamber. It was stained red with the blood of the many Druids she had killed there. Druids whose magic she had taken.

Dunmore had followed her and now stood at the entrance of the chamber as the wyrran half dragged, half carried the woman into the room. Deirdre merely watched as her wyrran tossed the *mie* onto the table and fastened the straps to her wrists and ankles.

Once the wyrran finished, Deirdre patted them on the head and stepped to the table. She looked down at the *mie*. She was young with sandy-blond hair and plain brown eyes.

"What are you going to do to me?" the Druid asked.

Deirdre smiled and ran the tip of one long fingernail along the *mie's* cheek. "I'm going to drain your blood. Slowly, painfully. Then I'm going to take your magic."

The Druid actually laughed through her tears.

Deirdre's rage spiked until she studied the Druid. There was magic within the *mie*, but it was so slight, there was no use trying to obtain it.

"You claim to be a Druid when you have so little magic? How dare you?" Deirdre demanded.

The young *mie* sniffed and blinked through her tears. Deirdre saw the courage and silently applauded her, though it would do the Druid little good.

"None from Loch Awe have much magic. You will get nothing from us."

Deirdre didn't like being denied. Anything. She wouldn't be deprived of the magic she required. "Oh, I will get your magic, you foolish *mie*. I will get it, but you will suffer unimaginable agony in the process."

As soon as the words left Deirdre's mouth, she lifted her hands over the Druid's prone body. The *mie* screamed as Deirdre's vengeful black magic lashed out.

This was the ceremonial chamber, the place where Deirdre would cut the Druids so their blood could pool in the valleys carved into the stone before filling the four goblets placed at each corner.

But she was too full of fury for a ceremony. She wanted blood, and the screams of the *mie* helped to soothe her wrath.

Deirdre used her magic to control her hair and brought it up to use as a weapon. Again and again her hair slashed across the *mie*'s skin like a blade, leaving trails of blood in its wake.

By the time the Druid stopped screaming, Deirdre's white hair was coated dark red.

A smile played upon Deirdre's lips as she closed her eyes and began the ancient chant taught to her by her mother, a chant which called forth the black magic and *diabhul*, Satan.

Deirdre opened her eyes to see the dark smoke surround the *mie* and snuff out the last bit of life in her body as it claimed her soul.

"I am yours!" Deirdre screamed as she plunged a dagger through the smoke into the *mie's* stomach.

The smoke vanished, but the ritual wasn't over. Deirdre went from corner to corner and lifted the goblets to her lips so she could drain them of the *mie's* blood.

Within the blood held the Druid's meager magic, but it was still magic and it would strengthen Deirdre.

As the magic mixed with hers, the wind began to howl around her, whipping her skirts about her legs and lifting the long white strands of her hair about her. She felt her power grow, felt her magic building as it always did when she took the magic of another Druid.

Even the little crumb of magic she had just taken bolstered her. By the time she was finished with the Druids in her dungeons, she would be ready for her vengeance.

"Get me another Druid, Dunmore," she called, and began to unbuckle the straps holding the dead *mie*.

She rolled the woman off the table and waited impatiently for the next Druid. Druid after Druid died on the sacrificial table to help strengthen her. Deirdre listened to none of their crying and pleas for mercy.

Until the last Druid was brought into the chamber.

"Please," the *mie* begged.

Deirdre stared at the older woman. Deep grooves of age and the hardship of life lined the woman's sagging skin. Her hair was gray and wiry as it stuck out at odd angles from her braid, which had come loose.

"Please what?" Deirdre demanded. "Do you think I will spare you as I did your friends?"

The woman glanced at the dead bodies and pushed against the wyrran's hold. She didn't appear to notice when the wyrran's claws dug into her skin and blood dripped from the wounds.

"Well?" Deirdre prompted. The killing of Druids always put her in a better mood. It was the only reason she toyed with the woman now.

"I was in MacLeod Castle for days. I can give you information."

Now Deirdre was intrigued. "In exchange for what?"

"Life," the woman answered without hesitation. "I don't want to die."

"How many more years do you think you have?"

"It doesn't matter."

Deirdre crossed her arms over her chest and realized all the Druids she'd killed would've had information about the occupants of MacLeod Castle. She should have gotten it before she killed them, but when her fury took hold, she never thought clearly.

Which is why she made sure to keep a tight rein on her anger.

"Speak," Deirdre commanded. "Tell me what you know."

"And you will spare me?"

"Depends on what details you impart."

The woman licked her lips. "There are twelve Warriors at the castle."

"That information I'm already privy to."

"There are six Druids at the castle, including three of our own who wouldn't leave."

"They were wiser than you. Who are the three?"

"Fiona, who is mother to wee Braden, and Reaghan."

Deirdre smiled. "Ah, Reaghan. The artifact you all protected so diligently?"

The woman slowly nodded. "Aye."

"I've been told she was dealt a mortal blow during the battle."

"Nay," the *mie* said with wide eyes.

Deirdre shrugged. "I will discover soon enough if Reaghan is dead. I learned a great deal about her while I occupied Mairi's mind."

The Druid's body began to tremble. "You were the cause of our elder spouting such hateful things."

"I was very convincing, was I not? Mairi's mind had weakened in her old age. If she'd had more magic, she might have been able to put up a little fight. It was almost too easy the way I was able to take over her mind and body."

The *mie* simply stared at Deirdre, as if only now realizing how dangerous Deirdre really was.

"Anyone else?" Deirdre asked.

"A man."

"Who?"

The woman's chin shook as tears gathered and spilled down her face. "His name was Monro. Malcolm Monro."

Deirdre closed her eyes. Malcolm was supposed to have been killed by her Warriors. Now she knew what happened to the Warriors she sent after the mortal. What she didn't know was who had saved Malcolm from the death she had ordered. But she would find out.

"Put her on the table," Deirdre ordered her wyrran.

The woman screamed and tried to jerk away, but she was no match for the strength of the wyrran. Besides, Deirdre had never told her she would be spared.

Once the woman was secured, Deirdre looked to the wyrran nearest her. "I want wyrran sent out separately to scout for Druids and any Warriors who might still be alive. They are to stay hidden, unseen by all. When they find a Druid or Warrior, they are to report back to me immediately. Especially if they find Broc."

The wyrran bowed his yellow head before he turned and raced out of the chamber. Deirdre turned to the woman, who was now a sobbing wretch.

"Now. Shall we begin?"

SEVEN

Sonya smoothed her hand down the pale blue gown she had donned and reached for the comb. Her hand still ached, so braiding her thick hair was going to be impossible.

She had awoken to find herself alone. Yet, she hadn't feared Broc had left. She knew he hadn't. He took his duties too seriously, and returning her to the castle was a priority.

A soft knock sounded, startling her. The door opened and Broc stepped inside. He closed the door behind him and leaned against it.

"Did you sleep well?" he asked.

Sonya turned her face away lest he see her embarrassment. She had dreamed of nothing but him all night. His lips on hers, his body pressed against her, his arms holding her tight. She had woken needy and aching. If he had been in the chamber, she wasn't sure what she would have done. All she had known was that she needed him with a hunger that went to her very soul.

"I did," she answered. "And you?"

"You know we doona need to sleep every night."

That got her attention. She ran her fingers along the small table as she walked around it. "So you stayed awake all night?"

"I kept watch."

"That's two nights you've not slept. You must sleep sometime."

He shrugged nonchalantly. "I'll rest when I need it."

Sonya blew out an exasperated breath and leaned against the wall. "So, what now? Is this where you try and talk me into returning with you?"

"This is where I try to convince you that MacLeod Castle is where you need to be."

"And if you cannot?"

His lips tilted in a lopsided grin. "Then I will continue to try and persuade you to my way of thinking."

She wanted to smile at him, to carry on as if everything was as it had been before the battle. But she couldn't. "What use am I to anyone if I don't have magic?"

"But you do," he argued. "I feel it."

There was such sincerity in his dark, compelling eyes that she believed him. How could she not? Broc would never lie about her magic. "All right. Then what use am I to anyone if I cannot *use* my magic?"

"You will use your magic again. Maybe once at MacLeod Castle with the other Druids you can discover what has happened."

Sonya looked at her injured hand. So much had changed in so little time. How could someone be so content in life and in the space of a heartbeat have everything crash around her?

"Did you no' tell Fallon the trees warned you to stay at MacLeod Castle?" Broc asked.

She nodded, unable to deny it. She didn't care why Fallon had told Broc. Obviously the eldest MacLeod brother had thought Broc needed to know.

Sonya swallowed and lifted her gaze to Broc. "I don't know why they wanted me at the castle, only that they said that's where I need to be."

"And you've always trusted them."

It was a statement, not a question. "Aye."

"Why question them now?"

Sonya smiled ruefully. "I'm not. I'm questioning myself."

He exhaled sharply and pushed off the door to slowly pace the confines of the chamber. "It's because of what I said to you, is it no'? It's about you finding me with Anice and learning that I knew her."

"It's partly why I ran, aye." There was no use hiding that information now. Broc already knew anyway. "Coupled with the fact I couldn't heal Reaghan when she was dying. If it wasn't for the spell she'd put on herself, she would be dead now."

"But she is alive." He stopped before her, daring her to deny his words.

Sonya had to tilt her head back to continue looking in his fathomless eyes. "A few days ago I knew who I was. I knew *what* I was. I knew the power of the magic inside me and all I could do. And then . . ."

She trailed off, unable to finish as she recalled the raw, heartbreaking agony she had felt when she could no longer call up her magic.

"And then Anice died," Broc concluded. "I know I hurt you by no' telling you the truth. I know I should have, but Anice wouldna know if she hadna stumbled upon me all those years ago."

Sonya had never been envious of her sister until she had seen her in Broc's arms. Not even knowing her sister was dead could halt the jealousy. It had been the complete suffering in Broc's voice and in his face which tore apart Sonya's heart.

"If it had been me instead of my sister who found you, would you have spoken to me as you did Anice?"

He stared at her, the muscle in his jaw jumping. "Nay."

"I see."

"You doona, Sonya."

"Then explain it."

His brow creased as his gaze dropped to the floor. "I . . . cannot."

Sonya hadn't thought she could hurt more than she already did, but those two simple words brought it all back and more. What had been so special about Anice that she lacked?

She would never know now.

Without a word, Sonya turned and walked out of the room. She needed to get out of the small chamber and away from Broc, away from the torment of wanting someone she couldn't have. Being that close to him was too much. It wasn't fair that she should endure such torture.

"Sonya," Broc said through clenched teeth as he grabbed her elbow.

She was brought to a stop with a firm jerk. Sonya pulled her arm from Broc's grasp. "You cannot hover around me all the time."

"I can and I will." His tone told her he didn't care what she wanted, he would do as he pleased.

"I'm going for a walk through the village. No harm can come to me from that."

Sonya didn't wait for him to answer. She spun around and walked down the corridor and descended the stairs. When she reached the bottom, she paused to look in the empty dining room.

"I'm glad to see ye up and about, milady," said a female voice.

Sonya shifted to see who spoke. The woman stood drying goblets behind the bar, a smile on her plump, round face. "Thank you," Sonya said.

"How is the wound on yer hand?"

"It's healing, Jean," Broc said as he came to stand behind Sonya.

Jean's smile grew. "Yer husband was verra worried about ye, lass. He didn't leave yer side."

Sonya didn't hear anything after "husband." Had Broc told everyone they were married? More frightening than that, why did a thrill race through Sonya at the prospect of being married to him?

He was a Warrior. Immortal. Dangerous.

Entirely too tempting.

"Jean cleaned your wound," Broc said, breaking the silence.

Sonya smiled at the woman. "Thank you. I'm feeling much better."

"Ah, but still a wee bit weary, I think. Ye shouldn't exert yerself, lass. Rest and allow yer body to mend."

"I will," Sonya said, and walked from the inn.

She didn't pause as she stepped outside. Sonya strolled leisurely through the village. Her body was still weak, but she needed the outdoors.

Four young lads raced down the street and parted to go around her. Sonya laughed at their antics as one gave her hair a soft tug. As she turned to watch them, she spotted Broc just steps behind her, a frown making him look angry and threatening.

Intent on ignoring him, Sonya immersed herself in the village. The sound of children laughing as they played helped to calm the resentment inside her. Women smiled at her, men nodded in greeting. It was as if she belonged there, as if she weren't a stranger.

Sonya stopped beside a cart full of vegetables. She picked up an apple and absently held it while she surveyed the village. She felt Broc move up beside her.

"This is only the second time I've been to a village," she said. "This is much larger than where I was raised. Things with the Dru . . . with my people were different."

"Magic is the difference," Broc whispered in her ear. "These people know nothing of Druids or Warriors. This is their life, and it's a hard one, Sonya."

She nodded and replaced the apple. "I know. It's just so different. Almost as if I walked into another world."

"You have in a way. You've been hidden all your life."

Sonya looked over her shoulder and into Broc's dark brown eyes, eyes that were mysterious, sultry, and altogether too fascinating. "How would you know how the others live? You've been in Deirdre's mountain for how long?"

He smiled tightly. "Lest you forget, I was able to get away from that cursed mound of rock frequently."

"Nay, you were referring to before Deirdre took you. Weren't you?"

His gaze slid away. "Aye."

For all the time Sonya had spent in the company of Warriors at MacLeod Castle, none of them spoke about their lives before their gods were unbound. At least, they didn't to her.

She found herself immensely curious about Broc's life before he became a Warrior. "Will you tell me?"

"What is the point in it?" he asked.

Sonya felt more than heard the hurt. "My days were spent in the forest or swimming in the loch when I wasn't learning mag . . . who I am," she amended.

"That was—is—a good life."

"But nothing like yours was."

Broc sighed and guided her away from the prying ears of the vendor to continue their stroll. "Nay, Sonya. It was nothing like mine. Until Deirdre, I never knew there was another, secret world living alongside mine."

"Was your world like this village?" she asked. She couldn't help herself. She had to know. "Did you live in a village much like this one?"

One side of his mouth tilted into a smile as he clasped his hands behind his back. "Nay, but one was nearby. I was there often enough causing trouble. My favorite thing to do was play jests on the merchants."

"Did you ever get caught?"

He chuckled, his eyes crinkling with laughter. "Oh, aye. Most every time, though I did learn to run away quicker."

Sonya stumbled when she caught sight of Broc's smile. His hand reached out to steady her, but she knew nothing would ever steady her heart again. Not after seeing something that transformed his face from handsome to heartstoppingly dazzling.

Broc's smile had been full of good memories, full of mirth and happiness, and it had changed his already striking face into one that took her breath away. He was an arresting male with his height, his long, fair hair, and his dark eyes, and his brooding only made him more so.

But the smile . . . the smile showed Sonya another side of Broc, a side she longed to learn more about.

They walked the rest of the village in silence. When they reached the end, Sonya turned to start back toward the inn when Broc pushed her up against a cottage.

His hard body pressed hers against the cottage wall, shielding her. Instinctively she braced her hands against his chest. Beneath her palms she could feel the strong, steady beat of his heart and the taut, hard muscles.

Fire licked beneath her skin, heating her blood and causing her heart to race erratically. It was always so when Broc touched her, and the more she stayed near him, the more her body yearned for his touch.

Sonya inhaled his scent of wind, of warm, sunny

skies. She waited for him to caress her, to kiss her as she had dreamed of him doing since the first moment she had seen him standing outside Quinn's chamber.

She could feel the heat of his skin through the tunic he wore. How she longed to be able to touch his bare flesh, to trace the line of muscles she felt beneath her hands, muscles she had seen countless times as he stood bare-chested before her in his Warrior form.

Slowly, Sonya raised her gaze from Broc's chest to his face. He wasn't looking at her as she had expected. His dark eyes weren't filled with passion and desire.

It was the way he stared off into the woods which told her something had alerted him to danger. He was there to protect her, to ensure she returned to MacLeod Castle without incident. Regardless of what Broc wanted, he would see to her safety first.

"What is it?" she whispered.

"Wyrran."

EIGHT

It was all Broc could do not to lean down and take Sonya's lips. Her hands on his chest, her body pressed so tightly against his. It was too much.

The yearning, the hunger for her was irresistible.

He had thought of nothing but protecting her when he'd caught sight of the yellow-skinned wyrran. But the moment their bodies had touched, Broc's need to stroke, to learn, to claim Sonya warred with that of protection.

Rage bubbled within him, rage he knew came from his god. Yet, he couldn't control it. He wanted to hunt the wyrran and rip it limb from limb for disturbing his time with Sonya.

"Are you sure?" Sonya murmured.

"Unfortunately. I couldna shake the feeling last night that something was near. Now I know what it was."

He could sense her fear by the way she shook. Her fingers, which had lain so gently on his chest, now dug into his skin as she tensed.

"Did it see us?"

"Most certainly," he replied grimly.

"Where are they?"

"It. I sense there is only one at the moment, and I doona know where it went. I also doona wish to leave you to find out."

"But you need to," she said, and tilted her face to him.

Broc shook his head as he gazed into her amber eyes. "I'm no' leaving you. There's no use arguing. It would be exactly what it would want so you would be left alone."

"Take me back to the inn. I'll be safe there."

"How will you protect yourself?" he demanded. He hated how gruff and entirely too harsh his voice was, but the thought of Sonya in the hands of Deirdre made his blood turn to ice. "You say you cannot use your magic, so what will you use?"

She lowered her eyes and shrugged. "I have nothing. No magic, no skill with a weapon. You've made your point."

"My point is to no' make you feel inferior. My point is that I cannot—and willna—leave you alone while there are wyrran about."

"Then how are you to kill it?"

Broc took a deep breath and took a step away from Sonya. "I doona know. Yet. But I will."

"In order to kill it, you're either going to have to take me with you or leave me alone in the inn. Those are your only choices."

He hated that she was right. Hated it more that the wyrran—and Deirdre—had put him in this position. But he'd always known it would come to this.

His life mattered not, but Sonya was another matter entirely. He didn't fear death, only that he wouldn't live long enough to ensure Sonya was protected at MacLeod Castle.

"There's another choice," he said as he thought of the Warriors and Druids. "We leave for MacLeod Castle. Immediately."

"And leave the wyrran to do whatever it wants with this village or another village it comes across? You know yourself what Deirdre has sent them to do."

Broc ran a hand down his face and turned to the forest. He knew all too well what the wyrran were capable of. He'd seen their destructive power on his family, had seen the death that lay in their wake after they swept through a village.

Could he leave this one behind? Did he dare to let it go on the chance it might not hurt anyone?

He knew he couldn't.

He put his hands on his hips and nodded. "All right. I'll kill it. Then we return to the castle. I doona know what is happening there and they could need me."

She hesitated for a brief moment before she said, "Agreed."

Broc curled his hands into fists as he felt his claws begin to grow. He wanted to hunt the wyrran straightaway. The sooner he killed it, the sooner he could get Sonya back to the castle.

And the sooner he could put some much-needed distance between them.

If the past few days had showed him anything, it was that being near her, alone with her, was testing the limits of his control. Which were fast unraveling.

"We need to return to the inn," Broc said as he took hold of her arm. "Act as if nothing is wrong, but be on guard."

"How did it find us so quickly?"

Broc kept his eyes moving around the village, looking for any signs a wyrran was still near. "I doona know. With Deirdre, almost anything is possible. After seeing her nearly take back control of Isla, it's obvious her magic has been restored."

"So she's looking for us."

"She's looking for the Warriors who were once allied with her and who are no' dead. I doona imagine there are many left. We killed most in the battle."

"The battle where everyone thought Deirdre had died," Sonya mumbled.

Broc opened the door to the inn and ushered Sonya inside. He gave a nod to Jean who still stood behind the counter, and walked Sonya up the stairs and into their chamber.

Once the door was shut and bolted behind him, Broc strode to the window. "Deirdre wanted the MacLeods before. She's no' accustomed to being betrayed. She will hunt and kill anyone associated with the MacLeods in retaliation."

"Including you."

"Aye. I know more than most. The only Warrior who was closer to Deirdre than me was William, and he was killed."

The bed creaked, signaling Sonya had sat. "I shouldn't have fought against returning to the castle. We'd be safe now."

Broc turned to Sonya. "This is no' your fault. We've seen the wyrran, and I will kill it. I willna allow it to harm anyone."

"And the others? You know there are others out there. You cannot kill them all."

"I can kill most. Finding them is no' the problem. It's getting to them before they can do any mischief."

Her amber gaze seemed to see right through him, as if she knew he longed to unleash his god and spread his wings to fly through the night, tracking each wyrran to kill it.

Warring with the need for the wyrran's death was his growing and ever-present longing for Sonya.

Just being alone in the room with her was the sweetest kind of torment. Her lavender scent made him think of wildflowers and forests. Her scent was on his clothes, on the linens of the bed, and forever in his memory.

With three steps he could close the distance between them. He could cover her lips with his, sinking into her kiss. Slowly. Thoroughly.

Completely.

To have her taste on his tongue, to know the essence of her, was what he dreamed about. Everything about her was magical and utterly breathtaking.

One of the best days of his long, exhaustive life was when she used her magic so he could hear the trees talk to her. It had been an experience that touched his very soul. An experience that only made him want her even more, if that were possible.

No one had shared anything so personal, so beautiful with him before. He hadn't mattered enough to anyone. Yet, Sonya had given him that small gift because she had wanted to share something with him.

He still didn't understand why she had chosen him, but he cherished it.

Her head cocked to the side as her red hair fell over her shoulder in a cascade of curls. "What are you thinking when you look at me like that?"

"I was thinking about when you allowed me to hear the trees. Why did you do that?"

She shrugged and picked at her skirts. "I'm not sure. You were there and I wanted you to hear them, to hear how lovely they were. How important they are to me."

"Everyone knows how important the trees are to you."

"Yet, you seemed surprised I would allow you to hear them. Why?"

Broc smiled wryly. "Do you forget where I was all those years? Do you think there was any kindness inside Cairn Toul?"

"How old are you?"

He blinked at her sudden change of topic. But he

didn't hesitate to tell her. "Two hundred and seventy-five since I was turned immortal."

"All of it spent with Deirdre?"

"All but the past few weeks, aye." He hated talking about his time with Deirdre, but since it took up most of his life, he had nothing else to talk about. And he knew Sonya was curious.

Sonya's tongue peeked out to wet her lips. "Then I'm glad I showed you the wonders of the trees."

Maybe it was the light in her amber eyes. Maybe it was the way she looked at him, but Broc almost went to her and took the kiss he had been fantasizing about.

She cleared her throat and gave a weak smile. "So, what do we do now? Wait?"

Broc glanced out the window as he tried to think of a reason a wyrran would be at the village. He felt no magic other than Sonya's, so the wyrran couldn't be here for a Druid. Unless there were Druids nearby.

"I'm going to go see how many wyrran are about. I want you to stay here."

"I will," she promised. "How many do you think there are?"

"If there are several, they've been sent to find someone and bring him back to Deirdre."

"And if there's only one?"

Broc blew out a breath. "That's another matter entirely. That means the wyrran was sent to scout for something or someone. Once it finds what it's searching for, it'll return to Deirdre."

"Who will then send more wyrran," Sonya finished.

"Aye."

"You think there's only one, don't you?"

He wouldn't lie to her, but how he wished she wouldn't figure things out so quickly. "I doona want to say until I've had a look around."

"Just tell me your thoughts. Please."

He would rather go look first, but Sonya was having none of that. "I think there's just one."

"I see," she murmured. "Then you had better go after it."

It wasn't yet noon. It would be easier if he waited until nightfall so he could fly, but waiting would allow the wyrran to put a great distance between them.

"I'll be fine," Sonya said, as if sensing his reluctance. "I'll stay here. In this chamber."

Broc looked around for a weapon—any weapon—he could give her. But there was nothing. As a Warrior, he didn't need a sword or other blade. His claws and superior strength and speed were all the weapons he needed.

Sonya watched Broc pace around the chamber as if he were searching for something. He stopped and glared at the door before he mumbled something about returning shortly and left.

She was too curious about where Broc had gone to be able to relax. What had him so troubled? What could propel him out of the chamber so quickly?

It hadn't been wyrran. That she was sure of. What, then?

Her answer presented itself when, a few moments later the door opened and Broc reentered. He walked to her and held out a short scabbard which held a dagger.

Broc slowly pulled the weapon from its sheath, and Sonya found herself staring at a wicked, deadly-looking curved blade that came to a vicious point.

"This is for you," Broc said.

Sonya took it, surprised to find that the dagger felt lighter than she had imagined. She studied, with astonishment, the detailed knot work etched into the wooden handle of the weapon. "Where did you find this?"

"I had Jean tell me where I could purchase a weapon for you."

"You realize what's on the hilt?"

He gave a small jerk of his head. "It's one of the reasons I chose it. Its light, and though the blade isna as long as a sword's, it's longer than some daggers."

Sonya couldn't stop looking at the weapon. "I'll keep it with me always. Thank you, Broc."

"If I didna have to leave, there'd be no need for you to have a blade. I'm no' sure you should thank me."

She took his hand in hers and gave it a small squeeze. "No one has ever given me anything before."

His warm fingers closed over hers. She lost herself in his dark eyes, wondering, wishing she knew what thoughts ran through his mind. There were times, like then, that she thought he might want her.

That he might desire her.

Then he would blink and it would disappear, as if she imagined all of it.

"I'll return as soon as I can. The wyrran willna have gone far. Hopefully I'll find it, kill it, and return before dark."

"And if you don't?"

"Jean already knows I have to leave. She's going to keep an eye on you. There are a few men she uses to guard the inn, and they will be here tonight."

Sonya nodded absently. "You will return."

"If for some reason I doona, here's coin," he said, and handed her a small bag. "Use it to buy a horse and men to ride with you to the MacLeod's.

"You'll return."

He stared at her a moment. "Aye, but just in case. Promise me you'll do as I've asked."

"I promise."

Sonya couldn't imagine Broc not returning, but then

again if Deirdre was out for revenge, Broc would be one of the first on her list.

He released her hand and turned away. Sonya stood and followed him. She didn't want him to leave, but she knew he had no choice. He had to kill the wyrran before it reported back to Deirdre.

"You will be careful," she said.

Broc turned to her with a smile. "I'm a Warrior, Sonya. It will take more than a wyrran to kill me."

"But you can be killed."

"No' today. No' by a wyrran," he said, confidence filling his voice.

Sonya blew out a breath and shrugged. "I will worry until you come back."

"Then I will return as soon as I can."

She had left MacLeod Castle to be alone and as far from Broc as she could get. Now the thought of being by herself and without him terrified her.

How odd that things could change so suddenly in such a short amount of time.

"Doona fear for me. I've lived nearly three centuries avoiding Deirdre and her machinations. I will survive a few hours hunting this wyrran."

Sonya believed him, and to prove it, she forced a smile. "I will wait and dine with you for supper."

"I would like that."

When he took a step closer, her heart began to pound. He lifted his hand to her face, making her breath catch in her lungs. His fingers slid into her hair and around her neck.

Sonya loved the feel of his calloused fingers, the way his large hand was gentle yet insistent when he touched her. She enjoyed looking into his eyes, seeing the emotions shift and fill his dark depths before he could close himself off to her.

Ever so slowly, he leaned toward her. His eyes held all the passion, all the yearning, she had ever hoped to see. His forehead touched hers, their breaths mingling as time halted.

Excitement blossomed and built within her, drowning her in the fervor of the desire that grew between them. It was palpable, tangible. Real.

She was afraid to move, afraid to speak lest she break whatever held her and Broc. For once, he was allowing her to see his feelings.

Her skin quivered and begged for more as his thumb stroked her cheek. He brought her closer so their bodies touched, brushed together.

Sonya's hands gripped his waist, unsure of what was going to happen and unwilling to release him.

She couldn't take her eyes off his mouth, couldn't stop thinking of kissing him. Of being kissed *by* him.

Then his hand lifted her chin and his lips covered hers. For an instant Sonya couldn't breathe, and then she was flooded with a whirlwind of sensation.

His soft, warm lips were firm as he kissed her, coaxing her closer, ever closer. Her arms wound around his waist of their own accord. And when his tongue skimmed along her lips, begging entry, Sonya never thought to refuse him.

The first stroke of his tongue against hers, the first wickedly intoxicating taste of him, was her undoing.

The kiss intensified, taking her deeper and deeper into the passion that had been calling for her, a passion she knew could only be with Broc.

Desire grew, swelled as Broc's arms tightened around her, holding her against him. Passion left a scorching trail through her as it wound in her blood and came to rest in the pit of her stomach, to build as their kisses deepened, the fire growing between them until it was an inferno.

All too soon, he ended the kiss and lifted his head. For long moments he stared into her eyes. Sonya waited for him to speak or to touch her.

His thumb grazed her bottom lip softly.

And then he was gone.

NINE

Broc leaned against the door in the hallway and closed his eyes. He shouldn't have given in and kissed Sonya. The sweet, blissful taste of her was in his mouth and on his tongue. Her scent was on him driving him wild with a need so primal, so primitive Broc shook with it.

The feel of her hands as they looped around his waist and her curves pressed against him, her passion as she returned his kiss. All of it would be his undoing.

He wanted nothing more than to walk back into the chamber and claim another kiss. He longed to kiss her through the night, learning her body and hearing her sighs of pleasure as he made love to her again and again.

But he couldn't. He had a wyrran to kill.

Broc's eyes opened and he felt his fangs fill his mouth. If he couldn't relieve his body, he would appease his god. It was time for death, time for blood. Anyone who dared to try and take Sonya would die.

Viciously. Violently. Brutally.

Broc pushed away from the door and made his feet walk away from Sonya. The sooner he left, the sooner he could return. The sooner he would have to confront her and the kiss they shared.

He walked out of the inn and into the forest with long, purposeful strides. No one dared to get in his way. As soon as he knew nobody could see him, Broc removed his tunic and tossed it on the limb of a tree.

Then, he unleashed his god.

His skin turned the darkest blue as claws sprouted from his fingertips and wings erupted from his back. Broc spread his wings and stretched his shoulders.

He might not like the god inside him, but he took pleasure in his speed and power, and certainly his ability to fly.

Broc felt the snarl of his god inside him, knew Poraxus wanted blood and death as much as Broc did to protect Sonya. And with Poraxus' gift, the wyrran wouldn't get far.

With a deep breath, Broc opened his power and began to hunt for the wyrran. In an instant he picked up the trail. It was like a thread glowing brightly in a world of gray.

Though he wanted to take to the skies, Broc couldn't chance being seen yet. So he ran, his wings clasped tight against him, ready for flight.

Once Broc caught the wyrran's trail, he would keep it until he found the vile creature. The beast was as fast as Broc, but it had no idea Broc was chasing it. Once it did, the wyrran would use all of its wily tricks to try and escape.

But nothing could elude Broc.

The silence of the chamber following Broc's departure was deafening. Sonya let out a shaky breath and ran her tongue over her lips.

They felt swollen. And sensitive. She'd had no idea kissing could feel so good or make her body come alive as if it had been sleeping for ages. One touch of Broc's mouth to hers and everything had changed, forever altered.

She didn't know why Broc had kissed her, and she didn't care. For those few moments he had wanted her. That's all that mattered.

Sonya walked to the bed and took the dagger in hand. She wasn't sure what to do with it. Broc hadn't showed her how to use it as Lucan had shown Cara, but Sonya would do her best regardless.

She buckled the scabbard around her waist and stroked the hilt as she sat. All she could do was wait. She tried not to worry. Broc was a Warrior, immortal and deadly in any attack. Yet, Sonya had seen what the wyrran could do. They were rarely alone since they preferred to attack in groups.

Broc had assured her the wyrran he'd seen was alone. How long before it joined others? And would Broc be able to fight them all? He knew them better than anyone after spending so much time in Cairn Toul.

Sonya rose and began to pace the chamber. She wished she had something to occupy her time. Too many hours were ahead of her to sit idly and let her mind race with possibilities.

She yanked open the door and paused. Broc had made her promise to stay in the chamber. But it wasn't as if she were going outside. She only wanted to go downstairs.

It was only for a moment. Nothing would happen while she was still inside the inn.

Her decision made, Sonya walked from the room. She found Jean behind the counter, though this time the portly woman was pouring ale into goblets.

"What can I do for ye, milady?" Jean asked with a smile. "I hope ye doona plan on leaving the inn. Yer husband made it clear you were to stay inside."

Sonya smiled as she imagined the conversation between Broc and Jean. "I'm not leaving. I have several long hours ahead of me. I wondered if there was anything I could help you with?"

Jean chuckled and reached for another goblet before yelling at a woman to take the ones filled into the dining room and the men waiting for them.

"Lady Sonya—"

"Please," Sonya interrupted her. "Call me Sonya."

Jean raised her brows, not believing a word. "I know nobility when I see it, milady, and Lord Broc is certainly nobility. As I was sayin', I wouldna give ye any of my work."

Sonya was still reeling with the notion of Broc as nobility, but now that Jean had mentioned it, there was a certain aspect about Broc which was different from other men. He had the same bearing as Fallon, who led the Warriors. But Broc's confidence went beyond even that.

"I cannot have idle hands," Sonya argued. "I will go daft as I await Broc's return. There has to be something I can do. Is there mending to be done?"

Jean set down the now full goblet and braced her hands on the bar as she looked Sonya over from head to toe. "Ye do look a wee bit better than this morning. The sewing willna tax your strength, but it will keep ye busy. If ye really want something to do, I'll bring it up to ye when I can."

"Thank you," Sonya said with a smile.

Sonya returned to the chamber and blew out a perturbed breath. She bolted the door behind her and went to the window. Being on the second floor gave her a good vantage point when peering out over the rest of the village. But not even being atop the rest of the inn would help her if the wyrran wanted inside.

They had claws, as all Warriors did, but the wyrran also had claws on their feet, which they used to help them scale walls and ceilings.

Sonya shuddered as she thought of the huge yellow eyes and the mouthful of sharp teeth that its lips couldn't close over. They were small, yellow creatures, about the height of a child, but they were as deadly as a Warrior.

In some ways more so because the only person the wyrran served was Deirdre. Her will was theirs, and nothing stood in the way of the wyrran completing a command made by Deirdre.

And Deirdre had a never-ending supply of wyrran. She created the wyrran, so when they were killed, she simply made more.

Sonya sank into the chair, her gaze focused on the forest and rolling foothills of the mountains. Broc was somewhere out there. So were the wyrran. And Deirdre. How long would it be before Deirdre began to seek revenge?

Or did she already?

Everyone said Deirdre never left her mountain, but Sonya had a suspicion that Deirdre's near death by the MacLeods had changed everything.

And Sonya feared the "everything" would be the world as they knew it.

TEN

Broc came to a halt when he sensed more than one wyrran near. He was nearly upon the first he'd been tracking, but somehow there were others. The glowing thread he saw had multiplied by six.

He cursed silently. It was still too light to take to the skies, where he could move above them for an attack. There would come a time in the not-too-distant future when mortals would know what he was. Until then, he would do his best to keep what he was a secret.

Broc crept downhill through the trees until he came to the edge of the forest. A half a league away was the beginning of a valley between the mountain they were on and another.

Though Broc had never heard the wyrran speak, obviously they could communicate with each other, which was evident by the way they stood together, their heads and hands moving.

Broc moved from behind the tree and walked out of the forest. It was but a heartbeat before a wyrran noticed him. The seven turned as one to him.

He grinned as he continued toward them. "You seem rather out of place, I think."

One opened its mouth and screeched.

The piercing sound didn't have the effect on Broc as they'd wished. He'd spent too long in their company.

"Was that supposed to frighten me? It didna," he said, his voice soft and casual. "Now, you realize I will have to kill all of you."

This time they all shrieked, the combined sound causing Broc's sensitive ears to ring. He jumped straight into the air and spread his wings as the seven attacked. Broc circled above the wyrran, just out of their reach as they leapt as high as they could, reaching for him.

Once they were clumped together, he folded his wings and dove toward them. He caught the first wyrran with the tip of his wing, severing the creature's head from its body while Broc's claws impaled another.

Broc flew the screaming beast toward the forest and slammed the wyrran against a tree. The impact shattered the wyrran's head.

Before Broc could yank out his claws, something vaulted on to his back, tearing and slashing at his wings. Broc landed on the ground with a roar of fury. He gave a jerk of his wing and sent the wyrran tumbling.

The remaining five wyrran began to circle him. Broc kept his wings outstretched, waiting for one of the creatures to move.

This time they changed their tactics. Instead of racing at him together, one sprang on him from behind and began clawing at Broc where his wings connected to his back.

The pain was terrible as the wyrran's claws cut through flesh and muscle. Broc could feel the blood spill down his back in rivulets. No matter how he tried to grab the wyrran, it was always just out of reach.

Two other wyrran each grabbed one of Broc's wings and tried to rip them from his body. When that didn't work, they began to shred his wings.

Broc's wings weren't made of feathers but instead resembled those of a bat. They were thick and healed as quickly as the rest of him. But his wings were more responsive than any other part of him. Each cut was like a thousand blades piercing him.

He stepped backward into the trees before he folded his wings and then snapped them out. The unsuspecting wyrran couldn't hang on and slammed into trees before they fell away.

With the other wyrran still on his back, Broc backed against a tree until the creature was caught between Broc and the tree trunk. He applied steady pressure to the wyrran's thin body. Almost immediately he could hear the creature's bones shattering one by one.

The wyrran was so desperate to get free, it forgot about tearing Broc's wings, which allowed Broc to grab hold of it.

Broc flipped it over his head and smashed it to the ground. He spun and jammed his knee into the wyrran's chest, then used his claws to sever its head.

He jumped up, ready to face more wyrran. Only to realize they had gone. All four had departed in different directions. They had distracted him in order to get to Deirdre, knowing that at least one of them would die in the process.

Broc launched himself into the air, his wings catching the wind and propelling him higher. No longer did he care who saw him. He had to find the four wyrran before they reached Deirdre.

It didn't take long for Broc to locate the first. He made quick work of killing the creature before he was back in the air, flying to the next.

The second wyrran was crafty, but not enough to evade Broc. It took longer than Broc would have liked to pull the damned creature out of the hollow tree where it was hiding and kill it.

Every moment wasted allowed the other two wyrran

to get closer to Deirdre. By the time Broc was flying toward the third wyrran, the sun had begun to set. With his heart pounding and his god demanding more blood, Broc flew faster.

The third wyrran was even cleverer than the last when he decided to duck into a cave in the mountains. Broc landed on the side of the mountain and glanced inside the cave. The ceiling was low, leaving no room for his wings, which arched over his head.

Broc tamped down his god, leaving only his claws and fangs visible before he ducked into the cave. The tunnel branched off several times, but Broc wasn't worried. It was only a matter of time before he caught the creature.

Except that moment dragged into hours as the wyrran took Broc through cave after cave and tunnel after tunnel. Being inside the mountain reminded Broc too much of Cairn Toul, except these stones didn't ooze with evil.

Broc was tired of hunting the wyrran and eager to catch the third. Yet, the farther back in the mountain he traveled, the lower the ceiling became, until Broc was on his hands and knees. The wyrran was putting distance between them as well.

But Broc wasn't about to give up. He would catch the creature.

The slope of the cave continued to plunge until Broc was on his stomach, scooting across the jagged rock, which cut into his skin and tore his breeches. He could see a small opening ahead with his enhanced vision.

The opening was so tiny, Broc had to scrunch his shoulders to get them through. Once his arms were free again, he was able to look around before pulling the rest of his body out. He was in a cavern with a bottom like a bowl. Broc used his hands to push himself farther out of the opening, then he was able to roll out of the gap.

He came to his feet in a rush and glanced around. There was no other way out. The wyrran was in the cavern, and it would be its tomb.

Out of the corner of Broc's eye, he caught movement. He turned just in time to see the wyrran scurrying through another opening.

Broc raced to the side and reached into the hole. He was able to latch onto the wyrran's ankle. For the next few moments Broc spent his time yanking the squirming creature out of the opening before flinging it in the center of the cavern.

The wyrran leapt to its feet and issued a long shriek. It echoed through the cavern, eliminating any other noise. Broc's rage had built with each cave he had walked through until he didn't hold back his god anymore.

He seized the wyrran's neck with one hand and punched it with the other. The wyrran clawed at Broc's arms and chest, trying desperately to get free. Broc bellowed as he ripped the wyrran's head off and tossed the lifeless body to the ground.

With his breaths coming in great gasps, Broc rushed to the opening he had pulled the wyrran from. It was larger than the one he had come through, making it easier to maneuver. He quickly crawled into the opening. Once he was back in the tunnels, he navigated his way out on the opposite side of the mountain.

Broc exited the last cave and stared at the moon with a grimace. He had lost all track of time while in the mountain, which is exactly what the wyrran had wanted. Broc thought of Sonya, of her beautiful smile and amazing amber eyes. It helped to calm his fury enough to find the last wyrran.

With his god once more unleashed, Broc took to the air. The chilly night wind helped to cool his heated flesh. He glided through the mountains, taking him farther and farther from Sonya.

As much as he hated that, Broc knew he had to kill the last wyrran. Once it was dead, he and Sonya could make their way to MacLeod Castle without Deirdre knowing where they were.

Broc flew over mountain after mountain. He wasn't surprised to find how far the wyrran had come. What stunned him was that the creature had caught up with others.

He could either engage the twelve wyrran he circled from high above, which could take hours. Especially if they split up the way the last ones did.

Or Broc could return to Sonya and get her to MacLeod Castle that night.

Broc didn't hesitate in returning to Sonya.

Sonya put her hands at the base of her back and stretched in the chair. She had no idea how many clothes she had mended. Jean would bring in a few at a time, returning later to bring more and take the ones that were finished.

It helped to pass the day, but as soon as the sun had set, Sonya couldn't concentrate on anything. Every sound she heard she prayed it was Broc.

When Jean brought a tray of food for the evening meal, Sonya couldn't eat. She had wanted to wait for Broc. But as the hours ticked by, Sonya couldn't shake the dread that filled her. Now every sound made her wonder if it was a wyrran coming for her.

Sonya set aside the tunic she had been sewing and rose to walk to the table. Her stomach growled in hunger. She knew she needed to eat. If Broc didn't return by morning, she would be on her way back to the castle. And she would need her strength.

She began to slowly put the food in her mouth, though she tasted nothing. Her mind was filled with Broc. Where was he? What was taking so long? Had Deirdre captured him? Was he injured? Even though his god healed him of injuries, she had learned there was something a Warrior's god couldn't heal—magic.

So many questions. Each one churned her stomach until it felt as if she would become ill.

With as much food in her belly as she could manage, Sonya stood before the window, her arms wrapped around her. It was well after midnight. The sky was clear, and no matter how hard she looked, she didn't see Broc.

Her window overlooked the village, but there were too many shadows for her to know if wyrran were waiting to attack. Below, she could see the men Jean had stationed to guard the inn. Their presence should have made Sonya feel better. But they didn't. She worried about them dying in an attack.

The fire in the hearth had died down to nothing but embers, and Sonya had no intention of building it back up. It allowed others to see into her chamber when she wanted to see out. If she was going to be attacked, she would be prepared for it.

After an hour of standing, Sonya moved the chair closer to the window so she could still maintain her position there. Fatigue and anxiety weighed heavily upon her, but she refused to give in.

Broc had risked his life going after the wyrran. The least she could do was stay awake through the night. She could rest once she was back at MacLeod Castle. If she made it back.

A shiver of dread raced down her spine.

How she wished she could use magic to talk to the trees once more. They could tell her where Broc was and if he was in trouble. The trees would also alert her if any wyrran were near. But both were difficult to do with her magic gone.

The trees had always been there to guide her in troubled times. Now, she had only herself, and that didn't inspire much confidence.

She had no magic to protect—or heal—herself, and she knew nothing about using the dagger Broc had given her. She was useless in defending herself, but she couldn't allow that to take away her focus in getting to MacLeod Castle.

If Broc had been taken, the others would free him just as they had freed Quinn.

Sonya gazed longingly at the forest. She didn't hear the whispers on the wind as she used to. Those whispers were the trees communicating with each other, and to her, one of the few who could understand them. Ever since she could remember, she had heard those whispers and felt the comfort of the trees as they watched over her.

All was quiet now, and it saddened her. Would she have to go through life without ever hearing the trees again? The thought left her feeling empty. Barren. Meaningless.

Was this how others felt? To those who had never experienced magic, they would never know the thrill of feeling it move inside them or the satisfaction that came from using it for good. They would never know how magic became a part of a Druid, much like breathing or eating.

But she would.

Magic had defined her life. Could she face her uncertain future without that magic? How did she even begin to try?

Sonya unwrapped her wound and stared at the cut. No longer was it tinged green with pus coming out of it. It was healing, but slowly. If there was still magic inside her as Broc said, she should be able to use it.

"Let's see," Sonya murmured.

Before, she hadn't even had to think of healing herself. It just happened. Maybe now she would have to concentrate as she did when she healed others.

Sonya held her right hand over her left and closed her eyes. She imagined her magic gathering inside her, imagined it building and coming up her arm and then being released through her hand as it had done countless times throughout her life.

But no matter how hard she focused, no matter how much she wanted to feel her magic rush through her body, there was nothing.

Tears spilled down Sonya's cheeks. She dropped her hand and stared in misery at her wound. She couldn't grip anything without tremendous pain, and it would be weeks yet before she could move her hand normally.

She had secretly hoped Broc had been right, that she did still have some magic. But she had just proven she didn't. No amount of wishing or praying would return it, and the only good thing was that it meant she wouldn't be in danger of being taken by Deirdre.

Without magic, she was insignificant. In more ways than one.

Sonya let out a shaky breath and leaned her head against the side of the window. The idea of no longer being able to call herself a Druid left a hole inside her, a hole she knew would never be filled.

She let her thoughts drift, and as usual they turned to Broc. He had filled her life so fully, so completely in just a few weeks that it seemed as if he had always been there.

When in fact he had. He had seen her grow from a small baby to the woman she was today. She wondered how she looked through his eyes. Sonya imagined throughout his nearly three hundred years he had seen many beautiful woman, and probably loved several of them.

She could mean very little in the grand scheme of things in a Warrior's life.

The door to her room suddenly burst open. Sonya jumped to her feet, her good hand on the hilt of the dagger. Until her eyes landed on the one man who could make her forget everything but him.

The sight of Broc sent her running to him. His arms wrapped around her as he held her against his bare chest, crushing her. But she didn't care. He was alive. He was with her.

"I was so worried," she said.

"I returned as soon as I could."

Sonya pulled out of his arms and looked over his body. His breeches were ripped. Dried blood coated his body as well as his breeches. "What happened?"

"There's no time. We need to leave."

Sonya took one look at him and knew Broc needed rest, but as a Warrior he would never admit it. This was his third night without sleep, which wasn't usually something that troubled a Warrior; but with the injuries he had sustained, he had no choice.

"Nay," she said. He didn't move with the same quickness as normal. He was sluggish and fighting to keep his eyes focused. Whatever had happened, he needed a respite. Yet, she knew he would argue against it. "I need a few hours of sleep first."

Broc shut the door behind him and walked to his

satchel by the bed. "I'll be flying you, so you can sleep on the way."

"Not until dawn."

"Sonya," he ground out as he wearily lifted his head to her. "Doona argue with me."

"A few hours rest, Broc. For you and me. You've evidently battled the wyrran. You need to eat as well."

He scoffed at her words and pulled out his last tunic from the satchel. "I'm a Warrior. I can go days without food or sleep."

"After you've been injured? It is just a few hours until dawn. Give me at least an hour. You can eat and tell me what has happened."

He raked a hand through his hair. "They'll be coming. I couldna get them all. By now, one of the wyrran has returned to Deirdre and told her where we are. If we doona leave now, we put everyone in danger."

Sonya fisted her hands to keep them from shaking. She could try to argue with Broc that she had no magic, and therefore was of no use to Deirdre, but she knew he wouldn't leave without her. Sleep would have to wait.

"There's a bowl of water. Wash the blood from you while I get some food and then we can leave."

He gave a simple nod and Sonya headed to the door. She gathered as much food as she could find and hurried back to their chamber.

"Do you have everything you need?" Broc asked as she entered their room.

"Aye. Eat this bread," she said as she handed him a portion she had torn from the loaf she'd taken. "Just take a bit or two before we leave."

He finished washing the blood from his upper body and tossed aside the towel before he turned to her. "I'm sorry. I thought I could get all the wyrran, but despite those years in the mountain, I never realized how intelligent the wyrran were."

"What happened?" she asked as she guided him into a chair and shoved the food at him.

"They split up." He fingered the bread a moment before he finally brought a piece of it to his mouth. "I tracked down one after the other, and each took longer because they were clever and hid in places I had trouble getting into. They kept me following them, kept just out of reach to give the others time to get ahead."

Sonya swallowed around the lump in her throat. She had been right to be worried. It was as dire as she had assumed it would be.

"I killed all but one," he continued. "By the time I found it, another eleven had met up with the creature. I knew I didna have time to kill all of them. I had to return to you."

"Eat, Broc. All will be well."

As she watched him, she saw the rage, the craze which could sometimes overtake a Warrior if he gave into the fury of the god inside him.

How close was he to losing himself to his god forever? She didn't know, but she wasn't going to let that happen without a fight.

He was too important. To everyone. But most especially to her.

ELEVEN

The bread was delicious, like an explosion of flavor in his mouth. Broc hadn't realized until he began to eat just how hungry he was.

He could go without food, but he was glad Sonya had forced him to eat the small bit of bread. Though, he knew he was taking a great risk by resting those few precious moments.

All he had been able to think about as he raced to the inn was Sonya. He feared the wyrran had already reached her. He hadn't wasted a moment in using his power to discern that she was right where he had left her.

Yet, he didn't feel true relief until he opened the door to the chamber and saw her.

When she had come running into his arms, it was the greatest moment of his life. Her body had trembled as he held her, and though he knew his hold was too tight, he couldn't release her. It felt too good, too right to have her in his arms.

Broc finished the last of his bread and stood. Sonya's amber eyes were filled with trepidation, but mixed with it was determination.

"We need to leave," he said. "It isna safe here anymore."

She nodded slowly. "I know."

"We'll travel on foot. At least until we get far enough

away from the village that no one will see me release my god. I'll fly the rest of the way."

"How far is it to MacLeod Castle?"

"I can get us there quick enough," he answered.

Sonya adjusted the dagger at her waist and grabbed the satchel. She slid the strap over her head and faced him. "I'm ready."

Broc smiled and took her hand. "Everything is going to be all right."

"All of this is my fault. Had I not left, the wyrran wouldn't have found us."

"The wyrran were looking, Sonya. They would have found another Druid if no' you. At least I was able to kill a few of them. They'll follow us now, leaving others safe."

Her gaze shifted around his shoulder to the window, and a moment later her face drained of color. Almost instantly Broc could feel the shift in the air.

The wyrran had come.

He had two choices. He could grab Sonya and leap from the window to escape into the sky. Or he could draw the wyrran away from the village and kill them.

As if Sonya knew his thoughts, she touched his arm gently and sighed. "We cannot leave the village to the wyrran."

"I know." Though he was seriously considering it. He didn't want anyone to fall victim to the wyrran, but Sonya and her magic were important. She was needed.

And he wouldn't let his curse touch her.

Sonya's gaze returned to the window. "What do we do now?"

"I need to hide you."

"Where?" she asked with a snort. "If there really is magic still inside me the wyrran can find me anywhere."

It was the truth, but he wasn't going to give up that

easily. "Can you protect yourself with a shield of magic as Isla protected the castle?"

"Nay."

That single word held a wealth of emotion. Frustration. Sadness. Despair.

Broc grabbed Sonya by the shoulders. "Doona worry. I've got a plan. Give me your cloak."

Sonya did as he asked without question. Her movements were quick and precise. She handed him the cloak and waited.

Broc gripped the fabric and prayed his plan worked. "When I leave, put whatever you can in front of the door. The wyrran will have to come in through either the door or the window. Give them only one choice."

"All right."

"I'm going to go downstairs and make sure Jean and her men are safely inside."

"Then what?" Sonya asked.

Broc looked at her cloak. "I'm going to make the wyrran think I have you. I will lead them away. It will take them a bit to realize they no longer sense your magic. By then, you and I will be on our way to MacLeod Castle."

"How long do I wait for you?"

"You doona." Broc saw her open her mouth to argue. "If I'm no' back in a couple of hours, take the coin and buy the horse just as we spoke about before. You ride for MacLeod Castle, Sonya."

She shook her head over his words. "I'm not leaving you."

"You have to."

"Broc—"

"I *will* find you."

A deep sighed passed her lips. "I will hold you to that vow, Broc MacLaughlin."

He was unable to hold back the smile, just as he couldn't stop his finger from caressing her cheek. "Stay safe."

Broc left before he kissed her. The temptation was so great that every fiber of his being told him he had to have a taste of her, had to feel her warmth against him one more time.

But he kept walking to the doorway. He glanced at her once more before he stepped into the corridor and closed the door behind him.

He waited a moment until he heard the unmistakable sound of furniture being scooted across the floor. Satisfied that Sonya was doing as he asked, Broc went to find Jean.

Just as he suspected, she was in the front of the inn. "Jean, you need to call your men inside."

She looked him over, her gaze pausing at the blood on his breeches. Instead of demanding to know what was going on, she walked to the door and gave a loud whistle. Almost immediately the men walked inside.

Broc touched Jean's arm. "Sonya is barricaded in her chamber. I'm leaving to take care of . . . something bad which is following us."

"Is there anything we can do to help?" Jean asked.

"Stay inside. It will be too dangerous to venture from the inn."

The men grumbled, their chests puffing in an attempt to prove their manhood. Broc silenced them with a glare. "You doona wish to tangle with what I'm going to kill. You would be dead before you could begin to realize what was happening."

Jean shivered and rubbed her arm with her hands. "All evening I've sensed great evil."

"More than you can begin to understand," Broc told her. "Stay inside. All of you, no matter what you hear.

If anything other than me comes through the door, kill it."

With Sonya's cloak still in his hand, he left the inn. He stood outside and listened. The night was quiet. Too quiet. The wyrran had surrounded the village. It was up to Broc to get them as far away from Sonya as he could.

Broc unleashed his god and let his wings stretch out to the side. In the next breath, he was in the air, his wings beating steadily.

Below, he could see movement scurrying around the village and through the forest. Broc let Sonya's cloak flap in the wind. He wanted the wyrran to think she was with him, wanted them to smell her scent.

Broc spotted a small clearing in the forest and dove toward it. He wanted away from the village, but not too far that he couldn't get to Sonya quickly.

Broc landed and folded his wings. The night erupted with the unholy shrieks of the wyrran. How he hated that sound. His disgust turned to glee when he realized the wyrran had taken the bait and were coming at him.

There could be one or two left at the village, but most likely all had followed him.

The wyrran crept from the forest. The moonlight glared off their pale yellow skin. Broc kept still as stone as he shifted his eyes to watch the wyrran station themselves on either side of him. More were to his back, but he didn't bother to face them.

The sound of a horse snorting drew Broc's attention. He watched the wyrran part as a horse emerged from the trees. And atop the animal was none other than Dunmore.

"I always knew there was something off about you," Dunmore said as he regarded Broc with disdain. "You were always too willing to aid Deirdre."

"You mean, like yourself?" Broc taunted.

Dunmore's lips shifted to a sneer. "Your glib tongue will not get you out of this, Broc. Deirdre knows you betrayed her."

"Deirdre betrayed everyone when she set out to conquer us. I never gave her my loyalty, only made her think I did. From the very beginning, I was a spy in her midst."

"You think you outwitted her, do you?"

Broc chuckled. "I know I did. Up until the moment I joined in the attack, she thought I was hers. For all her power, for all her knowledge, she was duped."

"She wants revenge." Dunmore shifted atop his mount and eyed the wyrran. "Deirdre has plans for you especially."

"And I have plans for her. We all do. Eventually we will win."

"Not all of you."

Broc shook his head. "Nay, there will some of us who die, but in the end, so will Deirdre. And the next time, it will be for good."

"I wouldna get too confident," Dunmore said. "You've left the mountain, Broc. There are things you doona know now. Things that if you did, you might no' be so willing to stand against her. In fact, if I were you, I'd be on my knees begging for her forgiveness."

Broc curled his hands into fists, his claws slicing his palms. All the rage that had built while tracking and fighting the wyrran had never dissipated, only simmered and waited. Now, it grew.

It overwhelmed.

It besieged.

And Broc did nothing to stop it.

He had always known he would die in his fight against Deirdre. Whether it was by death or his god taking over, he would be gone forever. His only regret was that he hadn't made sure Sonya was safe. At least with him gone, his "curse" wouldn't affect her now.

"But you are no' me, Dunmore. Nay, you're merely a mortal man. A man who has continued to age. I see the lines around your eyes and the gray in your hair. You are no' as strong as you used to be. You tire more easily than before."

"Shut up."

Broc smiled. "Deirdre has no one but these wyrran. She's using you. Once a Warrior returns to her, you will cease to be an asset. She'll kill you or send you away."

"She promised me immortality."

Broc threw back his head and laughed. "And you believed her? If there was a god inside you, she would have unbound it long ago. If she really was going to give you immortality, she would have done it while you were in your prime, no' aging as you are now."

Dunmore snarled and drew his sword from its scabbard. "I've heard enough from you. Deirdre wants you in her mountain, and I'm going to be the one who brings you to her. You'll see firsthand just how much I matter to her."

With a wave of Dunmore's hand the wyrran attacked. Broc killed the first three easily, but there were so many of them. He didn't understand how they could have gotten to the village so quickly.

He had a wyrran in each hand and one on his back when he saw Dunmore approach him. It must have been another signal, because suddenly all of the wyrran were on him, their slim bodies piling atop him as fast as they could.

Broc snapped the necks of the ones in his hands and reached for more, but their intent wasn't to harm him, it was to bring him to the ground.

The back of one of his knees was cut the same time a wyrran landed on his chest, sending him backwards. Broc roared as he fell to one knee and killed the wyrran before him.

He could feel the muscle and tendon mending in his knee, knew in just a moment he would be able to stand. But before that happened, Dunmore threw something at him.

The agony was immediate, consuming. He couldn't think, couldn't focus his mind as his god screamed furiously inside him. Broc knew then that *drough* blood, poisonous to Warriors, had been thrown into his many and various wounds.

He tried to get to his feet, tried to keep fighting, but the *drough* blood was too potent. His muscles seized as the poison worked its way through his body.

Broc could hear his god bellow inside him. Broc gave his own roar as he realized the wyrran hadn't come for Sonya.

They had come for him.

He fell backward hard as he tried to fight the effects of the *drough* blood. His body was immobilized, the pain blinding. He didn't care that he was being taken to Deirdre, to Cairn Toul Mountain, and most certainly his death. All he cared about was the Druid he had vowed to protect.

Sonya.

TWELVE

Sonya huddled behind a tree, her heart in her throat. It had cost her precious time talking her way past Jean and her men, but Sonya knew something was wrong. She felt it in the marrow of her bones. A feeling she couldn't dispel no matter how hard she tried.

The wyrran had followed Broc too easily if they had indeed come for her. And she saw why when the wyrran attacked him. It was a different attack than she had witnessed before. They weren't out to kill.

They were out to capture.

Sonya wiped away a lone tear from her cheek when she saw the wyrran lift Broc and carry him from the trees. His indigo skin of his god had faded and his wings had disappeared. From the way he held himself so rigid, it was clear that his body was wracked with pain.

She knew all too well what had happened to him. *Drough* blood. Sonya had helped Larena live through the nightmare. The poison had nearly killed Larena.

Sonya shifted the satchel and a limb cracked beneath her foot. A wyrran paused and lifted its head, its nose twitching as it sniffed the air.

She readied to run, thinking the wyrran would come for her. But the creature merely turned and followed the others and Dunmore through the trees.

If there was magic in her, the wyrran wouldn't have passed up an opportunity to bring a Druid to Deirdre. Yet, as empty as that knowledge made her feel, it allowed Sonya time to plan.

In an instant, Sonya made up her mind to follow Broc. She knew it wasn't what he wanted, but she wouldn't leave him. After she had learned what he had done for her and Anice, how much he had risked, how could she do anything different?

She might not have magic on her side anymore, but she had the element of surprise. Though she wasn't sure how she would get Broc away from Dunmore and so many wyrran, given the opportunity, she wouldn't hesitate to try.

Broc would be furious when he discovered she hadn't returned to MacLeod Castle, but she was willing to deal with his anger as long as he was alive and free of Deirdre.

Sonya stood and stared at the spot she had last seen Broc. He had always been so strong, so resolute. It was difficult for her to see him brought low by the *drough* blood. It was because he was such a great Warrior that they had to resort to such tactics.

She inhaled deeply and took a step. Her skirts were going to hamper her. She wished she would have thought to wear breeches as Larena did. It would be much easier to travel without having to worry about her skirts getting caught on anything.

Step after step, Sonya followed the wyrran. She traveled at a distance from them, keeping out of sight and hidden as much as she could. It was easy to follow them since they didn't try to cover their tracks. All Sonya had to do was track the wide path they cut through the forest.

Besides, she knew where they were going—Cairn

Toul. Though Sonya had never seen the mountain herself, she knew where it was.

She wasn't worried about getting to the mountain, or even gaining access inside. She was troubled about finding Broc and getting them both out alive. It was going to take some cunning, and she needed to form a plan quickly.

If she was lucky, there would be a way for her to free Broc before they reached Cairn Toul. The last thing Sonya wanted to do was go into that mountain surrounded by such evil.

With the satchel full of as much food as she could stuff inside, coin, and Broc's extra tunic he had left in the inn, Sonya was as prepared as she could be.

Her hand skimmed the dagger at her waist. Not to mention, she was armed.

Ramsey stood atop the battlements at MacLeod Castle, his gaze on the sky. He had expected Broc to return already with Sonya in tow.

"Do I have cause to be worried?" Fallon MacLeod asked as he came to stand beside him.

Ramsey shrugged and forced his fingers to loosen from the gray stones. "I thought Broc would be back by now."

"He has feelings for Sonya. Maybe he wanted some time alone with her."

"Nay," Ramsey said and faced the leader of their group of Warriors. "I know Broc. His first thought, regardless, and because of his feelings for Sonya, would be to bring her back. He wouldna waste any time in doing so."

Fallon sighed wearily, his dark green eyes troubled. "I feared as much. I had held out hope though. We have no idea where Sonya could have gone."

"Without Broc's power, we'd be searching blind."

"To have both Sonya and Malcolm leave at the same time." Fallon rubbed his chin and frowned. "I should have noticed they were gone much sooner than we did."

Ramsey laid a hand on Fallon's shoulder. "Doona blame yourself. We all knew Malcolm was going to leave. We just didna know when."

"Aye. Larena is determined to find her cousin. She wants him here."

"Malcolm has lost his way. He needs to find it before he can be happy anywhere."

"His surname is on the Scroll, Ramsey," Fallon reminded him.

Ramsey sighed as he thought of the ancient parchment the Druids had used to write down all the names of the men who had housed a god when the gods were first called up. "Do you think he could have the god?"

Fallon glanced at the castle. "There's a possibility. Larena willna admit it, but even she knows."

"Which is why she wanted Malcolm here. So Deirdre couldna get ahold of him."

"Aye."

Ramsey rubbed the stones of the castle wall with his thumb. "Deirdre has no idea Sonya has the Scroll or what names are on it. That is in our favor."

"You know as well as I Deirdre will be desperate for Warriors now. She will go back to the families she knows house a god and find their best warrior, but she will also look for anyone who is connected to us."

"Aye," Ramsey admitted softly. "She will."

"Add to that the fact that for some reason Sonya ran away." Fallon rubbed his eyes with his thumb and forefinger. "Why? Why would she run from us?"

Ramsey pressed his fist against the wall and heard

his knuckles pop. "Did you see Broc's face when he discovered she was gone?"

"I did," Fallon answered carefully.

"We have all seen the way Broc watches her."

"And how she looks at him."

Ramsey raised his brows.

"Shite," Fallon cursed. "He did something to make her leave. Does it have anything to do with her sister?"

Ramsey shrugged and said, "Perhaps. Broc was very distraught at Anice's death. I find it odd since he didna know her."

"Obviously he did."

"Indeed. How well, I'm no' sure, but I think Sonya figured it out."

Fallon slammed his hand into the stones, causing them to tremble with the force of his strength. "But to run? Sonya knew the danger awaiting her. She should have known better."

"Ah, but love rarely makes a person think straight when they are hurt, Fallon. You know this."

"I cannot sit by and just wait. If Broc hasna returned, then it's because of Deirdre."

Ramsey looked at the sky. "I left Broc once before in Cairn Toul. If Deirdre has somehow captured him, I willna leave him there again."

"None of us will," Fallon vowed. "But first, we need to find Broc and Sonya."

"The two people we would use for something like this are gone. There's no one else to ask the trees for help. There's no one else with wings."

This time it was Fallon who placed a hand on Ramsey's shoulder. "We will find them. This I swear."

Ramsey nodded his head once. "I know we will. But will we be too late?"

* * *

Broc wanted to roar his fury at opening his eyes to find himself once more in Cairn Toul, the one place he had never wanted to see again. But the *drough* blood in his system made it difficult to breathe, much less talk.

The stones above him blurred as he was carried haphazardly and carelessly by the wyrran. He wasn't sure how much time had passed since he had been taken by the wyrran. Whatever concoction Dunmore had in the animal skin which he made Broc drink kept him from dying, though it never lessened the pain of the *drough* blood.

So Deirdre wanted him to suffer. Didn't she know he suffered every day that he was near Sonya and didn't have her for his own?

Broc groaned just thinking of Sonya. He had to get her out of his mind, had to erase anything to do with her, Anice, or any of the Druids and Warriors at MacLeod Castle. If he didn't, Deirdre might learn of his attachment and use it against him.

Suddenly, he was dumped on the floor. The thud of his head striking the rock didn't diminish the pain of the poison in his system.

He thought he might be left on the cool stones of a dungeon to rot for a time, but he should have known Deirdre would want revenge. In blood.

Broc felt something cold and metal lock around his wrists. The sound of chains sliding against rock echoed around him. A heartbeat later, the chains were yanked, wrenching his arms out of their sockets as he was jerked to his feet.

It took everything Broc had to open his eyes. The poison was like a fire in his blood which licked at his skin, his bones, and every organ of his body.

He ground his teeth together to keep from bellowing from the unearthly, constant pain that ripped through him. His body was on fire and there was nothing he could do about it.

"It's so nice to have you back in my mountain, Broc."

He clenched his jaw as Deirdre's voice reached him. Broc lifted his head and looked around, startled to discover he was in the cavern deep below the mountain where he had been sure a Warrior had been held. By the time he had searched, there had been nothing but open shackles on the ground.

"You seem to be in a terrible amount of pain," Deirdre said. "Though I can attest it is nothing compared to what I endured at your hands."

Broc chuckled and gripped the chains to help him stand. He would not tremble at her feet or let her know just how much damage the *drough* blood was doing to him. "There is nothing you can do that will frighten me. You've already taken everything there was to take from me the first time you brought me here."

"Is that so?" Deirdre took a step toward him and held out Sonya's cloak. "Then who does this belong to?"

Broc was careful to keep his face passive and not bother glancing at the cloak. "I have no idea. Maybe Dunmore couldna find his cloak and decided to steal one."

He waited for Dunmore's angry rebuttal, but there was nothing.

"You have a woman."

It wasn't a question. Broc glared at Deirdre, his hatred burning bright. "You may kill me, but in the end, the MacLeods and their Warriors will win."

"Kill you?" Deirdre said, her hand over her chest as her white eyes pierced him. "Dear Broc, I'm not going to kill you. I'm going to make you suffer in ways you've never seen before. By the time I'm through with you, you will tell me everything I want to know about the MacLeods. And your woman."

"I'll see you in Hell first."

Deirdre threw back her head and laughed. Her floor-length white hair twitched around her ankles. "This *is* Hell, Broc."

THIRTEEN

Sonya finished tying off her braid with a strip of her chemise and ignored the pain of her wound. She'd been staring at Cairn Toul for some time. The wyrran had moved fast, only stopping because of Dunmore and his mount.

As she had feared, there had never been an opportunity to rescue Broc before they reached the mountain.

The few rest times had allowed Sonya to keep them in sight. The periods she had been exposed as she raced down the rolling hills had left her heart in her throat.

She had expected a wyrran to keep watch behind, to make sure no one followed. It was like they didn't care. Or didn't know she was there. Either way, she was glad.

The toughest part besides watching how roughly they handled Broc was the climb up the mountains. Her skirts constantly hampered her fast pace, and the cold air made her body stiff.

Sonya was ever thankful she had food and water in the satchel that she could eat as she walked. But the lack of sleep was taking its toll. Her body was exhausted, her mind weary. And her heart troubled. If she was going to help Broc she needed to be stronger—mentally and physically.

Sonya ducked behind a mound of boulders as she watched two wyrran come out of the mountain. It was as if they had walked through stone. Even if she had her magic, she couldn't walk through rock.

Then she spotted the door. It was made of the same stone, so blended with the mountain that it almost couldn't be seen.

The wyrran had moved faster, so they reached the castle well before she had. Broc had been in its depths for hours already. As much as Sonya wanted to rush inside, she knew in her present state she would only get herself captured.

Once again, the thought of being without her magic made her doubt herself. How could she, a mere female with no battle knowledge, help Broc who was inside the mountain, surrounded by God only knew how many wyrran?

If Deirdre found her, or she was captured, they'd use her against Broc, of that Sonya was certain.

She frowned and drew in a determined breath. Broc would never abandon her if Deirdre had captured her. She wouldn't leave him either. Regardless of what happened, she would do whatever she could, however she could, to find and free him.

With night falling, she decided to sleep for a few hours. Her body needed rest in order to be ready to rescue Broc. As fatigued as she was, her mind was on Broc and what Deirdre was doing to him.

Sonya leaned against a boulder as she finished the last of an oatcake before huddling against the rock, away from the cold wind. A plan was forming in her mind. A plan that would most likely get her killed.

But if she could give Broc time to get free, it would be worth it.

Broc ached everywhere, even his eyelids. It had been so long since he had felt anything other than minor irritation over a wound that it was taking everything he had to keep his mind focused and not give away more than he should.

Deirdre had kept the *drough* blood inside him. She used it to her advantage, threatening to kill him with it while trying to persuade him she wasn't his enemy.

Broc laughed every time.

Though it was becoming harder and harder to keep the smile on his face. It took great concentration to keep his lungs filling with air. And each time they did, the pain, the soul-shredding agony would make him question if it was worth it.

His skin burned from the inside out. His bones felt as if they were crumbling away. Pain. Misery. Torment. They were his only friends now, the only things which kept him from going stark raving mad.

And all of it had been done without Deirdre laying a finger on him.

He'd seen the use of *drough* blood used on Warriors before, but it had been a minute amount. Larena had nearly died because of *drough* blood.

He wasn't afraid of dying. He was afraid of Deirdre bringing him back.

It took powerful black magic to return a soul to its body, and a trace of evil always remained with that soul. Broc feared what he would become with Deirdre's evil inside him.

He had fought his god and learned to control it, but if his god got a taste of Deirdre's evil, Poraxus would take over. Completely.

And there would be nothing he could do about it.

It wouldn't happen the first time Deirdre brought him back. But he knew her. She would do it again and again until she got the results she wanted.

It had happened to a Warrior before.

What would happen to Sonya if his god did take over?

He hadn't allowed himself to think of her since he was first dragged into the dungeon, but now that she had come into his thoughts, he couldn't seem to stop thinking of her.

It was precarious for him to lose control so easily. But the image of her beautiful face, her red curls shining in the sun, and her amazing amber eyes helped to fortify him.

He lifted his head and opened his eyes. Behind him was part of the rock which had transformed for Deirdre so that it curved inward, away from him.

It was far enough behind him that Broc couldn't lean back, couldn't even kick backward with his foot and touch it. Before him was the huge cavern. The steps leading down to where he was being held were narrow and wound upward until he couldn't see them anymore. He had flown down that first time, not bothering with the stairs, but he knew he was far below anything else in Deirdre's mountain.

He also realized this was the place Phelan had been kept. The boy Deirdre had made Isla bring to the mountain. He had been chained for years until he had reached manhood. And then Deirdre had unbound his god.

Broc wished he had ventured here and found Phelan before the attack on Deirdre. Isla wanted Broc to find him, just as Larena wanted him to find Malcolm.

What would happen if Broc didn't return to the castle?

There's no if. I'm not going to ever leave the mountain again.

Broc knew it with a certainty that should have angered him, but one he accepted. He thought back to the first girl who had caught his eye. He'd been a lad of eight summers, she had only been six.

Ena had been shy, but even at such a young age, Broc

had known beauty when he saw it. It had taken him months, but he'd gradually gotten her to speak with him. He could still see her shy smile as she looked up at him with clear, blue eyes.

He also couldn't forget finding her body floating in the river.

The next lass to die had been two years later. Moyna had been the opposite of Ena in every way. She was as wild and reckless as Broc had been at the time. When he'd dared her to climb the cliff, she hadn't backed down.

It wasn't until they were standing at the top, near the edge, that the ground crumbled beneath her and she plummeted to her death.

There were others. Always some freak, unexplained accident or illness would take them, but always after spending months with Broc.

His clan began to look at him as if he were some evil soul. They whispered behind his back and kept their distance lest one of them be the next to die.

Broc had turned his attention to his sword. He spent hours training and becoming the best warrior his clan had ever seen. He'd never expected that would lead him to become something to truly be feared.

At least being locked in Deirdre's mountain had kept him away from anyone who might become attached to him. He chuckled inwardly as he foolishly thought he would be spared from the curse.

He should have known the moment he picked up Sonya and Anice as babies he was testing Fate.

Broc knew the instant Deirdre entered the cavern. He shut down his thoughts and focused on his hatred for her. By the time she walked down the thousand steps, Broc was ready for her.

"How is the *drough* blood feeling in your body?" Deirdre asked, her voice holding a note of excitement.

"I'm still standing."

She narrowed her unnatural white eyes. She wore the same black gown she always preferred, even after several centuries. "I can ease your discomfort."

He scoffed at her words. "In exchange for my fealty? Never."

"Such strong words. You've only been here for a little over a day. I wonder how you'll feel with *drough* blood in you for . . . decades."

"I will die before then."

She smiled, the gesture cruel and holding no ounce of kindness. "Without a doubt, my indigo Warrior. It is my magic which is keeping it from killing you."

"What color were your eyes before?" Broc asked to change the subject and keep in control. He had seen how Deirdre stared at herself in the mirror. He'd often wondered what went through her mind as she gazed at her reflection.

The smile vanished, replaced with a sneer. "What does it matter?"

"Curious," he said with a shrug of indifference. "It's twisted, that color of yours."

"Just as your Warrior eyes are. Have you seen what you become when you unleash your god?"

Broc laughed. "Aye. Have you seen what you've become? What color where your eyes? Hazel? Blue?"

"I don't see how this matters."

"Ah, but you're a vain bitch, Deirdre. As much as you love the black magic which runs through your soul, I've seen you stare into your mirror."

"My eyes frighten people. I use it to my advantage."

Broc smiled as he heard the lie in her words. He'd been right in thinking she didn't like the white color of her eyes. He'd continue this conversation to see what it brought him. "There are those who say you're beautiful. I doona see it."

In a flash she stood before him, her long white hair wrapped around his neck in a tight grip. "I *am* beautiful."

"Your conceit knows no bounds."

"Why do you wish to know what color my eyes used to be?"

Broc lifted his chin as he felt her hair tighten around his neck, cutting off what little air he had. "Idle conversation."

"Blue. They were blue," she said as her hair released him and fell back to the floor. "Before you ask, my hair was blonde. Are you satisfied?"

"Immensely. Now I know that hair and eye color can certainly make the woman. If you're so powerful, why can you no' turn your eyes back to what they were?"

He was baiting her, making her think of herself instead of him and her plan. It was working so far, but he wasn't sure how much longer it would last.

"Why would I?" she asked with a frown.

He shrugged. "A show of your mighty black magic. Can you do it, or are you no' as powerful as you would like us to believe? I doona think you have enough magic to do it."

"I know what you're doing," she said, her voice lowering.

Broc prepared himself for the worst. He had taken a huge risk. "What is that?"

"You want to see me as I was."

He was so surprised, he could only stare at her in silence. Amid all her delusions, he shouldn't be astonished that she had come up with something completely different than what he had imagined.

Deirdre moved to stand in front of him and rubbed

her lithe body against his. There was no doubt she could be beautiful, but the evil inside her made her repulsive.

Broc hid his shiver of revulsion. He needed to play along for as long as needed.

He had fooled her once. He could again.

"I never took you to my bed." She ran a hand up his bare chest. "I see I shouldn't have overlooked you as I did."

"Why did you?"

She shrugged, her black gown moving along her slim body. "I had my sights on Quinn."

"You still do."

Deirdre frowned and leaned in to kiss Broc's bare shoulder. "I always get what I want, Broc. Sooner or later the MacLeods will be mine in one form or fashion. They have escaped me twice, and I will have my vengeance."

"So you want them dead." He knew that look in Deirdre's eyes. She wanted blood.

Her hand halted its caress and her long, sharp nails pierced the skin over his heart. "I will see them suffer as I have suffered. I will take everything they have from them bit by bit until they have nothing but themselves once more. Then, I will kill Lucan and Fallon. Quinn will have naught to bargain with, naught to wish for. He will be mine."

Broc stared into her white eyes, the depth of her wickedness there for him to see.

"Until then," Deirdre continued, "there is a place in my bed for you. All you have to do is say the words, Broc. I can end all of this."

He took a step back, a small step which his chains instantly halted, but it was enough to break contact with her. "Nay."

"I could make you want me," she whispered. "I

couldn't use magic on Quinn if I wanted his child, but I can certainly use magic on you."

Broc's stomach churned with dread. He shouldn't have pushed Deirdre. He should have left well enough alone.

"Who do you want me to be? What woman has caught your fancy? Tell me, does she have blue eyes and blonde hair? Is that why you wanted to know if I could change my appearance?"

He kept silent, which was just as bad as telling her none of it was the truth. No matter what he said or didn't say, it would be used against him. Deirdre would see to that.

"You couldn't stop talking a moment ago," Deirdre said seductively. "Why so silent now?"

Broc looked over her head. He wouldn't answer her. He wouldn't give anything away. No names in his thoughts. No faces in his mind.

Deirdre leaned up on her tiptoes and tapped his jaw with a nail as she whispered in his ear, "There *is* someone. I will discover who she is. You know I will. Tell me now. Make it easier on yourself and her."

He thought of Phelan and all the other Warriors who had suffered at Deirdre's hands. He thought of the people he had killed in Deirdre's name, of the Druids he had brought before her.

"When I find her, I'm going to bring her before you and make you watch as I gut her," Deirdre said. "Then, I'm going to make you believe I'm her. You'll be my slave in every way, Broc. You'll share my bed and pleasure me night after night."

Broc swallowed the bile that rose in his throat. He thought of the wyrran and how he wanted to behead each and every one of them.

"You will not win this battle of wills. I will release

the full measure of *drough* blood until you are writhing on the floor. You'll be delirious. You'll tell me anything."

He thought of countless battles he had fought in Deirdre's name. He thought of the pain running through his body. He thought of anything but the one person who was forever in his heart.

FOURTEEN

Sonya came awake with a start, her body shivering in the cold, predawn hours. She had slept far longer than she had intended.

She wrapped her arms about herself and drew her legs up close to her body. Her hands hurt, they were so cold, and she couldn't feel her nose. Her lips were chapped from the chilling, bitter wind.

Her lips split open when she tried to bite into a piece of cold meat. Sonya hissed in a breath and cupped her hand around her lips. The water in her animal skin was so cold the top layer had begun to ice. It was time to get moving before she froze to death.

Sonya gathered her things and slipped the strap of the satchel over her head and across her body. She then stood and glanced around the boulder.

Nothing moved on the landscape. It was as if the world had stopped. There were no animals, no people, no wyrran.

"It's now or never," she whispered to herself, pushing aside the twinge of self-doubt that threatened to take root.

She took a deep, fortifying breath and moved around the boulders which had protected her. Sonya paused, waiting for wyrran to surround her.

When nothing happened, she proceeded toward the

hidden door, picking her way around the rocks and trying not to slip on the ice and snow.

The doorway she had spotted wasn't at the top of the mountain, but it was still quite a climb. She no longer felt pain in her injured hand, but she knew if she looked, the wound would be open and bleeding.

Both her hands were. Every time she reached a rock and used it to help herself up the mountain it would cut into her hands. Sonya didn't want to think about what condition her hands were in. At least not now.

Her first priority was reaching the door and getting inside the mountain. Once there, she would worry about her hands. And her lack of magic.

Sonya was just strides away from the door when she saw the blood. Most of it was old and black, but there were newer drops, thick and crimson.

Her heart lurched at the thought that it was Broc's blood. In order to heal Broc of the *drough* blood, she would need another Warrior's blood. As far as Sonya knew, the only thing that could reverse what the *drough* blood did to a Warrior was another Warrior's blood.

Sonya squared her shoulders and kept moving. When she reached the doorway, she pressed herself against the rock face of the mountain and waited until she caught her breath.

The view from where she stood was breathtaking. All around her were the magnificent mountains of the highlands. The sun was cresting over the horizon, its rays meeting first one peak, then another, and another.

The sight calmed Sonya. The light chased away the darkness, chased away the shadows and bathed everything in its golden radiance.

She knew in that instant she would get into the mountain. She would find Broc. And she would free him. Everything would be set to rights.

Sonya turned toward the door and tried to find a handle to open it. Her hands moved over the rock, searching for anything that could be used. But there was nothing.

She clawed at it, breaking fingernails so far down to the quick that she began to bleed. Tears gathered in her eyes, making her vision swim. It wasn't supposed to be this difficult. She had found the door. She should be able to find a way inside.

Sonya slapped her hands on the stone, her soul beaten down. To have come so far and failed. She laid her cheek against the rock and closed her eyes as she thought of Broc. Of his beautifully dark, sultry eyes. Of his wings. Of the indigo color of his god.

There was a whooshing sound, and the door creaked as it began to open. Sonya jumped out of the way and unsheathed the dagger. She stood in shock when she found a wyrran standing before her.

Before it could let out a shriek and alert others, she plunged the dagger into its chest. She then jerked the blade out and took a swing at its neck.

She had seen all the Warriors take wyrran heads, so she hadn't thought it would be too difficult. Her blade hit bone, and she realized too late she didn't have enough strength to behead the creature.

The wyrran crumpled to the ground, taking Sonya with it when she wouldn't release the hilt of her weapon. She scrambled to her feet and tried to remove the blade, but it wouldn't budge.

She didn't want to leave the dagger. It had been a gift from Broc, but no matter how much she tried to free the blade, it didn't move. She dragged the wee beast out of sight and hurried into the mountain before the door closed.

Sonya entered a short entryway and halted, her heart pounding hard and slow. Evil, menacing and ominous, enveloped her. She pushed it aside and refused to listen to the niggling uncertainty that played in her head.

As soon as she penetrated the mountain a shiver of dread and foreboding raced down her spine. Every instinct demanded she turn and run as far and as fast as she could.

Somehow, Sonya held her ground. The evil was so thick, so prevalent, she found it difficult to breathe.

"You cannot do it," a voice whispered in her mind. *"You have no magic. Nothing. How can you save Broc?"*

Sonya swallowed past the lump in her throat and squared her shoulders.

"It would take someone with magic in order to save Broc. Deirdre won't even look twice at you now that you aren't a Druid."

"Enough," Sonya whispered.

She closed her eyes and thought of the trees and how it felt to have them bend toward her and brush against her with their limbs. She thought of their whispers that would soothe her, comfort her.

And somehow, it blocked her mind from the incessant voice until it was no more.

Sonya opened her eyes. It was time to find Broc. She prayed she didn't run into any more wyrran, especially without her dagger.

It was much darker in the mountain than she had expected. The light from outside pierced the doorway, but it didn't go farther.

Sonya flattened herself against the stone wall and leaned to the side. She looked down to the left to see that the corridor that ran in front of her ended.

With a slow release of breath, Sonya peered around the corner of the entryway and into the hallway extending as far as she could see. Torches were mounted on the walls spaced evenly apart, but they still cast deep shadows around them.

From what she remembered hearing from the MacLeods and others who had been imprisoned in Cairn Toul, Deirdre's chambers were at the top. The many levels of dungeons filled the lower half of the mountain and extended far beneath the earth.

Sonya didn't know how long she would be able to search before getting caught, and she would never know, either, if she didn't start moving.

Feeling began to return to her hands as she warmed, causing them to feel as if needles were pricking her skin. The attack on the wyrran and her attempt to find the handle to the door had ripped the skin from her palms.

The pain, however, was small compared to whatever Broc was enduring. Sonya forgot about her injured hands and stepped into the corridor.

She saw more blood on the stones at her feet. The drops turning into small puddles. Whoever it was had lost a tremendous amount of blood and was in need of healing.

Sonya didn't tarry over the blood. She knew Deirdre's chambers were near the door, and she needed to get past Deirdre in order to have a chance at finding Broc.

The mountain was eerily silent. The other Warriors had talked about hearing the wails of the tortured and the cries of the dying.

There was nothing now.

During the rescue of Quinn the prisoners had been released and most of Deirdre's Warriors had been killed. Unfortunately, when the MacLeods had searched, they had found no Druids alive.

It hurt Sonya's heart to think of all her kin—the

Druids—dying at Deirdre's hands or while trying to find their way off the mountain.

Sonya expected to hear the cries of the Druids who had run from MacLeod Castle. The group from Loch Awe had been small, but they were Druids. Yet, their fear of the Warriors and Deirdre's infiltration into an elder's mind had sent all but a few of the group running away.

And into the wyrran's hands.

Those Druids had to be somewhere in the mountain. Sonya would have to search for them as well. After she found Broc.

Sonya moved as quickly and as quietly through the corridor as she could. There were several chambers where she would pause and glance inside. Once she knew no one saw her, and she saw no sign of Broc, she moved on.

The hallway stretched into eternity, curving as well as sloping downward. Sonya heard the unmistakable sounds of wyrran coming toward her. She ducked inside the first chamber she came to and held her breath until the wyrran had passed.

"Who are you?" came a broken male voice from across the chamber.

Sonya's heart missed a beat as she turned her head and found herself staring at Dunmore. She had seen him attack with the MacClures at MacLeod Castle, had seen him throw the *drough* blood on Broc.

But he had never seen her. He was mortal, so he had no idea if she was a Druid or not.

"You doona belong here," he said and grimaced as he clutched his stomach.

Sonya saw the blood oozing between his fingers. The drops of blood from the doorway led to him. So the blood she had seen outside the mountain and in the hallway had been Dunmore's and not Broc's. That alone caused a wealth of relief.

"Nay, I don't belong here, and I won't be staying long."

He smiled coldly. "You came for Broc."

Sonya raised her chin, proud of herself for getting as far as she had. Without magic. "I did."

"You'll never find him, and even if you do . . .," he paused to cough, "you willna be able to get near him."

"Where is Deirdre keeping him?"

Dunmore's beady eyes narrowed. "Why should I tell you?"

"Because I can heal you," Sonya lied.

That gave him pause. "Do it."

"Not until I get Broc free."

"You're going to need me. Heal me now, or I call for the wyrran and Deirdre."

Sonya knew by the stubborn way Dunmore looked at her he wouldn't tell her anything until he was healed. But if she healed him, he would most likely hand her over to Deirdre.

Then there was the fact she had lied. She had no magic to heal him. When she wasn't able to mend him, he would then call for Deirdre.

Sonya pushed from the wall and closed the door to the chamber. Once it was bolted, she turned to face Dunmore. "I know who you are. I know what you've done. I should let you bleed to death. You are very near it now."

"I can help you." The earnestness in his voice didn't soften her heart. He was a cold-blooded killer who had aligned himself with evil.

Unfortunately, she did need him.

Sonya knelt before him and pulled his hand away to see the wound. There were five deep gashes across his stomach. The cuts were long and spaced widely apart. Warrior's claws.

"Broc did this, didn't he?" Sonya asked with a satisfied grin.

Dunmore nodded his head as he coughed again. Blood trickled from the corner of his mouth. "He's a fighter, that one. Even with the poison in him, he fights."

"If I heal you, I want your word you will not tell Deirdre about me. That you will help me and Broc escape."

"Aye. If you heal me, I'll do as you ask."

"Does your word mean anything?"

"I suppose, Druid, that you'll find out."

Sonya stared at him for several moments. "Pray, Dunmore, that you don't deceive me, because if you do, you will regret it."

"Nothing you can do to me will be worse than what Deirdre has threatened. Now, get on with it. Unless you want Broc's torture to continue."

Sonya hated Dunmore. She would rather see him die, but the simple fact was he knew the mountain, and he most likely knew where Broc was being held.

She closed her eyes and thought of her magic. If Broc was right and there was still some inside her, she would find it. For him she would do the impossible.

Deeper and deeper Sonya went inside herself. She searched for the warmth of her magic, sought the glow of calmness which always filled her.

Sonya didn't rush it. She knew if there was any magic left inside her, she would have to look deeper than ever before. But the more she looked, the more she feared it was well and truly gone.

Then, just as she was about to give up, she caught a spark.

FIFTEEN

Sonya held her breath, willing her magic to grow and fill her as it used to. She expected to be flooded with it. Instead, there was just a small, tiny ribbon of magic that spiraled up inside her.

She could feel her hands healing, feel the skin mending together and her wound close up. She tried to make her magic ignore her wounds and tend to Dunmore, but it was already too late.

With her injuries mended, Sonya poured what little magic she had found into Dunmore. His wound was severe, and she feared the slight magic she had wouldn't be enough to repair him properly.

But she would do all that she could. For Broc.

The nagging fear about not having her magic when she would need it most roared to life within her again. Sonya didn't have time to let that panic take hold as it had in the past. Not when Broc's life was in jeopardy. She pushed the fear aside and focused on healing Dunmore.

She didn't move, didn't utter a sound until she became too exhausted to use any more magic. There were limits to her healing, and with the small spark she had found, Sonya was glad she had been able to do something.

It might well have been the last of her magic, but it would be worth it if Dunmore led her to Broc.

"Is that all you're going to do?" Dunmore demanded.

Sonya dropped her hands and opened her eyes. She pushed aside his hand to see the injury. It had stopped bleeding, and the wound had closed up, but it had not entirely healed as she should have been able to make it do.

"I thought you Druids could do magic!"

Sonya glared at him as she sat back on her heels. "Be glad you are no longer bleeding everywhere. The wounds are closed and mending."

"Heal me fully." His face twisted with rage.

Sonya raised her brows. "That is as good as I can heal you. If it isn't good enough, I will reverse it and leave you bleeding again."

She couldn't, but he didn't need to know that. It was a threat, and by the way his face went slack, it worked to her advantage.

"Once you get me and Broc out of the mountain, I'll finish healing you."

Dunmore wiped the blood from his hand on his tunic. "I doona suppose I have much of a choice."

"Nay, you don't."

Sonya climbed to her feet and waited impatiently for Dunmore to do the same. She knew she couldn't trust him, knew he would try to do something, but he was all she had. The mountain was too big and there were too many wyrran for her to try and search herself.

Dunmore rose slowly, testing his body. When he stood beside her, his eyes were too bright, too eager. Another shiver of dread raced down Sonya's back.

She would have to keep her guard up. At no time could she turn her back on Dunmore. She glanced at his hip to find his sword gone.

He smiled cruelly when he saw where her gaze had gone. "I gave you my word, Druid. Do you doubt it?"

"Most certainly. Tell me where Deirdre is keeping Broc."

Dunmore sighed and glanced at his wounds again. "He's been taken below."

" 'Below'? What does that mean?"

"Broc is well below the mountain. He's beneath all the dungeons. He's in a place where there is one way in and one way out."

And if Deirdre was there, Sonya knew the outcome wouldn't be favorable. "Take me to him."

"You doona want to go down there."

The truth shining in Dunmore's eyes made her stomach clench. Nay, she didn't want to do it, but she would. "Take me."

"As you wish." Dunmore walked past her to the door and opened it before he stepped into the corridor and turned left.

Sonya followed him, keeping just to his side and behind him. It was imperative she keep him in her sights at all times.

"Ah, Broc," Deirdre whispered. "You know what I can do. You know how far my knowledge stretches. I haven't lived this long and bound myself to the black magic for nothing."

"What do you think you know?" he asked. If he kept her talking it prolonged whatever she had in store for him and helped him to formulate a plan.

Since she wanted him coherent for their conversation, she had done something to hinder the pain of the *drough* blood inside him, but he didn't doubt for a moment that she would let it loose the first instant he made her angry.

She walked behind him, trailing her hands over his shoulders and back. "Oh, I know one of the artifacts I searched for is now being held at MacLeod Castle. I know the artifact is none other than a Druid named Reaghan."

"You think you know so much from being in Mairi's mind."

Deirdre laughed. "What little I didn't know from Mairi the Druids from Reaghan's village told me."

"Would you like me to clap for you?"

"This is a side of you I've never seen," she said as she came to stand in front of him. Her white gaze was curious and much too interested. "Have you kept this need for mockery and sarcasm inside all this time?"

"There is much you doona know of me."

"I know the important parts," she whispered.

Broc's nostrils flared in anger. Of course she would know the vital parts. She had been the cause of all of them.

"I'll tell you a little secret—"

"Why?" he interrupted her. Deirdre didn't tell anyone anything, and if she did, no good could come of it.

Deirdre's smile was slow as it spread across her face. Her gaze was calculating, her intent clear. "I've found the location of another artifact."

Now Broc was listening. This was information they could use. All he had to do was discover the spot and get to it before Deirdre. After freeing himself from Cairn Toul first, however.

"Ah, I see that got your attention." Deirdre once more rubbed her hands along Broc's chest. "I will find all the artifacts, and I will have Reaghan in my clutches. There is nothing you can do to stop me. I'm too powerful, Broc. There isn't a Druid alive who can compare to my magic. They all know it. Which is why they hide."

"They hide because you hunt and kill them."

She chuckled. "Thanks to you and the MacLeods,

my army of Warriors is gone. It's going to take me weeks to build it up again."

"My heart bleeds."

She cut her eyes to him and lifted her lip in a sneer. "You will be my first. You will take lead over my Warriors."

"I willna."

"You know I can make you. I will send you after the second artifact to ensure it's mine. Then, I will send you to the MacLeods. You can spy on them for a day or two before you kill the others and bring me the Druids and the MacLeods."

Broc shook his head. "Never."

"Few can withstand the evil once it seeps into your soul," she said as she leaned close. "With your god inside you it will only spread the evil quicker. You won't stand a chance."

"If the artifact is so important to you, why doona you get it yourself?"

"I cannot get to it."

Her confession surprised him. "The artifact must be of great importance if someone has gone to so much trouble to keep you out."

Then, a plan formed all of a sudden. It was reckless and would most likely turn his friends against him, but he had to try. "I'll get the artifact for you."

"Why would you do that?"

"You want it now. I will fight you as you waste precious days killing me and bringing me back, days the MacLeods could have learned where the artifact is and retrieve it themselves."

Deirdre's eyes were hard and icy. "Why are you so willing?"

"In exchange for leaving the MacLeods and all who reside at the castle alone."

"An appealing bargain, but one I'm not willing to accept. Those of you who betrayed me will be punished. The Druids who thought going to the MacLeods would save them will die at my hands. And you already know my plan for the MacLeods."

Broc gripped the chains and wished he could pull them from the wall. But they were held with magic, a magic too strong for even his strength to break through.

He remembered then that Isla had said there was a spell, a chant Deirdre used to unlock the shackles. Was it the same chant Deirdre used on other things? Broc's mind raced to remember the words, words he thought to never use.

"No quip, Broc? Nothing clever to say?" Deirdre said.

"Apparently no'."

She trailed her hand down his arm to where his hand gripped the chains. "You are a striking man, but I always did prefer you in your Warrior form. The indigo skin and those magnificent wings of yours. Very impressive."

"Where is the next artifact?" He figured he had nothing to lose.

Deirdre cocked her head to the side. "You think I will just tell you?"

"Aye. You are full of your own importance and think I will never get free."

"You won't," she stated. "You are mine now."

"Then what harm will come to tell me?"

For several moments Deirdre silently watched him, calculating. "Glencoe."

Broc hid his surprise. He had never expected her to reveal the location, especially not so easily. There had to be a reason. Deirdre was too manipulative, too shrewd to give away information so freely.

"Shocked?" Deirdre asked, her brows raised. "I realize you are correct. You will not leave my mountain until you are completely mine to control, so telling you does no harm. Besides, I want you to know just how futile it is to hope the MacLeods might learn of this artifact."

"Then tell me the rest," Broc urged. He knew there was more. There was always more where Deirdre was concerned.

"I found scrolls tucked away in an old Druid village. The occupants were long gone, the buildings falling to ruin."

"You mean a village you destroyed."

She grinned. "Of course. If I had known then what those *mies* were hiding, I might not have been so hasty to burn everything."

"If the scrolls burned, how did you find them?"

"They were protected by magic. Time and the elements did more to them than the fire I began."

Broc narrowed his gaze. "And you were able to read the scrolls?"

"After a bit of my own magic, aye."

"Are you going to tell me what's in Glencoe?"

"You really should work on your patience, Broc," she said with a grin.

He glared at her, wishing he could claw out her evil white eyes.

"All right," she said with a laugh. "It's a Celtic burial mound."

Broc shook his head. "They are no' to be disturbed, Deirdre. The Celts put great measures in place so that harm will come to those who enter."

"I know," Deirdre said and walked in a large circle away from Broc. She clasped her hands behind her back and looked at the stones as if they were the greatest work of art. "I assure you that as a Warrior, you will be able to get inside and acquire the artifact."

"And what is the artifact?"

She stopped and shrugged. "That I don't know."

"The mighty Deirdre absent information?"

Deirdre rolled her eyes. "The scrolls had magic, remember? They burst into flames when my magic came in contact with them."

Broc snorted. "Too bad they didna burn before you were able to get the information you do have."

"If that happened, I wouldn't be able to tell you that you alone can open the tomb. I also wouldn't be able to tell you there will be markings around the door, markings created by the Celts and filled with magic by the Druids."

"How does knowing of the markings help?"

"Do you know how many burial mounds there are?"

Broc shook his head, disgusted to even be having the conversation with Deirdre. The fact only he could open the tomb gave him a bit of an advantage. If he could get free, he could find the tomb and get the artifact.

"Why the interest in these artifacts?"

"To help me rule the world."

"It's a big world. You willna be able to conquer all of it."

"I have always made it clear I will do anything and everything to ensure I rule all."

"And you really think you will win?"

"I know I will. Shall I prove it to you?" she asked with a devious grin.

Broc saw her hand raise and instantly the blinding pain of the *drough* blood filled him again. He bellowed in fury as he fought against its power.

This time Deirdre let more of the poison take hold.

His knees buckled as he squeezed his eyes shut and ground his teeth together.

Nothing helped. The *drough* blood was slowing his body, halting his heart, and shriveling his insides.

"You will be mine," Deirdre said near his ear. "And it all begins now."

SIXTEEN

Sonya heard the enraged, pain-filled bellow and knew it was Broc. Her heart lurched in her chest, and her only thought was to reach him.

She realized the moment she moved past Dunmore that she'd made the costliest mistake of her life. She tried to duck when she saw him move toward her, but she wasn't fast enough to escape as his meaty hand closed around her neck and squeezed.

Sonya clawed at his hands, desperate for air.

"Stupid bitch," he ground out. "As if I would do anything against Deirdre. I'm no' a traitor."

He leered in her face, his features contorted with hate and malevolence. She barely registered that as her head was slammed into the rock wall and everything went black.

Dunmore watched the Druid's body crumple in a heap at his feet. It had been too easy. She had kept him in front of her, her gaze never wavering.

But one growl from Broc and she had forgotten all about Dunmore.

It had been to his advantage. He had grabbed the opportunity and knocked the Druid unconscious. Now he would take her to Deirdre. He knew he would be well rewarded.

Never mind the fact that Deirdre had known he was injured and hadn't helped him. She had needed to begin her torture of Broc. Dunmore understood Deirdre as no other could. It was why he had stayed loyal to her. Why he would always stay loyal to her.

He looked down at the redheaded Druid. She had wanted to see Broc. Dunmore smiled as he lifted the woman and tossed her over his shoulder. She would most certainly get to see Broc, but the outcome wouldn't be what the Druid wanted or expected.

Screams of pain, of torture would once more fill Cairn Toul.

Poraxus, Broc's god, raged and seethed inside him. His anger mixed with Broc's, sending Broc on a downward spiral of fury and uncontrollable craze. He could feel the reach of Poraxus as he tried to take control, tried to pull Broc under for good.

It was inevitable. But not yet, not this day.

Broc yanked on the chains. The shackles cut into his wrists, the blood spilling between his skin and the metal. He didn't pay it any heed. His gaze was locked on Deirdre's, on the evil he must end.

He had the information he needed. There was no reason to stay in the mountain. He would leave, but first, he would kill her.

Deirdre's eyes had grown huge when he began to jerk against his restraints. She did nothing but watch, expecting her magic to hold him.

It wouldn't be the first time she had been wrong.

The more he struggled with the chains, the more the *drough* blood inside him burned. He felt its poison, knew his body was badly damaged and might never recover.

The *drough* blood kept his god from taking over, and

Poraxus' rage kept the *drough* blood from debilitating Broc. The hours he had suffered with the poison had allowed his god to shield itself.

Broc felt the chains give way, but it wasn't nearly enough. He wanted free. Now!

With his gaze locked with Deirdre's, Broc began the chant that would release him from the bonds. The disbelief and confusion on Deirdre's face was worth all the pain he had suffered.

The shackles sprang open with a loud click before falling with a clank to the stones.

Deirdre held up a hand face out toward him. "I can kill you instantly."

Broc clenched his teeth and smiled. "Go ahead. Do it."

He felt her magic gather around her, felt the eerie, sinister magic that was opposite Sonya's noble and brilliant magic.

Broc focused his power on Deirdre. Just as when he hunted someone, he felt her heartbeat, felt the ferocity and a glimmer of panic churning inside her. It was how he knew when she was about to release her magic.

He dove to the side at the same time he called forth his god. His wings unfurled behind him the instant his fangs filled his mouth and his claws lengthened from his fingers.

Poraxus called for blood, demanded death. Deirdre's.

Broc was all too happy to give it to him. He jumped to his feet as Deirdre's white hair whipped out and wrapped around his neck. He grabbed it with one hand while he severed the strands with the other.

He tossed aside the remnants and ducked as her hair, fully regenerated, snaked out for him again. Broc managed to get away from the strands reaching for his neck, but he couldn't move fast enough to stop them from slashing through his wings.

Broc roared and jumped toward Deirdre. A blast of her magic sent him tumbling head over heels backward to land with a bone-jarring thud against the rocks.

But Broc didn't stay down. He was up and running back to her when the sound of someone—a mortal—approaching reached him.

"Mistress?"

Broc smiled when he heard Dunmore's voice. He was going to make that bastard suffer, but first Broc was going to finish Deirdre.

He spread his wings and flew upward so that only a portion of her magic touched him, not enough to do more than sting his skin. Broc quickly dove toward Deirdre and punched her in the middle of her back.

She screamed and went flying forward, to sprawl on the ground. Broc landed and stepped on her arms so she couldn't move. He reared back his hand, ready to sever her head with his claws.

Decapitating her hadn't killed her the first time, but it would be a start.

"Mistress, I have a surprise. A Druid has come looking for Br . . ."

Dunmore's voice trailed away as he caught sight of Broc standing over Deirdre.

All thoughts of killing vanished as Broc thought of Sonya. She had followed him, had ventured into Cairn Toul. For him.

His rage was replaced with urgency. He had to find Sonya before she was hurt. Or worse, before Deirdre got to her. Broc severed Deirdre's head before he turned and flew toward Dunmore, who waited on the stairway.

Dunmore nervously crawled backward as Broc approached him. Broc landed before Dunmore and grabbed his throat. "Where is she?" he demanded.

"The wyrran took her."

Dunmore, the great and mighty mortal who always did as Deirdre wished, now shook and clawed at the hand that held him.

"Did you harm her?"

Dunmore shook his head, his eyes wild. The lie was there for Broc to see, and it sent him over the edge.

"Doona fear, you witless fool. Deirdre will be joining you soon." With that, Broc broke his neck with a twist of his hands.

He tossed Dunmore's body down the stairs and flew to the entrance. Broc landed in the doorway and listened. He didn't have long before Deirdre's magic mended her. He had to find Sonya and get her away from the mountain before then.

Broc thought of the curse, of how it was getting ready to strike again. This time with Sonya.

He couldn't let that happen. He *wouldn't* let that happen. He'd find her and take her far from Cairn Toul. He'd take her to someone who could heal whatever injuries she had.

And he would leave her.

He had no choice. It was evident the longer she stayed near him, the more likely she was to die. He wouldn't live through that. The past few days had sent him teetering on the edge of oblivion with his god.

If Sonya died . . . there would be nothing holding him back from giving in.

With his plan formed, he used his power and located Sonya in the dungeons. He hurried to her, afraid he would be too late and hopeful the wyrran were still with her so he could kill them.

He heard a faint sound of distress when he reached the dungeons. Sonya was alive, but scared and hurt. He could feel her magic, feel the pull of it.

He didn't deny what he was, or the need to feed his god. What was coming was Deirdre's and the wyrran's fault. And they would pay dearly for every scratch on Sonya's beautiful body.

Broc walked into the dungeon ready for battle. He growled as he found seven wyrran circling Sonya. She lay on her side, her arms over her head for protection.

Fury began to burn in his chest. The wyrran hadn't noticed him as they continued to taunt Sonya, their shrieks bouncing off the walls. Rage exploded in Broc when a wyrran reached down and scratched her with its claws.

Broc roared as the frenzy overtook him. The need to protect Sonya, to kill those who would dare to harm her. He couldn't stop it.

And he didn't want to.

One by one he killed the wyrran. He didn't feel their claws, never heard their screams. He was intent on their blood and death.

Kill. Kill. Kill.

Until he stood alone.

Broc's chest heaved, his breathing harsh to his ears. Gradually the frenzy died. His god was appeased. Death had been dealt.

The dungeon was alarmingly silent. He slowly turned to find Sonya lying still as stone. Panic began to snake up his spine that he had accidentally killed her. The thought paralyzed him for one heartbeat, two.

His gaze raked her from head to foot, hoping she was all right, praying he hadn't hurt her. He tried to make himself go to her so he could see for himself, but fear of what he might have done while he was crazed held him rooted.

"Broc?"

The sweetest sound he had ever heard was her voice at that moment. He dropped to his knees and gathered her in his arms. "Are you hurt?"

"My head aches. How . . ."

"Later. Now, we need to get out of the mountain. Can you walk?"

Her chin lifted. "Of course."

Broc hid a smile as he helped her to her feet. Warmth spread through him at having her near again. It seemed right, as if it had always been destined that they would be together.

He didn't believe in destiny, but the thought felt too good to dismiss, especially after thinking he might have killed her.

"This way," he said, and took her hand as he led her from the dungeon.

Her grip was tight, her body steady. That in itself gave Broc more relief than checking her himself for injuries.

The stairs out of the dungeon were steep and slick from the dampness of the mountain. Broc couldn't fly to the top, since the narrow stairway switchbacked to the top, leaving him no room to spread his wings.

They reached the top without incident, but almost immediately were beset by wyrran. Broc kept Sonya at his back and used his wings to protect her.

Her hands, small and warm, upon his wings as he fought made him shiver with need, with a hunger that demanded he take more. Demanded that he ignore the curse and make Sonya his. But now wasn't the time for his mind to think such thoughts. Too much danger was near.

With the wyrran quickly dispatched, they were running again. Broc kept his pace slow so Sonya could keep up. There were supposed to be only two exits in the entire mountain. But Broc had made a third only he knew about.

And it would be the one that saved their lives.

"This way," he said as he veered down another hallway.

Sonya never questioned him. She kept hold of his hand and didn't stop. The fact she trusted him so completely made him feel like the man he had been before his god was unbound. A man Broc had never thought to be again.

They snaked their way through the hallways and up stairs. Only twice did they have to stop and kill more wyrran. Each time Broc used his wings to safeguard Sonya.

"Here." He slid to a halt and directed her into a small chamber.

Broc followed her into the storage room and shoved aside sacks of grain, baskets of wheat, and barrels of ale until he found what he was looking for.

Sonya leaned forward. "Is that an exit?"

"One I spent years digging. It'll get us out, but we have to hurry."

She didn't hesitate to climb through the opening. Broc tamped down his god and quickly followed Sonya. They would have to crawl, which would slow them.

"I see light," Sonya whispered.

Broc smiled. "You're almost there. When you get to the opening, be careful. It's a wee bit of a drop."

He watched, ready to spring forward and grab Sonya as she reached the end and used the tunnel wall to gain her footing. He heard her indrawn breath and knew she was looking down.

Broc climbed out beside her and took her hand. The

view before him was awe-inspiring. The clouds cast shadows on the mountains in various shapes as they soared across the sky. But a look down showed they had a narrow ledge half the width of his foot on which to stand.

"Are you ready?" he asked.

Her smile was wide as she met his gaze. "I do love to fly."

Broc turned and grabbed her as he fell sideways. He called forth his god and flapped his wings to take them high into the clouds.

Somehow they had gotten free of Deirdre. It had been almost too easy, point in fact. Broc had no doubt she would redouble her efforts to find them, especially when she knew where he was headed.

Glencoe.

SEVENTEEN

The wind howled around Sonya as Broc took her in his arms and fell from the mountain. Not once did she doubt she was safe. Never would she doubt it again as long as Broc was near.

She watched as his sun-kissed skin turned the deepest, darkest blue beneath her fingertips. One moment they were falling, and the next, his wings were unfurled and lifting them higher.

Sonya stared, transfixed at Broc's wings. She'd always found them fascinating. They were smooth as leather, and just as tough and thick. And they were massive, rising well above his head and falling past his knees.

The steady beat of the wings as they flew was reassuring. Soothing. Sonya didn't see any of the beauty that surrounded her. She was focused on Broc, on the man who could seemingly do anything.

He had been captured by Deirdre a second time, yet somehow he had gotten free. She couldn't wait to hear how.

Sonya laid her head on his shoulder. Her head ached fiercely from Dunmore's vicious shove. But she would do it all again as long as Broc was released.

She closed her eyes and let her mind drift. The wind whistled by her ears, the only sound other than the pounding of Broc's wings and his heart.

His arms held her securely against him, their bodies molded as one from hip to shoulder. For a brief moment, Sonya could allow herself to think she and Broc were something more.

For a brief moment, she allowed herself to think nothing evil would ever touch them again.

Broc circled the Glencoe area several times looking for wyrran as well as a safe place to land. He let his eyes feast upon the Aonach Eagach on the northern side, a pinnacled ridge which linked three peaks and spanned at least three leagues.

The mountains on the southern side were strikingly beautiful. But the grandest and highest peak of Glencoe was the Bidean nam Bian, hidden behind the three truncated crests called The Three Sisters of Glencoe.

Water tumbled from those high mountains to fall in an array of spectacular waterfalls. Broc found the perfect spot near a stream with several small cascades.

The rocky, rolling landscape would provide the cover they needed. Broc dove from the cover of the clouds to swoop low over the land.

A startled buck raced away from him as he flew by. He reached the stream and hovered over the spot a moment before allowing his feet to touch the ground. An instant later, his indigo skin and wings had disappeared.

"Where are we?" Sonya asked as she blinked and looked around.

Broc gently pushed her down to sit on a flat rock. He took the satchel from her and reached inside for the water skin. "Near Glencoe."

"Glencoe," she repeated. "I thought we were returning to MacLeod Castle."

"We probably should have, but as I flew from Cairn Toul, I knew we had to come here first." Broc filled the water skin before handing it to her. "Drink. Then we'll talk."

He squatted across from her and waited as she drank her fill. She never stopped gazing around them. He wanted to see to the wound on her head as well as her previous injury on her hand. He couldn't imagine either were doing well at this point.

She lowered the water skin. "Now, tell me why Glencoe?"

Broc shook his head slowly. "Nay. First, you will tell me what you were doing in Cairn Toul as well as how you became injured."

"When you left the inn, I saw you. I saw you land in the woods, and I knew that at any moment there would be wyrran barging into the inn. None came."

"You should have stayed put."

She cocked an eyebrow. "It took some doing, but I was able to convince Jean to let me leave the inn."

"Tell me you didna go into the forest." The thought of her near so many wyrran left him fuming. He had warned her to stay away.

She shrugged. "I had to know what was going on. Before I ever heard Dunmore, I knew they weren't there for me. It had been too easy for you to lure them away if they had been after me. They had come for you."

"So you saw them take me?"

"I did," she answered with a quick nod. "And I followed."

Broc ran a hand down his face. Sonya was going to be the death of him. Didn't she understand the danger? Didn't she realize how much it meant to him that she stay alive?

"I had to, Broc. I wasn't going to let her hurt you again."

He looked into her amber eyes and felt something

shift inside his chest. He saw the depth of fear and worry she had for him. All the anger dissipated, replaced with . . . awe.

She had risked her life for him. It was almost too much to believe.

"What happened?" he finally managed to get past his lips.

"I found the door into Cairn Toul but couldn't get in. Then, it opened and there was a wyrran in front of me. I used the dagger to cut off its head, but the blade got stuck in the bone and I couldn't free it."

Broc inwardly groaned. "You went into that mountain without a weapon?"

She lifted a slim shoulder in a shrug. "I wasn't inside long when I stumbled upon Dunmore. He was mortally wounded and dying."

"He wasna wounded when I saw him. But he willna be able to harm anyone ever again." Broc frowned as he began to put things together. "It was Dunmore who hurt you, wa it no'?"

"We had made a pact. I would heal him if he took me to you."

Broc could only stare at her. "I thought you said you couldna heal anymore."

"I knew I couldn't, but I was willing to try."

For you went left unsaid. But Broc knew that's what she had meant. He could see it in her eyes, hear it in her voice. And it left him rejoicing. Still angry she had put herself in danger, but overjoyed nonetheless.

"I tried to convince him to bring me to you first," Sonya continued, unaware of his inner turmoil. "Dunmore refused. I had no choice but to try."

"You obviously healed him."

"Not wholly. I found a small thread of magic somehow. I stopped the bleeding and managed to mend the wound together, but he was still in a great amount of pain."

Broc blew out a breath. The longer the tale went on, the more irritated he became. She had done it for him, though. No one had ever done such a thing for him, and that was the only thing which kept him from telling her how he never wanted her to put herself in that kind of danger again.

"So, what happened?" he asked. He had to know the rest.

"I was able to feel a small portion of my magic. It repaired my hands before it began to heal Dunmore."

"Good," Broc said quickly.

Sonya smiled. "He wasn't pleased. Once I had convinced him I had healed him all I could, we went in search of you. I kept him in front of me at all times so I could see him. But then I heard you."

"Ah," Broc said. It must have been when he'd bellowed.

"I knew which direction to go in then. I forgot about Dunmore, which I shouldn't have done. I realized my error right as I began to pass him. He shoved me into the wall and my head hit a stone. I don't remember anything after that until I woke with wyrran around me."

Broc shifted so that he sat on a large, flat rock and braced his elbows on his knees. "So you can heal yourself now?"

She reached up and touched her head. "I think so. It's odd. I can feel my magic again, but it isn't as great as before. It takes a lot for me to be able to use it. I thought I had used what little I had left on Dunmore, but when I awoke in the dungeons, I could feel my magic."

"I'm no' going to question how you can feel it again, I'm just glad you can."

She grinned. "I thought I was half a woman after my

magic left me. Odd how when I thought I could possibly be going to my death to free you, I realized I was still the same person. Magic or not."

"Magic doesna make you special, Sonya. You are special because you are you." He held her gaze before he cleared his throat. "And your head? How does it feel?"

"It still aches, but not as much as before. It's also stopped bleeding."

Broc was pleased. He had never ceased feeling Sonya's magic, and now she could once again feel it giving her the confidence he had come to associate with her. "Come, wash the blood from your face."

She rose and walked to the edge of the stream. There was a short waterfall just to the right of them, the water running over and around the countless and varied rocks that lined the stream. The water flowed down the mountain, creating the many waterfalls.

Broc never took his eyes from Sonya as she knelt on a long, mostly level rock and dipped her hands into the cool water. She splashed her face, the water droplets trickling over her jaw and down her throat before disappearing into her gown.

He had never been so envious of water before. It was touching her as Broc had never dared, but he had certainly dreamed about. He knew her kiss, but he wanted to know all of her. Every wonderful, delightful inch of her.

As if sensing his gaze, she looked over her shoulder at him. The hair around her face was damp and curling into thick ringlets. The sun peeked from behind a cloud and set her locks on fire.

Sonya smoothed her hair from her face and returned to Broc. "Tell me how you got loose from Deirdre. And why they took you."

"They took me because Deirdre wanted revenge. I

betrayed her. She always suspected Quinn would, but I had fooled her."

Sonya nodded, her lips twisting wryly. "I see."

"She was going to kill me and bring me back to life as many times as it took for the evil to take root and my god to seize control."

"Could that really happen?"

He frowned. "Aye."

"By all that's holy," Sonya murmured. "How many times did she kill you?"

"None."

Sonya's eyes grew large. "What did you do?"

"She's vain. I was able to get her to talk about herself. She has always been too confident, too certain of the outcomes. She began to tell me about another artifact she has located."

Sonya smiled. "Ah, the reason we are in Glencoe."

"Exactly. I doona know where precisely the artifact is, but I know it is in a Celtic burial mound."

"Tell me you're jesting," Sonya said with a shiver. "You know no one can go inside the mounds."

"I wish I were jesting."

"She could be lying."

Broc shook his head. "I know her, Sonya. She wasna."

"Forget the tomb right now. I want to know how you got free of her."

"She had me far below the mountain where she kept Phelan all those years."

Sonya's face crinkled with disgust. "Isla told me that place is desolate."

"The entire mountain is. But I was isolated there, and that's what she wanted. I was to be the leader of her new Warriors. She threatened to harm those I cared about, and with her magical chains holding me, I couldna get free."

"Did you convince her to release you?"

He smiled. "Somehow through the agony of the *drough* blood I recalled the spell I heard her use to unlock doors and chains. I knew I had nothing to lose in trying it."

"But you aren't a Druid. How could the magic work for you?"

Broc shrugged. "It's just a spell."

"Anyone can say a spell, but you if don't have magic, it won't work."

"I suppose there's some in my god then, because the chains released me."

Sonya bit her lip with her teeth. "There must be some magic in your god, in all the gods. It would explain how the Warriors can sense Druid magic."

"It certainly would."

"I cannot imagine Deirdre was happy when the chains released you."

Broc chuckled as he recalled Deirdre's fury. "She was more surprised than I that it actually worked. I attacked her and beheaded her before I turned to Dunmore. I killed him and went looking for you."

"That's quite a story."

"As was yours."

She ducked her head and smiled. "We were lucky, Broc."

"Verra lucky."

"Almost too lucky, some would say."

Broc sighed, Sonya's words echoing his from earlier. "If she captures us again, neither of us will be so fortunate."

"Precisely," Sonya said. "Which is why I think it would be wiser to return to MacLeod Castle and gather more Warriors to search for the tomb."

Broc shook his head. "We doona have the time.

Deirdre knows Reaghan is the first artifact. If Deirdre amasses the artifacts, we've failed. We have to try. I've gotten us here before them. If we hurry, we should be able to find the burial mound and retrieve the artifact well before Deirdre arrives."

For long moments Sonya stared at him before she smiled and stood. "I suppose we need to begin searching then."

EIGHTEEN

Deirdre rose up on her elbows and wiped the blood from her lips with the back of her hand. She rolled over and sat up only to find Dunmore's body, twisted and broken, beside her.

Somehow Broc had gotten free of her chains. How could a Warrior use her spell? She had never thought any of them paid attention to her spells, or would realize how valuable they would be.

Apparently she had been wrong.

And she loathed being wrong.

Once more she was without a Warrior. It would have taken weeks to break Broc into the Warrior she wanted and needed, but it would have been worth it. Broc was a leader, had been a leader in his former life.

He would have been the perfect Warrior to challenge Fallon MacLeod to rule the others. But she knew exactly where to begin searching for Broc.

"Deirdre," whispered a voice in the cavern.

The deep, gravelly voice bounced off the stone walls and echoed around her. The black smoke came from nowhere and encircled her, constricting her breathing and hampering her movements.

"My lord," she whispered, because she could barely talk.

The voice tsked several times. "Deirdre, you had him

within your grasp. I told you all you needed to do to convert him and have his god take control."

"I didn't realize he knew my spell."

"Or that he could use it," the voice said stonily.

Deirdre refused to show fear. This was *diabhul*, Satan, her master. She had given her soul to him and would do all that he commanded. "I have failed you now, but he will be mine."

"You need him and Quinn. There are others, but for now, concentrate on those two."

Deirdre nodded. "I will see it done, my lord."

"I want this world covered in darkness. For death and fear to fill the air. You will rule it, Deirdre. I choose you from all the *drough* because you are the only one who has the boldness to see this through."

"I have done everything you asked."

"No!" the voice boomed around her. "Your insolence allowed the MacLeods to escape again and again. Now, you have no Warriors and Broc is gone."

Her skin prickled where his anger coated her. It felt as if she were on fire. "There are the artifacts still."

The annoyance disappeared as he chuckled. "Do you really believe those will help you? The MacLeods already have one, and your overconfidence has given Broc the means to acquire the second."

"I will stop him."

"Forget the artifacts. They are nothing. No amount of magic can compare to my power. And yours. You know this."

"Aye, my lord, but the Seer said if I am to succeed, I need the artifacts."

The smoke began to drift upward. "I command you again, Deirdre. Forget the artifacts. Find more Warriors. You will need them."

Deirdre waited until the smoke was gone before she

rose to her feet. She had always listened to her lord, but this time she could not. She knew in the depths of her black soul she needed those artifacts.

And she would have them.

Deirdre left the cavern, her mind forming multiple plans as she walked the never-ending stairway to the top. Once she reached the doorway, she called to her wyrran. She sent groups of six of them to the clans where she knew a god was passed down through their blood.

Once the wyrran had departed, she hurried to create more. She had lost so many in her battle with the MacLeods, but the wyrran were easy to form. She would have her army.

How many hours passed as she worked, she didn't know.

Deirdre leaned her hands against the stones as exhaustion weighed upon her. She had been creating wyrran for hours. The stones, however, gave her the relief and strength she needed to fortify her.

And as much as she didn't want to, she knew she had to leave her precious mountain to seek Broc.

Sonya walked beside Broc in companionable silence. The hills they crossed had been easy to climb. So far they hadn't seen any burial mounds, but with the landscape, they could easily pass near one and not know it.

She glanced at the mountains. "I don't think the mound would be in the mountains."

"Nay," Broc agreed. "Too much rock."

"It could be anywhere. Should we go to the village and ask?"

Broc shook his head. "I doona want anyone to know we're looking for it."

"Then we could be searching for weeks."

"Let's hope no'. It willna be too much longer before Deirdre arrives."

Sonya frowned. "Deirdre? She never leaves her mountain."

"Things have changed. I suspect since losing the first artifact she'll come for this one herself."

Sonya hoped Broc was wrong. She didn't want to encounter Deirdre, not with her magic as low as it was. "Maybe you should take a look from above. Fly around and see if you can see anything."

"No' without you," he said.

"I'll stay right here."

He stopped to look around them before he turned dark eyes filled with reluctance and determination on her. "In the open? Where anyone could see you? I doona think so."

"You said yourself a wyrran can smell my magic. What difference does it make where I am?"

Broc clenched his jaw and narrowed his eyes. "I'm no' leaving you."

"You want to find the tomb, and we need to hurry. What other choice do we have?"

"Nay. This isna a debate, Sonya."

Sonya faced him, an idea taking root. "What if you use your power? You can find anyone. Why not whoever is buried in the mound?"

"Because I doona know who this person was. I have to know who I'm searching for or it doesna work."

"Oh," she said, and began walking again. She had thought she had solved their dilemma.

Broc caught up with her in two strides. "It was a good thought. Verra clever thinking."

Such words shouldn't make her so happy, but they did. Deliriously so.

They walked for another quarter hour before Broc turned them off their course.

"What are you doing?"

"There's a storm coming," he said and pointed to the sky.

Sonya glanced up and saw the clouds gathering overhead. She hadn't even noticed them. The Highlands were notorious for sudden, freak storms and disorienting mists which descended from the mountains when least expected.

No sooner had Broc mentioned the storm than it began to drizzle rain. Sonya gripped his hand when he took hold of her and led her toward the mountains.

The last thing she wanted to do was try to climb on the wet rocks, but she followed Broc. By the time they reached the edge of the mountain she was soaked through and shivering.

"Here," Broc shouted over the din of the rain.

Sonya followed him into the cave and stopped at the entrance as he let the satchel drop from his hands. She couldn't see in the dark as he could with his advanced eyesight, and until she knew nothing lurked in the gloom, like a wolf, she wasn't going to move.

Broc glanced at her and grinned. "There's nothing in the cave, Sonya."

"How far back does it go?"

"A ways. Stay here and I will take a look."

Before she could tell him nay, he was gone.

Sonya turned and put her back against the wall of the cave. She wrapped her arms around her middle and tried to keep warm. Her eyes felt as if sand coated them. She rubbed them, then immediately wished she hadn't since it only made them burn worse.

"Nothing," Broc said as he walked toward her from

out of the darkness. "I did find a few pieces of wood. They're small, but they'll start a fire."

Sonya took the wood from him. "I'll get this going. Go look for more before it gets too wet."

She set about stacking the wood and had just got the fire lit when Broc returned with more wood. "This is going to have to last us."

"We can begin looking again as soon as the storm lets up," she said and huddled as close to the fire as she could.

Broc tugged his tunic over his head and spread it out to dry. "You need to remove your clothes so they can dry. I doona want to chance you becoming ill and no' being able to heal yourself."

She swallowed nervously and glanced at his mouth, a mouth that had kissed her softly, sensuously. Thoroughly. She had done well in not letting him realize just how much that kiss had affected her, but she couldn't lie to herself. Not when she craved more of him.

Sonya cleared her throat and tugged at the clinging, wet material as it stuck to her. There was nothing for her to cover herself with. Broc had taken her cloak, and as far as she knew, it was still out in the woods somewhere.

His dark, soulful eyes turned to her. She couldn't read his emotions, never knew what he was thinking, because he kept himself closed off and apart from everyone else. He'd had to in order to survive in Deirdre's mountain.

Sonya shifted onto her bottom and removed her shoes. Broc held her gaze the entire time. He didn't look away when she pulled her skirts up to her calves so she could remove her wool stockings.

He didn't look away when she rose up on her knees

and began to gather her skirts in her hand. It wasn't until the cool air hit her legs that he dropped his gaze and turned his back to her.

She was disappointed he had turned away. Maybe the kiss had just been a kindness. Maybe it meant nothing and she was simply making a fool of herself.

Sonya spread out her stockings and her gown near the fire. She shivered in her wet chemise, but when she turned around, Broc held out a tartan, his face angled away.

"Warm yourself with this," he said.

She hastily removed her chemise and grabbed the tartan to wrap around her shoulders, thankful someone had thought to pack it in the satchel. She sat before the fire and hoped it chased the chill away.

Broc sat across from her and stirred the fire with a long stick. "You should probably rest."

"You as well."

"I will."

"How did you know the cave was here?"

He shrugged. "I spotted it when I noticed the storm."

"I'm glad."

His fathomless eyes shifted to her. They beckoned her, lured her. Some unnamed emotion, dark and full of longing and need flashed in his gaze. It made her stomach flip and her breathing quicken.

When his eyes dropped to her mouth, Sonya sucked in a breath that locked in her lungs. No one had ever looked at her before with such desire, such yearning.

She was drowning in his brown eyes.

Engulfed.

Overwhelmed.

Immersed.

And she never wanted to be anywhere else again.

What was it about Broc that drew her? He tried to

keep himself withdrawn, but she had seen the kindness of his soul, knew what lengths he would go to for those he cared about.

But what drew her from the first moment she had seen him was the way he looked at her.

As if she mattered. As if she was important.

To him.

NINETEEN

Broc knew he should look away from Sonya. But he couldn't.

She consumed his thoughts, his dreams. His desires. He knew the feel of her tall form against his, knew the way she fit alongside him. He knew the scent of her skin, the warmth of her body.

He knew there were seven freckles across the bridge of her nose and she had flecks of gold in her amber eyes. He knew the intense and sensual feel of her magic.

Broc had thought he knew all there was to know about Sonya. Then he had kissed her.

If he had yearned for her before, now he burned.

That one simple, soul-stealing taste of her was seared on his being forever.

Desire blazed within him as he thought of kissing her again, of holding her body against his. Of hearing her soft sighs of pleasure.

His balls tightened, urging him to go to her. To taste her again. Longer, more leisurely. His gaze dropped to her lips, and he bit back a moan when he saw them part.

Could she want him? Did the same raging need fill her veins that did his?

Broc desperately wanted to find out. He wanted to go to her, to pull her into his arms and kiss her until they were both lost in the passion that controlled him.

Then, he remembered his curse.

The fire burning through his veins cooled instantly.

Broc pulled his gaze from Sonya and jabbed at the fire with the stick. He turned his mind from her tantalizing body to the burial mound and how they would find it.

Maybe Sonya was correct. Maybe he should take to the sky and see if he could locate the mound. It would certainly help save time.

"I think your idea of me looking for the mound is a solid one," Broc said.

"When will you begin your search?"

He glanced out of the cave into the rain. "As soon as the rain begins to lessen."

"Have you thought about what will happen if we don't find it?"

"The only way that will be acceptable is if Deirdre doesna find it either."

Sonya sighed softly. "Does she know where it's located?"

"She might. She didna say anything about it, but then again, she could have purposefully left that part out."

"What aren't you telling me, Broc?"

He glanced at her and shrugged. "I doona know what you're talking about."

"You do. If Deirdre has known about this second artifact and where it is, why hasn't she sent her wyrran or Dunmore after it before now?"

He should have known Sonya would figure out he was hiding something. There was no other choice but to tell her now. Maybe she would know something he didn't.

"Do you know anything of the burial mounds?" he asked.

She shook her head, her brow furrowing in thought.

"Only what they are and that they aren't to be disturbed."

"The Celts used the Druids to inscribe spells around the doors to some of their tombs."

"As a means to keep people out?"

He licked his lips and chuckled. "In a manner of speaking. The few who have these spells etched on their doorways did it because they have something of importance inside, something they doona want anyone to get. They made sure that some people could get inside, but they might never find the one thing which was meant to be kept hidden."

"In other words, Deirdre cannot get into the tomb."

"Precisely."

Sonya drew her legs up to her chest. When she did, the tartan fell open to reveal her foot and most of her calf. Broc thought of reaching over, of laying his hands along her skin and slowly caressing up her leg to her thigh, then the swell of her hip.

"How did she expect to reach the artifact?" Sonya asked, jerking Broc out of his thoughts.

Broc cleared his throat and tried to take control of the desire that burned intensely. "She was going to use me."

"I don't understand." Sonya's brow was creased, her eyes filled with doubt and uncertainty. "How did she expect you to get in?"

"I'm no' sure. She was certain I would be able to, though."

"Before or after she released all the evil in you?"

"After."

Sonya shook her head, her flame-colored curls coming loose from her braid. "Could it be just *droughs* which are kept out of the tomb?"

"If she didna send wyrran or Dunmore, it has to be more than that."

"What, then? It cannot be evil. If that were the case, then once your god had control of you, you would be recognized as evil as well."

"I doona think we'll understand any of it until we reach the burial mound. Until then, we are doing nothing but speculating."

She grinned, her eyes crinkling at the corners. "I know, but I find myself vastly curious. Obviously, Deirdre has known about this artifact for some time but hasn't been able to obtain it. If she's so formidable, what would cancel that power?"

"I'm guessing whatever is in the tomb."

Sonya reached inside the satchel and drew out their last two oatcakes. She handed one to Broc and began to eat hers as she watched him. He was a keeper of secrets, but just what kind of secrets? "You know so much of me and my life, yet I know almost nothing of you."

"There's nothing to know."

She suspected he might not want to tell her, and she didn't want to push. She might never know who Broc was before Deirdre had first captured him.

Despite his reserved nature, she had seen a glimmer of something in Broc made more obvious by Jean's statement that Broc was a nobleman.

Since she had been kept in isolation with the Druids most of her life, she wasn't sure she would know the difference between a noble and a commoner, except for the obvious clothes and jewels.

Sonya finished her oatcake and tried again. "As much as I've enjoyed my time at MacLeod Castle, I would like to visit another village soon. Maybe even travel to Edinburgh and see the king's castle."

"You think you've missed out on things being raised by the Druids, do you no'?" Broc asked, his voice soft, mellow.

"In some ways. There is much of the world I know nothing about."

"You havna missed anything. People are cruel and savage. They steal and murder at the least provocation, and think nothing of betraying their friends."

"That is true of everyone. Mortals, Druids, and Warriors alike," Sonya said.

Broc grunted and his lips twisted in a sneer of anger and bitterness. "You have no' seen the wars I have, Sonya. Hundreds of men dying because their lords told them to. A war simply because one man thought the other purposefully served him soured wine."

There was something in Broc's voice, something in his face that told Sonya he had not only known this but experienced it. "That must have been difficult to watch."

"No' watch. I was in the middle of the damned battle."

Her heart ached for him, for the resentment he still carried. "You survived."

"Ah, but so many good men didna. Both my brothers fell, as did my father, three cousins, and uncle."

Sonya reached out and placed her hand on his arm. "I'm sorry, Broc."

"It was a long time ago."

"Maybe, but it still bothers you."

"It took less than a day for my life to turn on its side. One moment for Hugh, the laird of the Ferguson clan and friend of my father, to declare Da had given him spoiled wine on purpose. It wasna like Hugh to act so rashly."

Sonya lowered her hand when he shifted away from her. So Broc had been a laird's son. A noble. Jean had been correct. "That statement caused the rift between your clans?"

"Aye. Clans which had been allies for generations were now enemies. Men I had called friends suddenly refused to acknowledge me. The next morning, we met on the battlefield."

She shivered at the desolation in his voice.

"I thought I would never see such death again. But it wasna long after that the wyrran took me."

"And your god was unbound."

"Aye."

"Who became laird when you went missing?"

His head swiveled to hers. With eyes staring hard, Broc said, "A younger cousin."

"Have you seen your clan since Deirdre took you?"

"Once. They are thriving, which is all I could have hoped for."

Sonya rearranged the tartan across her shoulders. "Why didn't you want me to learn you were nobility?"

"I never said I was."

"You didn't have to. Jean did. And it's the way you act. Why deny it?"

"Because I'm no' the man I was."

"You may not be as naïve, but you are a better man than the one who watched his father and brothers die on the battlefield."

Broc scrubbed a hand down his face. "I've done terrible things, Sonya. If I was such a good man, why would I have done them?"

"You were a spy. You had no choice if you were to have Deirdre trust and confide in you."

"There was a point, no' long ago, that I forgot who I was. I wasna sure if I was really spying for Deirdre or if I had aligned with her. The lines had begun to blur."

Sonya could only imagine what he had gone through at Deirdre's hands, and the many things he had done in service to her. "You didn't give in. Instead, you did things others wouldn't have. You saved me and Anice. You helped the MacLeods."

"I could have done more."

"Everyone can look back into their pasts and say that."

He suddenly grinned at her. "For one so young, you are certainly wise."

"I am a Druid," she teased.

"That you are."

They fell silent, and Sonya once more found herself longing to kiss Broc. She wanted to be in his arms, to feel his strength surround her.

If the past few days had showed her anything, it was that life could be snatched away at any moment. For so long, Sonya had let her fears rule her.

Not anymore.

She would take the risks she had longed to take, say the words she had wanted to say, and kiss an indigo Warrior who filled her thoughts.

Sonya rose to her feet. Broc tilted his head in question, a small frown marring his forehead. She wanted to smooth her fingers across his brow and erase those lines.

"There have been very few times in my life when I've done as I wished," she said and walked around the fire.

"What are you talking about?"

She grinned. "Me. Anice was the one who did as she pleased, uncaring of how it affected others. Whereas I always did what was expected. No more."

"Sonya . . ." Broc's voice trailed away when she continued around the fire.

She stopped in front of him. "No one knows what tomorrow will bring or if we'll survive this day. I don't want to regret anything anymore."

Before he could say a word, she let the tartan drop to her feet.

TWENTY

In all his two hundred and seventy-five years, no one had surprised him like Sonya did.

He let his gaze run over her stunning body at his leisure, from her full pink-tipped breasts to her narrow waist. To the flare of her hips to the triangle of red curls that hid her sex and down her long, lean legs.

And back up again.

Broc was on his feet and standing before her in the next heartbeat. He looked into her amber eyes and saw the desire, the need that beat within himself.

"Sonya," he whispered.

He put his hands on her elbows then caressed up her arms to her shoulders. A small sigh, barely discernible except to his hearing, was the only sound.

Everything was just as he had imagined it would be, except for one thing.

Broc reached behind her back and grasped her braid. He unwound the strip of fabric and spread her hair about her shoulders.

He traced her lips with his thumb, eager to plunder her depths again. Her scent surrounded him. Lulled him. Appeased him.

But it was the feel of her magic that drove him wild.

It was unlike any other magic he had ever felt. Commanding. Imposing. Dominating. Pure, raw *mie* magic at its most powerful.

And she had no idea just how strong her magic was. Which is what made her so special. Special enough that he shouldn't touch her, taint her with the deeds of his past or the curse.

Yet, he couldn't walk away.

Deep inside, he had known the moment he had found her with the wolf that their paths would lead to this. He had thought to dissuade her, to keep his distance. But that wasn't possible.

Broc took the small step which separated them and pulled her body against his. Sonya placed her hands on his chest. His skin burned wherever she touched.

Her caress was feather light as she worked her way up to his shoulders, then around his neck. It was Broc's turn to bite back a moan when her fingers toyed with his hair at the nape of his neck.

She rose up on tiptoe and used one finger to move a strand of blond hair out of his face.

Broc could take no more. He leaned down and took her mouth in a kiss. It was violent, raw, and passionate. But the need, the ferocious hunger that tore at Broc's soul would not be denied the sweet taste of Sonya's lips another moment.

He rejoiced when she melted against him and opened her lips. He delved into her mouth, stroking her tongue with his. With every sweep of his tongue, he claimed more of her, demanded more of her.

And she gave freely.

Broc's hands roamed her back and cupped her bottom so he could grind against her. Her soft body cushioned his and enflamed his mounting desire. She moaned into his mouth, her fingers digging into his neck each time he pushed his throbbing cock against her.

He deepened the kiss, taking them higher, driving them further and further toward the sweetest reward. She clung to him, her breathing as ragged and broken as his own, but there were no thoughts of stopping running through his mind.

Too many nights he had dreamed of holding her thus. Too many days he had looked at her lips and wondered about her kiss. Too many times he had thought of spreading her legs and filling her.

Broc broke the kiss and stepped out of her arms. "Doona move," he told her.

He hurried to spread the tartan at her feet. Then he pulled off his boots and reached for her again.

"Aren't you forgetting something?" Sonya asked and glanced down at his breeches.

"Have you been with a man before?"

A slight blush stained her cheeks. "Nay. But I know enough that you won't need those."

Broc smiled but shook his head. "I think they need to stay on a wee longer."

"I disagree."

He sucked in a breath when her hands reached for the waist of his breeches. Her fingers glided between his skin and the leather, tempting him. Teasing him. Enticing him.

"Sonya," he whispered as her fingers skimmed the head of his arousal.

She unfastened his breeches and pushed them down his hips to puddle around his ankles. There was a sensual smile pulling at her lips when she stepped back to look at him.

Sonya stood in awe. Broc was a masterpiece of striking male beauty. With his wings, he often went without a tunic, so she knew the raw masculinity of his upper body. The way the muscles moved in his chest and arms, the thick sinew of his neck and shoulders.

She let her gaze drift down his powerful chest to the rippled muscles of his stomach. His chest narrowed to slim hips, but that's not what got her attention.

It was the strip of golden hair that ran from his navel down to his arousal. Sonya swallowed as she got her first look at him.

Broc's rod was thick and jutted upward. It jumped as if sensing how eager she was to feel it inside her.

She barely got a look at Broc's powerful legs before he had her crushed against him, her breasts pressed flat to his chest. She tilted her head and opened her mouth for his kiss.

In the next instant she was on her back, Broc looming above her. His dark brown eyes met hers for a moment before he kissed her once more.

Sonya welcomed his weight, the hard length of his body against hers. She had never known something could feel so good. And his hot shaft against her leg only fueled her need to touch him.

She reached between their bodies and wrapped her fingers around his rod. He moaned and thrust his hips. Sonya loved the feel of him. Like silk over iron. The skin of his cock was smooth and soft, but the heat of him, the hardness enthralled her.

Suddenly, he shifted and moved out of her reach. Sonya didn't have time to argue as his hands came up to cup her breasts. His fingers swirled around her nipples, coming ever closer to the peaks.

Until finally he touched them.

Sonya gave a whimper as heat bubbled and spread

through her body. Her breasts swelled and ached for more. He rolled her nipples between his fingers and lightly pinched them, causing her to moan.

Her sex pulsed and wound tighter with each caress. Sonya lifted her hips until she could rub against him, adding fuel to her already rampant desire.

And then Broc's mouth closed over a straining nipple.

Sonya's back arched when he began to suckle. His tongue stroked the peak until she was panting and begging for more. When he moved to her other breast, she cried out at the delicious feel of his mouth.

Time ceased. The only thing in the entire world was Sonya and Broc and the passion that raged out of control.

The sensations wracking her body were strong and fantastic. As he kissed down her stomach, all Sonya could think about was giving him as much pleasure as he gave her.

She tried to rub against him again, but he had moved down her body and now lay between her legs. His hands gripped her hips as he kissed first one thigh, then the other.

Sonya couldn't take her eyes off him. No one man had ever seen her without clothes, and the way Broc stared at her sex should have embarrassed her. Yet, it made her blood heat and her passion rise.

The longing, the yearning in his gaze took her breath away.

When he opened her thighs wider, she didn't stop him. A low moan escaped her lips when his fingers ran through the triangle of curls between her legs.

His fingers touched the sensitive flesh of her sex, urging her to open for him. Sonya never thought to deny him. She could feel her own dampness, knew Broc was the cause of it.

"So beautiful," he whispered before he spread her sex and put his mouth to her.

Sonya screamed at the first brush of his tongue against her clitoris. Her body was flooded with pleasure, inundated with the need for more.

His tongue stroked her, sending her higher and higher. Sonya was mindless with desire. Her body reacted instinctively and opened wider for him, silently begging for more. She got her wish when he pushed one long, thick finger inside her.

It was just what she needed. She moaned and began to rock her hips. His finger moved in and out of her, slowly at first to match his tongue. Her desire built, winding tighter and tighter.

He gradually increased the tempo until all Sonya could do was lie there as his experienced hands and mouth continued to pleasure her.

She had never felt so desperately needy, never felt such fire and hunger.

And then it all shattered.

Sonya cried out as her world broke apart. It sent her spiraling down an abyss, the waves of pleasure rolling over her again and again.

Broc rose over Sonya and watched as she peaked. She knew the touch of no other man, but she had trusted him, given herself to him.

Her eyes slowly opened, and she smiled up at him. No words were needed. He knew exactly how she felt by the contented way she looked at him. Her hands lightly caressed his back, inviting him.

She gave a small nod. It was what he had been waiting for. Broc grasped his cock and rubbed it against her sex. She moaned and whispered his name.

It was almost too much. He had been too long without

a woman, and his hunger for Sonya was too great. If he didn't get inside her soon, he would spill.

He guided himself to her opening and slowly pushed inside her. He felt the resistance of her maidenhead and paused.

"Don't you dare stop," she said.

Broc grinned. "Never."

With one thrust he seated himself inside her. She stiffened beneath him, her indrawn breath like a blade to his heart. He hadn't wanted to hurt her, but he'd had no choice.

"Sonya?"

"I'm all right," she whispered, her hands gripping his back.

He didn't believe her, but he'd make sure she felt pleasure again. Broc began to move within her. She was so tight, so hot. He had never dreamed she could feel so good. She soon relaxed beneath him and lifted her legs.

Her moans turned to cries of pleasure as he plunged deeper, harder into her tight sheath. Sweat glistened on their bodies, their breathing harsh as it echoed around them.

His need stretched endlessly, his hunger knew no bounds. Sonya matched his thrusts with equal fervor. He relentlessly, ruthlessly took her body, and she opened for him, accepting everything he demanded and taking her own.

The hunger, the consuming ache for Sonya urged him to claim more of her. He lifted first one knee, then her other. She gasped and rocked beneath him as he went even deeper.

She clung to him, her nails scouring his flesh as she wordlessly urged him onward.

He thrust harder, faster as he felt her body rise for

another orgasm. He wanted to look into her eyes and see her body surrender, to feel her body as she succumbed to the climax.

Sonya screamed his name as her back arched and she peaked. Her slick walls clutched him, convulsing around him until he could hold back no longer.

Broc gave a final thrust and gave in to the release.

He was swept away by the force of it, surprised by the strength of it.

Then he looked into Sonya's eyes and saw the fulfillment. She wrapped her arms around him.

Broc rolled to the side and pulled her against him. He hadn't meant to take Sonya, to mark her body with his. But now that he had, nothing was going to stand between them.

TWENTY-ONE

Phelan Stewart stood atop the hill and gazed out at the tall grass over the rolling landscape. He had no idea where he was.

And he didn't care.

Behind and to the side of him were the majestic mountains, with peaks arching to the clouds. He had explored only a portion of the mountains so far. Yet, he planned to climb each one. After all, he had eternity stretching before him.

A lengthy, leisurely, and, he was sure, lonesome expanse of years.

Phelan raised his head to the sky and closed his eyes against the onslaught of rain. He had almost forgotten what the rain felt like after one hundred and fifty years in Deirdre's mountain as her prisoner. Not counting the score of years she'd held him until she released his god.

The rain came down at a steady pace, enveloping the world in gray. The wind cut across the valley, causing the grass to sway and bend to its will.

He loved the feel of the elements on his skin, no matter how harsh they were.

Ever since Phelan had left Cairn Toul, he had been walking. So many years he'd been locked away in that dark mountain with Deirdre taking his blood and keeping him chained. It had been the cruelest torture.

But she had freed his god, and with his god was a power he had learned quickly to use. He had shown Isla his power by turning his prison into a sun-drenched day in the Highlands. How many times had he used his power to chase away the darkness and gloom of that cursed mountain?

So many times, but his power had been the only thing that had kept him from going insane.

He had missed the wind ruffling his hair and the rain upon his face. He had missed the smell of the heather and the way the sun and clouds would cast shadows over the mountains. He had missed the first snow of winter and the first sprouts of green in the spring.

If he could envision it, his power could create it. It was believable enough. But Phelan had known the truth. There was nothing like the feel of the real sun upon his skin or the sight of a full moon hanging low in the sky.

Isla had cautioned him that the world had changed in the years he had been held prisoner. He hadn't believed her. After all, she was the one who had lied to him as a lad. She was the one who had brought him to Cairn Toul to be kept there, locked away and tormented until he reached manhood.

Then Deirdre had unbound his god.

After that, he was chained, never to leave the hated cavern.

Isla did free you.

Phelan grimaced. She had freed him, and at a grave cost to herself. She had been dying. Her wounds were severe and she had lost a terrible amount of blood. But she had ventured down to his prison, down all those stairs to release him.

He supposed there was no use hating her anymore. She was dead. It was his loathing of her which kept him fighting Deirdre's pull. His need to exact his vengeance on Isla for taking him from his home and family had kept his mind from giving in to Deirdre's constant rhetoric to ally with her.

Phelan blew out a breath. It was all over now. Deirdre was gone. Isla was dead.

And he was learning of this new world.

He took in a deep breath and looked forward. There was a future out there waiting for him. He just needed to find it.

As Phelan started forward, the distinctive feel of magic washed over him. Druid magic. He froze, his god bellowing furiously inside him.

If there was one thing he had learned, it was that no Druid could be trusted. He swiftly lowered himself to his belly and looked around to locate the Druids.

He would keep his distance from them, but he had no qualms about killing them if he had to. They were evil and needed to be destroyed.

Phelan's gaze turned to the mountain on his right. There. A Druid was there. He could feel her magic, feel the weight of it around him, suffocating him.

He was contemplating his course when Phelan saw the indigo Warrior walk to the cave's entrance. He had wings which towered over his head.

Few mortals knew Warriors existed, so the fact this one stood in his Warrior form for anyone to see stunned Phelan. A moment later a female came to stand beside the Warrior. She was wrapped in a tartan, her flame-colored hair falling over her shoulders.

Phelan watched in amazement as the Warrior turned to the Druid and caressed her cheek with the backs of his fingers. The Druid leaned her head against the Warrior's dark blue hand.

There were no words, just a long look that passed

between the two before the Warrior turned and spread his wings as he leapt into the air.

Phelan took a moment to watch the Warrior fly before he jumped to his feet and rushed to hide behind a group of small boulders.

The Warrior was looking for something, but what? More importantly, what was the Warrior doing with a Druid?

Phelan wanted to find out. He could get the Warrior's attention, but how did he know the Warrior wasn't in league with Deirdre?

It was better to keep moving, to keep to himself. Never again would he allow himself to be captured. The world was a cruel, vicious place. Except now, he could defend himself. And he would do it without hesitation.

As for the Druid . . . Phelan looked to the cave entrance, but the Druid was no longer there. He needed to get moving. He'd already spent too much time watching the couple.

Phelan didn't look back as he scrambled over the rocky terrain and up the mountain to the future that called to him. A future without Druids, torture, or dark, dank prisons.

Sonya watched Broc fly away before she returned to the fire. They had only half an oatcake left, which he had demanded she eat, with the promise that he would return with food.

She smiled as she thought of what they had shared, of the few hours that had been theirs. On her lips was a smile she couldn't wipe away. Being with Broc had been wonderful. Amazing. Astonishing.

Just thinking of how his hot, hard body had felt against hers caused Sonya to sigh in pleasure. The way his hands had caressed her, branded her left her with an ache she knew only Broc could quench.

He was simply all she wanted. All she would ever need.

Yet, she had seen the hesitation in his eyes. He might have shared a part of his past with her, but it was a small part. Whatever dark secrets he kept plagued him in ways Sonya couldn't begin to imagine.

Broc doubted himself, but she didn't. She had seen for herself the kind of man he was. And if it took her the rest of her life, however long that might be, she would prove it to him.

Sonya adjusted the tartan and looked about the cave. It was only a little past midday, but the rain had kept them inside.

They had spoken little since they had made love. Sonya wasn't sure what there was to say. She and Broc were worlds apart.

It wasn't as though Sonya expected anything from him. They didn't have to worry over a pregnancy either since she used a spell to prevent it. She had gotten what she wanted. Him. For those precious hours they had been the only two people in the world. He had made her feel special and beautiful.

Her body felt different, as if it had awakened after years of slumber.

A slow smile pulled at Sonya's lips. Aye, Broc had certainly awakened her. She knew she loved his touch, but she hadn't expected to crave it as she did now. Or hunger for his body against hers.

Sonya absently rubbed her left palm where her wound had been. Her mind was occupied with thoughts of Broc and how he had kissed and touched her body. So, it took a moment for her to realize her magic had healed her completely, leaving not a trace of a scar.

Her magic wasn't as strong as it once was. It didn't

fill her, infuse her as it had in the past. She had thought to never feel it again, so just knowing it was there, sensing it made her feel better.

She had doubted herself ever since she had been unable to help Reaghan as Galen had asked. Yet, how could she help her fellow Druids with the measly amount of magic she had?

It's better than having none.

But how much did she have? Her healing took more time than it used to. What about the trees? Could she still communicate with them?

Sonya hurried to change and went to the cave's entrance. She strained to hear the whispers of the trees. There were few around her, but still she tried.

Heaviness weighed upon her heart when she heard nothing, but she cast it aside. Until she stood in a forest and didn't hear the trees she would hold out hope.

After all, the wounds on her hands were completely healed.

Her magic had done that. Without her having to command to do it.

She couldn't wait to tell Broc. He had told her she still had her magic. Maybe it had just been her own doubt which began to decline her magic.

If she was going to help Broc or anyone else in their fight against Deirdre, then Sonya had to trust herself. It was going to be difficult, but as long as Broc believed in her, she knew she could face anything.

As she stood at the mouth of the cave, the rain began to pour again. She could see the mist descend from the mountains and blanket everything. It would make it that much more difficult for Broc to see the mound.

If he was able to see anything at all.

Sonya returned to the fire and added another few pieces of wood. She rubbed her hands up and down her arms in an attempt to warm herself. Her gown wasn't completely dry, and with the dampness of the cave and the storm, a chill settled in her bones.

She curled up on the tartan and let the heat of the fire lull her.

Broc cursed and cursed again as he flew over more mist. The damned mist had descended as quickly as the rain, and it was everywhere.

Even with his enhanced eyesight, he couldn't see through the haze. Instead, he had focused on finding food, which he now carried back to Sonya.

He landed outside the cave and used his claws to skin the hare. Broc had expected Sonya to greet him as soon as he landed. He'd found it nearly impossible to concentrate on finding the burial mound when all he could think about was Sonya and her stunning body.

A body which had been under him, opening for him just hours ago.

Broc wanted her again. That instant. He had always known taking her body would make him only crave her more. The fact that she had gifted him with her innocence only added fuel to his need to make sure no other man touched her. Ever.

How will you do that with the curse?

Broc didn't want to think about the curse. Yet, it wouldn't leave his mind. He clenched his jaw and finished with the rabbit. Then he stood and shook off as much of the rain as he could before he pushed his god down.

When he walked into the cave his gaze sought out—and found—Sonya. She was asleep on her side, an arm curled beneath her head.

He didn't wake her as he set the hare up to roast over the fire. Once that chore was done, he sat back and watched her, watched how the glow of the flames danced over her skin and hair.

For once, she had left her hair unbound. Hair he longed to run his fingers through. The thick, untamed curls were at odds with the woman who attempted to keep everything in order. If only she would understand that she couldn't keep life as tidy as she wanted. Then she might see herself as Broc saw her.

Wild. Wanton.

His.

Broc ran a hand over his jaw. He wasn't surprised he now thought of her as his. He had taken her. Left his mark on her body. It might not be a mark anyone could see, but Broc knew it. And Sonya knew it.

He had kept his distance from her, never let himself think of her as anything other than someone to watch over.

He should have known that couldn't last.

Not when someone so lovely and alluring tempted him beyond measure. It was wrong to hunger for her as he did, not after the life he had led and the atrocities he hadn't stopped Deirdre from committing.

There would be no forgiveness. Broc would have to live with the things he had done. And those he hadn't.

It was one of the reasons he fought alongside the MacLeods now. It was his way of trying to atone for some of his sins. The rest . . . the rest he would carry all the days of his life.

Sonya's eyes opened and met his gaze. She smiled, her face softening. "You've returned."

"Aye. With food, as I promised."

She inhaled and rolled to her back. "It smells delicious."

Broc fisted his hands as he watched her back arch and her breasts push into the air as she stretched. She yawned and used her hand to help herself sit up.

"You didn't find the mound, did you?"

He shook his head and grimaced. "The mist didna help. If I didna know how temperamental the weather in this region was, I'd say Deirdre had something to do with it."

"It wouldn't be the first time she interfered."

"She will interfere this time. Never think for an instant that she willna. However, I doona think she'll do it until she arrives. It's why we need to find the mound and be gone before then."

Not to mention Deirdre now knew there was someone important in his life. It wouldn't take Deirdre long to realize that someone was Sonya. Deirdre's arrival would only spur the curse into action.

Sonya had been lucky to be shielded from the things Deirdre had done, and he wanted it kept that way. Sonya didn't know what Deirdre looked like. Which was fine with Broc. There were enough of them who knew Deirdre entirely too well.

"What are you thinking?" Sonya asked.

"I'm thinking we need the mist to clear," he lied. "I had hoped by this afternoon we could begin our search again."

"So we go out in the mist."

Broc scowled and poked at the fire with his stick. "You doona know the terrain, Sonya. I'll no' risk it."

"It's my risk. We have to find it, don't we? The longer we wait, the more time we give Deirdre to arrive."

He hated that she was right. Hated more that he couldn't stop her if he tried.

But that's what drew him to Sonya. Her passion and her desire to do whatever was necessary in order to defeat Deirdre.

Broc just prayed they would find the tomb soon.

TWENTY-TWO

Sonya once again wished she had breeches to wear in place of her gown. With the mist surrounding them in the oppressive grayness, she couldn't see her hand in front of her face.

"I knew we should have waited," Broc grumbled from beside her.

She rolled her eyes and pretended not to hear him. He'd a grip on her arm ever since they'd left the cave. Nothing she said would get him to release her.

And though she hated to admit it, she was glad he had a hold of her. Twice already she had stumbled over rocks she couldn't see, and each time he mumbled something underneath his breath she didn't quite catch.

"It will get better once we're off the mountain."

Broc grunted in response. "What makes you so sure the mound isna on the mountain?"

"Would you like to dig through all this rock?"

There was a long pause before he said, "Nay."

"I don't imagine it was much easier in the valleys, but I cannot think of another place."

Her foot slid off the edge of a rock, causing her to tilt away from Broc. In a blink he pulled her against his bare chest to steady her.

The moment she had felt herself lose her balance,

her stomach had dropped to her feet. Sonya listened to the steady beat of his heart while hers hammered in her chest. She clung to him, letting the heat of his skin help to calm her.

Sonya wanted to lay her head on his chest and forget their dangerous mission. She wanted him to fly her somewhere no one could find them where they could spend days, years locked in each other's arms with nothing of the world touching them.

Instead, she took a deep breath and gave herself another moment to enjoy the feel of Broc's arms around her, holding her. Shielding her.

"Thank you," she said, hating how her voice shook. It was probably a short drop. Nothing to be frightened of.

Or you could have taken a tumble down the mountain.

Sonya shivered. Broc's large hand rubbed up and down her back.

"I should have brought you to MacLeod Castle," he mumbled against the top of her head.

"There wasn't time, remember?" But there was something in his voice, something that told her there was more going on inside his mind than he was telling her. "What is it? What is bothering you?"

"You nearly fell."

She tried to pull back so she could see him, but he held her still. "The rocks are wet. Anyone would slip on them."

"Aye. But you're with me."

The more he talked, the more confused she became. "I'm glad you're here. You caught me before I could tumble down the mountain."

He squeezed her tighter. "Shite. Doona remind me."

"Broc. Enough. Tell me what's wrong."

Silence stretched between them, and Sonya could imagine Broc was trying to find a way out of telling her what had him in knots. But she wasn't going to allow that.

Always there had been a part of Broc he'd kept to himself. A secret part. Whatever that was is what was bothering him now, and she knew it had something to do with his life before he turned immortal. Why it would still trouble him after so many decades was the question.

"Broc?"

"I'm no' sure you want to know," he finally said.

"You don't want to tell me." It wasn't a question. She could hear it in his voice.

He blew out a harsh breath. "Nay, but you've a right to know since you are with me."

She wanted to think he meant that she was his, but she suspected he meant because she was there alone with him. "Please. Tell me."

Another sigh. "I'm cursed."

She wasn't sure she heard him right. He couldn't have said "cursed." Could he? "Cursed?"

"Aye. Since I was but a young lad."

"How? Why?"

"The why of it I'm no' sure. It began when I was eight. A lass drowned after spending time with me. Two years later, when I again took an interest in a girl, the edge of the cliff fell out from beneath her and she plummeted to her death. One died from a mysterious fever that affected no one else. Another got thrown from my horse, which I had trained from a foal. It broke the lass's neck instantly. There are others as well."

Sonya leaned her head back to look at him. "And you believe because of these . . . accidents you are cursed?"

"There isna a female I've taken an interest in who hasn't died within months of me spending time with her."

"Broc, there has to be another explanation."

"There isna. It was my grandmother who realized I was cursed. I thought once my god was released the curse would leave me, but it didna. Anice died. I cannot allow that to happen to you."

The feverish gleam in his eyes made her chest constrict with emotion. "I don't believe in curses. Nor do I believe being with you will bring upon my death."

"Sonya—"

"Nay," she interrupted him. "I was nearly killed by the wolf. You saved me. I walked into Deirdre's mountain. You brought me out. Without you, I would be dead."

"That was before I could no' ignore my need for you. Now . . . now every moment you are with me I risk your life."

"Deirdre is coming. She will bring wyrran. She will find us. If you don't want me to die, then we need to find the tomb before she does. We can discuss this curse later."

Broc was as stubborn as they came. She could stand there and argue with him for weeks and she knew he'd never budge in his thinking. So she gave him a reason to forget the curse. For now.

Deirdre.

It always worked on the Warriors. She hated to be so devious, but the facts were the facts. Meanwhile, she would show Broc that, curse or not, she wanted him.

She stepped out of his arms, but this time she was more careful about where she placed her feet. With a smile, she took his hand in hers and together they maneuvered the rocks. Fortunately, it wasn't long before they were in the valley.

"We'll start with this valley first. Which direction?" Broc asked as he looked first one way and then the other.

Sonya glanced to the right, the way Broc had flown them earlier. "To the left. I suspect if this tomb is so important the Celts made it very difficult to find."

"Aye. I'm sure you've the right of it. With as many mountains and valleys around us, I fear we'll be here for a verra long time."

"What if someone has already entered the tomb?"

Broc blew out a harsh breath. "Let's hope they have no'. It might keep the artifact out of Deirdre's hands, but it willna put it in ours."

Sonya hadn't thought of that. She stubbed her toe on a rock and bit back a cry of pain. "It would make things much easier if the mist would leave."

"Aye."

She turned and looked at Broc, but she could only see his outline. She could have sworn she heard laughter in his voice.

It seemed they walked forever. Searching to no avail. The mist hampered them with every move. They ambled slowly over the land, Sonya's frustration growing with every passing moment. Until Broc slid into a small indention in the earth.

For a heartbeat they both grew excited, thinking it might be the entrance to the burial mound. But in the end it was nothing.

"I doona like this," Broc grumbled.

Sonya dusted off her hands and waited for Broc to return his grip to her arm. "You mean not being able to use the power of your god? Do you mean feeling as though you are a mortal again?"

A short chuckle came from beside her. "Aye. Exactly that."

But his grumbling gave her an idea. "Leave me to look for the tomb while you see how close Deirdre is."

She expected him to reject her idea immediately. Instead, he stood quietly contemplating her words.

"What if you encounter trouble?" he asked. "You no longer have a weapon."

"The sooner you leave, the sooner you can return."

He moved to stand in front of her as his other hand came up to hold her arm. Sonya's hands rested on his chest as she raised her face to his.

"I doona want to return and find you hurt in any way."

She smiled and nodded, knowing the thought of his supposed curse was making him worry. "I will be here waiting."

"Make sure of it."

His head came down and his lips fastened on hers. She sank into his kiss, wrapping her arms around his neck as he pulled her roughly against him.

The kiss was all ravenous passion and scorching heat. Sonya felt the unquenchable desire that stirred to life between them, the irresistible longing which couldn't—and wouldn't—be ignored. She was swept along and engulfed by his urgent, hungry kiss.

Heat filled her veins, flooded her body. She threaded her fingers in Broc's blond locks. Her stomach quivered when she heard his low, hungry moan.

All too soon he broke the kiss and took a step back. The flare of yearning in his eyes and his hard arousal against her stomach only fanned the flames of her desire.

"Hurry," she whispered.

He gave a small, reluctant jerk of his head, and then he was gone with the whooshing beat of his wings. She hadn't even seen him call up his god.

Sonya licked her lips and took a deep breath. She was on her own, but she wasn't afraid. There wasn't time to be scared.

She put one foot in front of the other in slow, measured steps. The valley was wide, leaving various places the mound could be. She walked forward, careful of where she was going, but for all she knew the tomb could be right beside her.

Sonya stopped and put her hands on her hips. She decided to walk from one side of the valley to the other and back again. Sooner or later, in this valley or the next, she would find it.

An hour later and Sonya had made little progress. She had fallen twice, scraped her hand once, and banged her knee so hard on a rock she knew there would be a bruise. Each time her body had healed her after she had urged her magic. She could feel the steady pulse of her magic growing inside her bit by bit.

And every time it did, her confidence in herself and her magic grew.

She cocked her head to the side and closed her eyes to concentrate. There, with the barest of sounds she heard the whisper of trees on the wind. She couldn't discern what they said because she was too far away, but she heard them. That in itself was enough to bring a smile to her lips.

Sonya must have walked another half hour when the ground suddenly dropped at a steep angle off to her side. She followed it down, surprised to find there were steps.

"The burial mound," she whispered as she stopped in front of a stone door.

She leaned close to see if something might be etched into the stone, but she didn't glimpse anything. Time could have eroded the markings, however. She tried to push against the door to open it, but the heavy stone didn't budge.

Sonya sank onto the steps and waited for Broc. She bounced her leg and drummed her fingers on her knee. She'd never been good at waiting. Patience wasn't a virtue that came naturally to her, and she hadn't tried to cultivate it.

She didn't know how long she sat before she heard the sound of Broc's wings above her. An instant later he was standing before her.

"I'm not hurt," she said as she stood.

He walked down the steps with barely a glance at the door of the tomb. His gaze raked her up and down. "Nay, you are no'."

"I found the tomb."

"A good thing too." Broc's Warrior eyes looked over her head. Gone were his dark, sultry eyes. In their place were ones of the darkest blue covering every inch of his eye, even the whites. Warrior eyes. "Deirdre isna far."

"I tried to open the door."

Broc nodded and turned to it. He looked around the door and shook his head. "This is a burial mound, but I doona believe it's the one we're looking for."

"Are you sure?" Sonya wasn't ready to give up. With Deirdre arriving soon, their time was running out.

"I'm certain. Deirdre told me about the markings."

Sonya took a deep breath and walked up the steps. "Then we need to keep looking."

Broc couldn't stop the smile as he followed Sonya. Her disappointment was great, but she wasn't giving up. It was her tenacity which would work to their benefit.

He knew she was tired, but she was ready to continue. For as long as it took. He followed her as they searched. She had set up a system that seemed to work.

Thrice more they found burial mounds—mounds he hadn't seen from the sky, they were so well hidden—but each time they turned out not to be the one they hunted.

The sun was setting, creating more shadows in the mist and making it even more difficult to see. Broc was half a step behind Sonya when he heard her gasp. He grabbed hold of her arm as he saw her pitch forward, his heart in his throat.

He pulled her up beside him and just held her. He fought against the instinct to take her far away from him, but then he remembered her argument. If he left now, Deirdre might find the tomb before he returned. He had no choice. For the moment. But he would keep her safe.

With his speed and enhanced senses, he was better equipped to keep Sonya safe than any before her, save Anice. He'd learned his lesson there, however. He would make sure it was a different outcome with Sonya.

Broc forced his hands to drop from Sonya. He knelt and peered through the mist inside the hole. "It's another tomb."

"Where are the stairs?" Sonya asked.

"I doona see any." He jumped into the indentation and reached up to swing her down beside him.

Sonya groaned. "I can barely see anything."

Fortunately for Broc, he could see as well in the dark as he could in the light. The stairs down to the entrance of the tomb had been taken over by the earth. "This is a verra old burial mound."

"Broc."

He heard a thread of excitement and apprehension in her voice. "What is it?"

"Feel," she said.

He didn't need to. He could see what her fingers traced. "Celtic markings."

"This is it, isn't it? We've found the tomb."

Her face was turned toward him, a huge smile on her lips. Her eyes danced with anticipation as her fingers moved from one marking to the next.

"I want to have a look inside first," he said.

"We have no idea what the artifact is. How can you look inside and know if this is the correct tomb or not?"

Broc shrugged. When he realized she couldn't see, he said, "I doona know. This is an old burial mound, but . . ."

"But what?"

"I expected more."

"You mean you expected it to be more difficult to get inside?"

"Aye."

She sighed. "But you haven't tried the door yet."

Broc eyed the square stones that formed the entry before disappearing into the earth on either side and on top. The door itself was made of a solid piece of boulder with a huge spiral carved at its center and smaller ones around it.

He gripped the rock and pulled. It groaned and creaked as it began to gradually slide open. Broc halted Sonya when she began to step around him to enter first.

"Let me," he said and ducked into the mound.

The chamber was made up of the same square stones to construct a perfect circle. The ground continued its descent another foot, and above him the roof rose and narrowed to resemble a beehive.

"Broc," Sonya whispered.

He looked around at the broken remains of pottery and the scattered bones. "Come see."

She stepped through and covered her mouth with her hand as she coughed.

"You'll get used to the smell. It has been closed up for a long time," he said.

"Someone moved the body."

He nodded and walked around the small chamber. "Most likely someone came to see if there was anything of value."

"Which there isn't."

"Or if there was, it was taken."

She knelt beside the skull. "This was our fifth burial mound. There has to be more."

"I'm sure there are. We'll find the one we're looking for, Sonya."

"I have no doubt," she said as she stood and walked from the tomb.

Broc gave the tomb one more look before he followed her.

TWENTY-THREE

Deirdre hadn't realized how difficult it would be for her to leave Cairn Toul. It had been centuries since the last time she had ventured from her mountain.

The day the MacLeods were destroyed, to be exact.

How she missed the cool, hard feel of the stones, how they spoke to her, calmed her. They gave her magic even more strength.

Now, with every step she traveled farther and farther from her home.

She lifted her chin and lengthened her stride. Her Warriors and wyrran were meant to carry out her orders and ensure her victory. The MacLeods and their allies had put an end to that.

Fury burned deep and true within her, fury at the MacLeods for daring to attack her and ruining all she had built. Soon, they would feel her wrath. They would know the full strength of her magic.

She would see each of the Warriors who had allied with the MacLeods punished. After much suffering they would be hers. Never again would a Warrior dare to think of opposing her by the time she was finished with them.

It hadn't been an idle threat she had given Broc. She would torture and kill the Warriors, only to bring them back. No one, least of all a Warrior with a primeval god inside him, could withstand such evil.

The army she would build would be better and stronger, and more importantly, *hers*.

Her infatuation with Quinn had led to this. She knew that now. She had wanted the power of the MacLeods, to have all three brothers fighting for her instead of against her. She had thought she could convince Quinn to fulfill the prophecy and give her a child.

Then it would only be a matter of time before the other two brothers became hers. Instead, everything had fallen apart.

All because of Marcail.

Deirdre had never hated a Druid more. Marcail had ruined everything. Not even throwing the interfering bitch into the black flames had stopped whatever hold Marcail had on Quinn. It seemed only to fuel Quinn's need to kill her.

And kill her they had. Only, Deirdre had put spells in place that ensured it took more than just physical harm to end her existence. She hadn't given her soul to *diabhul* for nothing.

Deirdre paused and lifted her head as she heard the sound of water. She turned and started for the stream. Around her, twenty wyrran waited for her orders. They followed her blindly, just as her new Warriors would do.

If you can control the gods. You know you cannot let them have too much control.

She knew just how dangerous it was to allow the gods inside the Warriors full control. The stories of how the first Warriors had killed anything and everything once the Romans were driven from Britain's shores were not ones she had forgotten.

The spell she used to unbind the gods was one which

made certain the gods were able to demonstrate their power, but didn't overtake the men in doing so.

She hadn't known this at first, but as she searched for the MacLeod Warriors, she had learned much about the original spell as well as the alternate one she had.

Some of the Warriors did give in to their gods. Quinn had been so close. He would have been difficult to restrain, like any who allowed their god control, but she could have done it.

Deirdre stopped next to the stream and knelt to put her hands in the icy water. She splashed some of the liquid on her face before cupping her hands for a drink.

When finished, she raised her head and looked toward Glencoe. She should reach it within a day or two. She knew Broc was already there.

She had underestimated him. A mistake she wouldn't make again.

Deirdre blew out an annoyed breath and straightened. With a wave of her hand she sent two wyrran ahead of her to keep watch on Broc. He wouldn't escape her a second time.

"I wonder, my dark Warrior, if you have discovered just how many burial mounds there are," she said with a smile.

She didn't know exactly which mound held the artifact. But she had no doubt she would find it. Even if Broc happened to discover the mound before her, there were ways to ensure her victory.

Deirdre continued onward, her gaze focused ahead. A few wyrran stayed close to her while the others spread out to alert her to anything.

All those years Broc had spied on her. Had she been as overconfident as he had said? She should have known he would betray her. She should have realized what he was about.

But she had learned her lesson. The only one she could trust was herself. And her wyrran.

Deirdre smiled as she recalled how agitated Broc became when she had mentioned making herself appear as anyone he wished. There was a woman he cared for. But who?

"No doubt someone at MacLeod Castle."

Which meant this woman was a Druid.

Deirdre threw back her head and laughed. "How utterly perfect," she said as she petted the wyrran's head closest to her.

The creature tipped its face back and made a sound of pleasure at the back of its throat.

"Aye, my darling," Deirdre murmured. "I'm going to find whoever this woman is. Then, I'm going to make Broc watch as I kill her and take her magic."

The wyrran smiled, showing its mouthful of teeth.

Deirdre couldn't wait to find Broc and his woman.

Broc didn't give Sonya a chance to argue as he took her in his arms and flew back to the cave.

"There is still light enough to keep looking," she yelled over the beating of his wings.

"Nay, there isna. We've searched enough for today. Hopefully by the morn the mist and rain will be gone."

He landed outside the cave and released her. Sonya's lips were pinched as she strode inside to the dying embers of their fire.

Broc watched her. He understood her frustration. He felt it himself, but she had been out searching for hours in the mist and rain. She needed to rest.

"I'm going to find more wood and hunt," he said.

She lifted a hand in acknowledgment but didn't speak. Broc blew out a deep breath and flew away. He had to travel farther away than he wanted to find wood for the fire, but he was lucky enough to locate that as well as two pheasants.

By the time he returned to the cave, the sun had already sunk into the horizon. Broc dropped the birds at the entrance to the cave and walked to the fire.

"You must have traveled out of the area in order to find dry wood," Sonya said.

Broc grinned and jerked his chin to his wings. "They do come in handy."

"Aye, they certainly do." She smiled and dusted off her hands as she stood.

He built the fire up again and observed as she cleaned the pheasants. Broc loved to watch Sonya. Everything she did was poised and purposeful.

She glanced up and grinned. "You look bored."

"No' at all." And he meant it. He shouldn't get such pleasure from watching her do such a menial job. But he did.

She laughed and shook her head. "With that lopsided grin, I think I believe you."

He hadn't even realized he was smiling. It brought to mind the realization that as often as he had studied Sonya throughout the years, and as much as he claimed to know her, he didn't know as much as he would like.

"Were you happy with the Druids?"

She cocked her head to the side at his question. "What?"

"The times I saw you, you looked happy. Yet I know there were long periods I didn't look in on you."

She finished with the second bird and took one in each hand as she strode to the fire. "I was happy. The Druids never mistreated us. Though I knew they weren't my real family, they cared for us as if they were."

"I'm relieved to hear it." He had often worried about the girls.

"Just how often did you spy on me?"

He frowned at her words. "I wouldna call it spying."

"What was it then?" she asked with a grin.

Broc took the birds and set them over the fire to cook. "I'd call it assessing."

Her bark of laughter caused him to chuckle as he leaned back on one hand while he rested his other arm on his bent knee.

"Assessing, was it?" Sonya asked. "So how often?"

His smile faded as he thought of all the times the darkness had threatened to consume him, how easy it would have been to forget who he was and give in to Deirdre. "Whenever I needed to remember who I was."

"You put yourself in a situation which helped to fight Deirdre. It proves how strong you are that you survived."

The only reason he hadn't submitted to Deirdre was because of Sonya. How he wanted to tell her the truth. It had begun because of his pledge to the girls.

He had vowed to make sure they were safe. He had kept to that vow by looking in on them from time to time. Whereas Anice had been content to be by herself, Sonya had been vivacious and so alive surrounded by others. Anice had faded into the background while Sonya shone as bright as the sun.

Broc sometimes forgot how quickly time could move when he was stuck in Cairn Toul. There were times Deirdre didn't allow him to leave, as if she knew he had a secret.

There was one occasion he had seen Sonya as a girl of six summers, laughing with her red curls streaming behind her as she ran through the forest. Then the next time he saw her she was much older, her body already showing the curves of womanhood.

That's when everything had changed for him. No

longer could he look at Sonya and think of her as his ward. Lust had flared strong and true.

Every time Broc returned to Cairn Toul after seeing Sonya, he would think of her when things became too dismal, when he began to forget who he was and who he was supposed to be spying upon.

"Broc?"

He jerked and raised his gaze from the flames. He hadn't realized how lost in thought he had become. "My apologies."

"You are free of her now."

"I doona think I will ever be free of Deirdre until she is well and truly gone. There will always be a part of me that is in her damned mountain, a part of me that knows I must make amends for the things I've done."

Sonya moved to kneel in front of him and took his hand in hers. His heart missed a beat as she freely touched him. He had made it a point in Cairn Toul not to touch anyone he didn't have to, nor did he wish to be touched by anyone in the mountain. Least of all Deirdre.

But Sonya's touch was . . . wonderful. She caressed up and down the length of his fingers before she lifted her gaze to meet his.

"You have atoned for any deeds you think you need absolution for by standing with the MacLeods."

"If only it were that simple."

"Then let me make it easy," she whispered and leaned toward him.

The first touch of her lips sent a rush of driving need straight through him. He wrapped his arms around her and deepened the kiss as he slowly fell backward, taking her with him.

Her lips were as soft as silk and tasted as good as sin. Broc let his hands glide up and down her back, over her buttocks and along her hips, to the indentation of her waist.

He claimed her breast with his hand and gently squeezed. Her moan filled his ears and urged him onward as her fingers tightened in his hair.

The taut bud of her nipple pressed into his palm through her gown. He wanted to rip the clothes off her and feast upon her breasts and have her screaming his name as he thrust inside her.

His claws began to lengthen just thinking about it. And before he knew it, the tip of one had already cut the material at her neck.

Broc instantly ended the kiss before he hurt her. He'd never forgive himself if he did.

She blinked down at him and smoothed his hair away from his forehead. She then took his hand and put a finger where his claw had ripped her gown.

"You will not hurt me, Broc. Do not hold back. Please."

Her words tore through his mind, and his god bellowed inside him, urging Broc to take Sonya again, to devour her as he so desperately wanted to. The need to flip her onto her back and show her how effortless it would be for him to let go of everything.

But did he dare?

He would be giving a part of himself to Sonya he had never given anyone before.

A part of the man he had once been.

TWENTY-FOUR

Sonya saw Broc's hesitation and felt a resounding ache in her heart. The years with Deirdre had left scars on Broc that no one could see, scars that might never go away or mend.

All Sonya knew to do was heal him as her magic urged her to do. It wasn't an open wound she was healing, but the man himself. If he would let her.

She twirled a lock of his long blond hair around her finger. "Do you think I fear you?"

"Nay," he answered without pause.

"Have you changed your mind about wanting me?"

"God's blood, nay," he said through clenched teeth. "Sonya, I fear I will hurt you. No' even the threat of the curse can hold back my need for you. Whenever we touch or kiss, I begin to lose control in ways I cannot explain."

She smiled and urged, "Try."

He closed his eyes and sighed, but his hands never stopped touching her, caressing her. "If you knew the things I had done, you wouldna allow me to touch you."

"I know you saved me and Anice when you didn't have to. I know you betrayed Deirdre and stood with the MacLeods when you could have run. That's all I need to know. The things you did for Deirdre are in the past. Let them go."

His eyes opened, and his brown depths searched her amber ones. "And you would absolve me of the sins of my past?"

"I would." She kissed first one cheek, then the other. "Let go of your past. It's only through the sins you hold yourself accountable for that Deirdre still has a hold on you. You've seen she isn't as all-powerful as she has told everyone."

"She isna all-powerful, but I've seen the things she can do."

And that's when Sonya understood what really drove Broc. "You're afraid of what she'll do to me."

"I am. If we're still here when she arrives, she will do anything to take you from me. You have no' seen what she does to Druids. I have. I willna have that happen to you." His hands came up on either side of her face. "I couldna live if she took you."

She didn't want Broc to know how scared she was of Deirdre. What Druid in their right mind wouldn't fear someone who hunted and killed them?

"We will find the tomb and the artifact," Sonya declared. "And we will be on our way to MacLeod Castle before Deirdre ever arrives in Glencoe."

"What makes you so sure?" he asked as the corners of his lips began to lift.

"I have you."

His thumbs caressed her skin near her mouth. "Is that so?"

"It certainly is."

Broc looked around her and chuckled. "Our meal is burning."

Sonya would rather have forgotten the pheasants and

kissed Broc again, but they had to eat. Or, at least, she did. She rolled off Broc as he sat up and lifted one of the birds over the fire. He handed it to her and took the second.

She tried to peel of a section of meat and burned her fingers. Sonya blew on them before she did the same to the meat in an effort to cool it down enough so she could eat.

Finally, she was able to tear off some of the meat and bit into it. She glanced up to find Broc watching her. She stopped, startled by the intensity of his gaze and the longing that flared in his depths.

If there had ever been a question of whether Broc desired her or not, she had her answer right then.

Fallon MacLeod paced the battlements. There was still no sign of Broc or Sonya. He had a bad feeling in his gut, a feeling which told him Deirdre was somehow involved.

"Don't even think about it," said a feminine voice behind him.

He turned to his wife and forced a smile. "I doona know what you're talking about."

Larena put her hands on her hips and raised a blond brow. Her golden locks where pulled back in a braid, and she wore her usual tunic and breeches. As the lone female Warrior who had the power to turn invisible, it was easier for her to fight without skirts hindering her.

And Fallon needed all the Warriors he could find. Even if it meant putting the most precious thing in the world to him in harm's way.

Besides, Larena had a mind of her own.

"You know exactly what I speak of." She dodged his hands as he tried to pull her against him. "You think Deirdre has Broc and possibly Sonya. You're contemplating, even as I speak, about jumping to Cairn Toul to see for yourself."

Fallon grimaced. His wife knew him entirely too well. "Aye, I'm thinking of doing just that. I cannot leave either of them in Deirdre's hands. You know that."

"I do," she said in a softer tone. She closed the distance between them and took his hands in hers. "I also know how deeply Broc feels for Sonya, even if he will not admit it. I have no doubt he's found her."

"And if Deirdre has Sonya, Broc went after her."

"Precisely. If anyone knows their way about that mountain as well as Deirdre, it's Broc."

"How long do I give him before I begin to search?"

Larena turned her smoky blue eyes to the distance before she looked back at Fallon. "Another day. We're all worried, Fallon. Sonya is like a sister to me, to all the women. And the only Warrior able to find her is with her."

"I ken we have no idea where to begin searching, but I have to try."

"We all have to try. They are family."

"I knew I chose you for a reason."

She playfully punched his shoulder. "You chose me? If I remember correctly, Fallon MacLeod—and I always remember correctly—I was the one who picked you. You wanted nothing to do with me."

"I was a fool," he admitted as he wrapped his arms around her. "But it didna take me long to realize my mistake."

She smiled and rose up on her toes to give him a quick kiss. "That is the truth, my Warrior laird."

Fallon was content to hold her as the world continued to fall apart around them. He knew Larena worried about her cousin, Malcolm, as well, but she hadn't spoken of him since Fallon had tried to convince her it was best to let Malcolm alone.

"Quinn and Arran are with Ramsey trying to calm him," Larena said. "Lucan said he's never seen Ramsey so distraught."

Fallon sighed and squeezed his eyes closed for a moment. "Ramsey willna wait much longer before he sets out to find Broc."

"That may be exactly what Deirdre wants."

"It's crossed my mind. She could capture us one by one if she's a mind to."

Larena leaned back to look at Fallon. "If Ramsey leaves, you know Hayden and Logan will go with him."

"I will go with him also," Fallon said.

"Then we all go."

"And who will be here to protect the Druids? We cannot bring them with us."

Larena's eyes narrowed. "You will not leave me behind, Fallon MacLeod. I've proven how beneficial I can be in gaining entrance to Deirdre's mountain."

"I'd never dream of leaving you behind," he promised. "With Marcail expecting, I imagine Quinn willna want to leave."

"Arran, Ian, and Duncan will stay with Quinn as well then."

"Most likely."

She cupped his cheek, her brow furrowed. "You've already thought all of this out, haven't you?"

"It's my duty."

"And you do it so well."

Fallon basked in her praise as he escorted her inside the castle. But his good mood soon vanished. He needed to talk to Ramsey before Ramsey did something rash. They could ill afford for Deirdre to capture any one of them.

* * *

Sonya sat with her knees against her chest, her arms wrapped around her legs as she studied Broc at the cave's entrance. Ever since their conversation he had been withdrawn. Almost as if he regretted the intimacy they had shared. Or worse, it could be the curse he was so sure of.

She hoped it wasn't the case.

The way Broc stared at the stars fascinated her. She wanted so desperately to join him, but she had a sense he needed to be alone.

Sonya rested her chin on her knees while she picked at her skirts.

"Do you know Deirdre didna allow any of us out of our Warrior form? She wanted to be able to see our god."

She looked up at Broc's words. His back was still to her, but his words had carried easily enough through the cave. "Why?"

"At first I thought it was to prove to her what we were. In fact, it was because the longer we stayed in our god form, the harder it is to control when our god is visible."

"You don't have a problem controlling your god."

He snorted and lowered his head to his chest. "I spent so many years with my god visible that it doesna feel right no' to look down and see the blue skin or my claws, no' to feel the fangs in my mouth or the weight of the wings upon my back."

"You are both a man and a Warrior."

"Am I?"

"Aye. Do you not believe me?"

Finally he turned to face her. "When I look into your eyes, I can forget everything."

"Then come look," Sonya said and held out her hand.

Broc walked in slow, measured steps until he stood

before her. He squatted and lifted a lock of her hair to his nose.

Shivers raced over her skin as he inhaled. She would never have guessed he hid such horrors inside him, but she had gotten a glimpse of them. It was no wonder he held himself away from everyone.

"You're a stunning woman, Sonya. Why would you want me?"

"Why not you?"

He rubbed the curl between his fingers before he let it drop beside her breast. "I should try and convince you to turn away from me."

"I wouldn't listen."

His brow furrowed, his dark brown eyes troubled as he stared at her. "It would be best. For both of us. I couldna live with myself if the curse took you."

"What do you want? What is it that you want out of life?"

"You."

Sonya was taken aback by his words. She swallowed as warmth spread through her chest. Hope. Happiness. Anticipation.

She saw the heat in Broc's eyes, felt the desire which drew her to him. This thing that was between them, that had always been between them, strengthened, tightened, pulling them closer and closer.

"Desire this hot can burn out fast," Broc murmured as he shifted to his knees.

Sonya also moved to her knees, their bodies a hand's width apart. "Possibly. I'd like to find out."

"I fear there's no turning back for me."

She had no time to respond as his head lowered. And he covered her lips with his.

TWENTY-FIVE

Broc claimed her, claimed her body. The need to touch her had been irresistible. The hunger to taste her too tempting. The ache to fill her uncontrollable.

Desire burned powerful and all too alluring through him.

He deepened the kiss even as his own world spun about him. Sonya's lips were petal soft, and oh, so willing. She met his kiss with fervor, her fingers delving into his hair and skimming the skin at the back of his neck.

Broc could feel his control slipping away, could feel his god, Poraxus, nearly purr in contentment with each stroke and kiss from Sonya. Soon Broc forgot about everything but the woman in his arms.

He wanted to feel the smoothness of her skin against him. This time he didn't hesitate to lengthen a claw and slice her gown and chemise down the middle.

Sonya let out a surprised gasp, her eyes wide as they searched his. Her clothing slid sensuously off her shoulders, tempting Broc with the sight of her creamy skin. He pushed the material down her arm until it fell to the ground.

Broc's hand spanned her back as he crushed her against him. And kissed her again.

Urging. Seeking. Fulfilling.

His hands already knew every inch of her body, but

he needed her. Needed her sighs, her warmth . . . her tenderness.

She arched against him, pressing her breasts into his chest. Broc slid a hand between them and covered one of her breasts. Sonya moaned into his mouth as her nails raked his back.

Broc kneaded her breast before rolling her turgid nipple between his fingers. He ground his hips against her, his hunger consuming him. All he could think about was her slickness and heat, of thrusting into her hard and fast.

He laid her down and covered her body with his. Her fingers joined his as he jerked his breeches down and kicked them off with his feet.

Then they were skin to skin.

Broc looked down into the beautiful face he had dreamed of for so long. Sonya's eyes burned bright with passion, her skin flushed with desire. Her lips were swollen from his kisses, enticing him to kiss her again.

She opened her arms and pulled him down for another kiss. With a knee he spread her legs so he lay between them. He sucked in a breath at the feel of her heat against his cock.

He wanted inside her with a desperation that bordered on insanity. Yet, he cautioned himself. She was new to lovemaking, her body needed time.

But the hunger inside him wouldn't release its hold.

Broc broke the kiss and rolled onto his back. Sonya was special. If he couldn't get more than a tenuous hold over his control then he didn't need to touch her.

He stared up at the cave's ceiling and watched the light from the fire dance over the rock. Nothing diminished his yearning or cooled his hunger.

"Broc?" she asked as she leaned up on an elbow to look at him.

"It's too soon for you."

He thought she might believe the lie, but when she laid her hand on his chest, whatever control he thought he had slipped from his grasp like water.

"You fear losing control with me. I want you to."

Broc closed his eyes and prayed he hadn't heard her correctly. Surely she couldn't have said those words, and even if she had, she couldn't know what they meant.

His eyes flew open when she straddled him. "Sonya, please."

The sight of her flaming curls draped over her pale skin was breathtaking. Broc's chest constricted, and a low moan erupted from his lips as she took his rod in hand and stroked him. She had no idea how wonderful her hands felt, how desperately he had craved her touch.

She pumped her fist up and down his length, slow and steady. Broc lifted his hips in time with her hand. Desire burned his blood, passion fueled his need.

He had nearly lost control the night before. A Warrior's appetites could be extreme. He had no wish to turn Sonya's interest into something she feared or hated. Yet, each stroke of her hand was leading him down that path.

"I've never felt anything so wonderful," she whispered as her second hand joined the first.

Sweat beaded Broc's brow as she pumped her fists faster. If she could tease and tempt him, he could do the same to her. He reached up and cupped her breasts. He squeezed one nipple while he rolled the other between his fingers.

Her head dropped back and her lips parted as a breathy sigh escaped her. She shifted her hips and he felt the evidence of her arousal.

And his control snapped.

Sonya's sex throbbed with need, but she wasn't ready

to release Broc's rod. She liked the way he watched her with heavy-lidded eyes. She enjoyed the sound of his moans and the way his hips shifted as she learned him.

"Sonya," he growled and dragged her down for a kiss.

She braced her hands on either side of his head as he took her lips. The kiss was rough and fiery, fueled by need and longing. His cock ground against her with each stroke of his tongue, teasing her, tempting her.

His hands were everywhere. She broke the kiss and cried out when he pushed a finger inside her. It was just what her body needed.

Sonya moved against his hand, urging his finger deeper. There was a moan mixed with a growl as Broc's mouth closed over a nipple and he began to suckle. Hard.

With his lips pulling at her breast and his finger moving in and out of her, Sonya could do nothing but let the pleasure overtake her.

Broc's hands gripped her hips and suddenly he lifted her so that she knelt over his arousal. She met his gaze and gave him a small smile. It seemed to be all he needed as he lowered her onto his thick shaft.

Her eyes closed as he filled her, stretched her completely. He shifted her hips forward, and the friction sent new and wonderfully pleasurable sensations running through her.

Sonya then took control. She moved her hips from side to side, varying the tempo. Broc continued to knead her breasts, teasing her nipples by running his fingers around them, but never touching the small buds.

She braced her hands on his chest and leaned forward so he would take the peaks in his mouth. As soon as she did, he pulled out of her, only to plunge deeper than before.

Pleasure erupted in Sonya, and she cried out. Again

and again Broc thrust inside her. She loved the feel of him sliding in and out of her, of him going deeper and harder each time.

She heard him whisper her name, the sound filled with yearning and awe. The next instant she was on her hands and knees and he was behind her. She looked over her shoulder at him, and her heart missed a beat.

If she had thought she'd seen desire in his eyes before, it was nothing compared to what flared in his dark depths now. She saw the hunger and need there, felt the same emotions in herself.

She cried out his name as he slid inside her. He gripped her hips and began to thrust deep. Desire spiraled out of control as her climax came closer and closer.

The feel of him brushing against her exposed bottom was new and different, and she loved it. His hips pumped hard and fast, his arousal pushing repetitively into her.

When she tried to move with him, he tightened his grasp, holding her still, motionless. She closed her eyes and let him fill her body, her soul with inconceivable pleasure.

Sensual delights she could have only wondered about swarmed her, filled her. He thrust harder, faster, ever more powerfully.

The need to move against him, to play a part in their lovemaking grew, but he wouldn't release his hold. She surrendered to instinct and clamped around him. She heard him drag in a broken breath, felt a tremor run through him.

Each time he pounded into her desire tightened, passion sizzled.

She felt the same burning need tense inside him, expand and swell. He gasped as his hips pumped desperately, urging her to follow him.

Her senses shattered as release swept her in a tide of sharp, dazzling sensation that exploded, splintering her into a million pieces.

Lights flared behind her eyelids. She had never felt anything so profound, so primal. It was as if Broc had opened an entirely new world for her, one she never wanted to leave.

Pleasure erupted around them, over them, through them as Broc succumbed to his release. He kissed the back of her neck and whispered her name as the wonder, the splendor of what they had shared engulfed them.

His breathing was harsh as he curved over her. He lowered them onto the tartan, her body tucked protectively against his. She felt the beat of his heart against her back, felt the heat of him still inside her.

She had never been so sated, so content.

"I lost control," he said after several heartbeats of silence.

"And I loved it."

"Sonya—"

"Broc," she interrupted him. "You didn't hurt me. Not once. I've never felt anything so wonderful in my life."

He sighed, but said no more. She knew he didn't believe her because she was mortal. But she would make Broc understand he wouldn't hurt her. She wanted him to lose control when they made love, because she certainly did.

She snuggled against Broc's warmth, against the man, the Warrior who was now a part of her body, her soul.

Broc folded his wings as he landed next to the cave. He tamped down his god and walked to the fire where Sonya slept. Dawn was breaking, but he didn't want to wake her. They would have a long day, and she needed rest.

He laid down the two bundles in his hand and added more wood to the fire.

"Good morn," Sonya said as she rolled over and yawned.

He smiled, still unable to believe he had taken her again, taken her and lost control. And she enjoyed it. The thought made Broc want to spread her legs and take her again.

"Good morn," he answered.

She sat up and ran her fingers through her tangled curls. "Where did you go?"

"You needed a gown to replace the one I ruined."

Sonya laughed, the sound hitting him square in the chest. "I don't suppose I could walk around naked."

"I wouldna mind."

She grinned and licked her lips. "I'm sure you wouldn't."

"I also got us some food."

"Good. I'm famished."

Broc untied the first bundle and pulled out a new chemise and a gown of the darkest red.

"Oh," Sonya whispered.

He feared she wouldn't like it, but as he looked at her face and saw the surprise, he knew he had chosen correctly.

"I've never had anything so lovely," she said as she touched the gown.

"Put it on."

She didn't need urging twice as she jumped to her feet and reached for the chemise. She rubbed the thin material against her cheek before she slid it over her head and arms.

The gauzy material fell over her body without a sound. She hurried to put on her wool stockings before she took the gown from him.

He couldn't take his eyes off her as she dressed. The skirts made a soft whooshing sound as they fell to her feet. "Stunning," he said.

"I wish I could see for myself."

"Trust me. You look amazing."

"Thank you. For everything."

He gave a nod and cleared his throat at the emotion that welled inside him. He'd never bought a gown for a woman before, and suddenly he found he wanted to be the one to clothe Sonya. He wanted to buy her jewels and ribbons and anything else she wanted.

"Bread and cheese," she said with a smile as she looked in the second bundle. "How did you manage it?"

"Anything is possible with coin."

"You act as though you have as much coin as you need."

He shrugged and leaned against the cave wall as he accepted the food from Sonya. "I do. I amassed quite a bit through the years. I've several places throughout Scotland in which I've kept coin hidden in case I needed it."

"Aren't you afraid someone might find them?"

"No' unless they have wings."

TWENTY-SIX

Sonya held onto Broc's shoulders as she turned her head to peer at the ground below them. The mist and rain had disappeared overnight, just as he had predicted.

She'd expected to see evidence of the burial mounds they had discovered the day before, but with the undulations and rocky outcroppings in the wide valley, she couldn't see any.

"Have we already past the mounds from yesterday?"

Broc nodded. "We're over them now."

"I cannot even see them."

"I know," Broc said, his voice flat.

In other words, he didn't like that for once, being in the air wouldn't give them an advantage. They were going to have to search on foot.

Sonya blinked when a strand of hair flew into her eye as Broc dove to the ground. Her stomach jumped into her throat, but she wasn't afraid. She loved the thrill of flying. It made her blood pound and her heart race.

Broc landed softly and folded his wings, but he didn't release her. Sonya looked into his dark eyes and tugged a strand of his blond hair near his jaw.

"You don't have to say it," she said. "I will be careful."

He frowned, a muscle in his jaw jumping. "Stay near me."

It didn't take her but a moment to realize why Broc was so tense. "You expect Deirdre to arrive today."

"I doona know when or where, but aye."

"We cannot leave without the artifact."

Broc sighed and looked over her head. "We'll discuss that when the time comes."

"We'll discuss it now." If Sonya had learned anything about Warriors it was how stubborn they could be, and Broc most of all.

"We've had this discussion. I realize how important the artifact is to our cause."

"Precisely," she said. "Above all else, we must secure it and bring it back to MacLeod Castle."

"It could well mean your capture by Deirdre."

"I'm ready to die."

"I refuse to let you die!" he shouted.

Sonya didn't know who was more surprised by his outburst, her or him. He swore and dropped his arms from her as he raked a hand through his hair.

"Broc," she said and touched his arm to halt him. "I vow I will do anything and everything to stay out of Deirdre's hands."

His gaze was hard, cold when he turned it to her. "Even if it means leaving the artifact?"

"You know her and the wyrran better than most. You know how they will attack. You may need to take the artifact and leave me."

"Nay."

"Don't be hasty in your response. I'm just one person. Compared to thousands, my life is meaningless."

Broc knew in his heart he would sacrifice the artifact for Sonya. She meant that much to him. Yet, he couldn't tell her that. She would continue to argue the artifact was more important.

He kept silent, which seemed to be all the answer she needed.

"Good," Sonya said with a smile. "Now let us begin our search."

He watched her turn away, her hands on her hips as she looked over the land. Her red hair was pulled back in another braid, but wisps of tendrils had escaped and curled becomingly about her face and neck.

"Now that I know what we are looking for, I think I see a couple of entrances," she said.

Broc moved beside her and looked to where she pointed. "I believe you're correct."

"I'll begin checking and you can go see how close Deirdre is."

He raised a brow and waited for her to look at him before he said, "You do enjoy ordering me about."

A slow smile spread over her lips. "Ah, but you won't argue about it because you know I'm right."

"This time. I'll do a sweep of the area first looking for wyrran before I leave you."

She stroked his shoulder and down his arm before she lifted his large hand in hers. One of her fingers curved slowly over an indigo claw. She raised her amber gaze to his. "Be careful."

"I ask the same."

"Hurry back."

He would fly faster than he ever had just to return to her. After a quick, hard kiss, he jumped into the air.

Sonya took a fortifying breath as Broc disappeared from sight. She knew he needed to check on how close Deirdre was, but she hated being without him. He would have stayed with her had he known, which is why she broached the subject first.

She kept to the same plan as the day before, except

now she could walk faster since she could see where she was going. If the weather had held the day before, they could have covered at least double the distance they had.

The first mound she found had markings around the door, but the tomb itself didn't look old enough to be the one Deirdre had spoken about.

Since she couldn't move the massive rock blocking the entrance into the burial mound, Sonya marked it by stacking three rocks atop each other near the steps before moving on to the next one.

So it continued for the next hour. She had just found her fourth tomb when she heard the familiar sound of wings and looked up to find Broc landing beside her.

His angular face was set in hard lines. "She'll reach this valley in a matter of hours."

"But she still needs to search the tombs as we have."

Broc glanced away, which made Sonya's stomach fill with lead. "Possibly. Or she will set about searching for us since she knows I'm here."

"I see." Sonya had foolishly thought Deirdre would have to go about her search just as they had. Sonya should have known better.

"Doona be too hard on yourself," Broc said.

"I don't think like her, and I could put myself or others in jeopardy one day because of it."

"You doona think like her because you've had no contact with her. You doona know what she's like, and for that you can be pleased. Let me think like her."

"And if you aren't around?"

"I'll be around," he vowed.

Sonya nodded woodenly.

"What have you found?"

She swallowed. "This is the fourth mound. There are no markings on it."

"And the others?" he asked as his Warrior form vanished before her eyes.

"There is one which might be a possibility. It's over there," she said and pointed. "I have three stones stacked on top of each other."

He nodded and smiled at her. "Clever. I'll go see if it could be our tomb."

Sonya continued walking as she watched him. Broc didn't fly this time, he ran. She could never get used to the speed in which a Warrior could move.

He was at the burial mound and back again before she found her next one. "The one you discovered isn't old enough. The carvings speak of a Celtic tribal leader, but that is all."

Sonya lifted her skirts with a nod and continued on. "We are only halfway through the valley."

"And easy to spot as well."

"If you have a better idea how to find this burial mound, now is the time to speak of it."

He chuckled. "I have nothing."

"Me either," Sonya said, not able to mask the feeling of doom that began to sweep over her.

"We will find it."

She smiled as his fingers closed around hers. Just having him beside her gave her the strength she needed to keep going. Sonya squared her shoulders and lengthened her stride.

It wasn't long before they stopped beside what looked like a small tunnel in the ground. There were no steps, just a slight slope. Grass hung over the edge of the tunnel and rocks almost covered it.

"I'll have a quick look," Broc said as he moved the last rock. He glanced back at her with a grin before going into the tunnel feetfirst.

She winced when his wide shoulders almost didn't

squeeze through. He had to angle his body and hunch his shoulders just to make it.

Sonya stepped up to the entrance and peered inside, but without a Warrior's eyesight, she couldn't penetrate the darkness.

"It's a burial mound," Broc said. His voice echoed slightly as it reached her.

"Is it the one we are looking for?"

"Nay."

Sonya glanced at the sky and let out a breath. There was a scraping noise and then Broc was squirming out of the tunnel.

"So the passageway is the entrance?" she asked.

"Of a sort. Once you are through it you are inside the earth, but there was room enough for me to stand. It is built like the others. This one, however, has no' been disturbed."

She glanced at the hole which he had come out of and grimaced. "And now I know why."

Dirt and debris smudged Broc's bare chest and arms, but he didn't seem to mind. "Come," he bade her as they moved on.

The sun rose higher as they continued their search to no avail. Sweat trickled down the side of Sonya's face, her only relief the cool wind that came off the mountains.

Broc left her again to ascertain Deirdre's position. He returned looking grimmer than before. Sonya didn't have to ask what he had seen. The answer was there in his gaze.

She couldn't believe they were going to fail. "I thought for sure we would have found the mound by now."

"Me as well," Broc confessed. "There isna much of this valley left for us to explore. We can then move onto another valley."

"You move faster than I. Finish our search."

Broc handed her the water skin and nodded. "Doona stay here. Keep walking to me."

"Of course."

Once he was gone, Sonya let her shoulders droop. She had been so sure they would leave Glencoe with the artifact because they had reached the area before Deirdre.

Soon they would have to decide whether to leave or fight Deirdre for the artifact. A tremor of dread went through Sonya at the prospect. A month earlier she might have stood against Deirdre, but now, she knew her magic wasn't strong enough.

And she had Broc. That made all the difference.

Sonya glanced over to find Broc running across the land, pausing when he found a mound. What was it about this area which called to the Celts to bury their dead? It was beautiful, no doubt, but there wasn't a place in the Highlands that wasn't awe-inspiring.

Sonya started after Broc. She walked in a straight line toward him while he continued to zigzag across the valley. Sonya glanced over her shoulder as she remembered Broc stating how easily they could be spotted.

She quickened her steps and leapt over a rock when Broc called her name. It was the catch in his voice, the hope and surprise and excitement that made her dash to him.

They were at the end of the valley, where two other mountains joined. Broc stood beside what looked like a jumble of rocks, but as Sonya drew closer she saw the squared stones.

Her lips parted in wonder as she realized that what she had thought was a small hill in the valley was actually the burial mound.

Broc's smile was huge, infectious. "We found it."

TWENTY-SEVEN

"I knew we would," Sonya whispered.

Broc could well understand her astonishment. He pointed in front of them about five paces. "Look at the long, oval rock there. Do you see the spirals?"

"I do."

"That's how I knew it was a burial mound. I almost missed it, the markings are so faded."

Sonya knelt before the rock and ran her fingers along the etchings. The Celts used the spirals to symbolize growth, expansion, as well as cosmic energy. "This feels . . . different."

"How?"

"Older than any of the others we have found, but it's also the hint of magic I feel. Don't you feel it?"

Broc concentrated, but shook his head. "The only magic I feel is yours. Come, let us see the rest."

They walked around the long boulder. An archway of stone that was nearly covered by grass and weeds was their next find. It led into the huge mound, drowning out most of the light.

"No carvings," Sonya said.

Broc used his claws and cut away some of the grass. "Nay, nothing."

They stepped beneath the archway, and that's when

Broc felt the magic. It pulsed around him like a heartbeat, steady and strong.

Beside him, Sonya paused as well, a smile of contentment on her face. "You feel it now, don't you?" she asked.

"I do."

"This is the tomb," she said as she turned her head to him. "I know it."

Broc's eyesight let him see into the semidarkness of the mound. This was different from the others they had seen. There was a feeling of a great passage of time, as though the mound had been waiting to be discovered.

"The doorway is there," Sonya said and pointed to her left.

Broc was able to see the door, but he knew Sonya's eyesight wouldn't allow her to. "How?"

"The magic," she whispered. "It is very strong. Strong, old, and so very pure. It is *mie* magic which protects this place. I've never felt any magic other than my own before."

Broc didn't want to disturb the tomb. Not because he feared what might happen to him, but because the magic and the artifact within were special.

So many Druids had died over the years. There weren't many left, and a place that held such magic should be left alone.

"Deirdre may no' find the tomb," he said.

Sonya tucked a curl behind her ear and smiled sadly. "The wyrran can smell magic. It will lead them here."

"The magic is felt more inside the archway. Outside, I barely felt it. Maybe the wyrran willna feel it either."

Her brow furrowed. "You don't want to open the tomb."

It wasn't a question. Broc shook his head. "It doesna seem right."

"Nay, it doesn't, but we must. If we don't, Deirdre will find a way, regardless that she cannot enter herself. She will destroy all that is within. We will only take the artifact."

He knew she was right, but he would rather have left the tomb undisturbed. Broc walked to the doorway and saw the many and various etchings around the door. Time had not touched them. They were as deep and clear as if they had been made the day before.

"Amazing," Sonya said as she ran her hands over them.

Broc stood just a stride away but it was as if he was immersed in magic. It made his skin prickle and itch as it ran from his head down to his toes. Almost as if it were learning him.

Sonya moved closer and took his hand. Her magic mixed with the other. As soon as her magic touched the other, Broc felt the heaviness which had surrounded him begin to ebb.

"What did you do?" he asked.

Sonya shrugged. "Nothing. Why? What happened?"

"I could have sworn the magic was learning me and trying to decide if I was friend or foe."

"And you think my being here helped?"

Broc looked at the etchings. "I know it did."

"What do the markings say?"

He leaned in to read. "They are spells. They speak of violent death and certain doom if anyone enters the tomb."

"A Druid would not put such spells around a tomb lightly. For a *mie* to have crafted such enchantments is unheard-of. We do not harm others. This would be something a *drough* would do."

"But you felt *mie* magic."

She nodded. "There's no doubt as to what I felt. It is *mie* magic."

Once again doubt spread through Broc about opening the tomb. "Deirdre cannot get inside. Neither can her wyrran. If we leave now, she might find it, but she will no' be able to get inside."

"She will eventually." Sonya squeezed his hand and lifted her face to his. "The battle with Deirdre needs to end. Everyone who fights against her tyranny—Druid, mortal and Warrior alike—knows our lives could end in the fight. We have to do this."

Broc sighed, knowing her logic was sound. "You're right. We need to do this."

"I need you to read me exactly what the spells say."

Broc wasted no time in deciphering the ancient language. The more he told Sonya, the more her brow furrowed and her lips pinched. By the time he was done, she didn't look quite as eager as before.

"It is a good thing I'm here with you," Sonya said as she rubbed her hands together.

"Why is that?"

"Because without me you wouldn't be able to touch the door without dying."

Broc eyed the stone that acted as the door. "How so?"

"You were correct when you said the magic was studying you. It knows you are a Warrior. To the ancients, all Warriors were evil. They never thought there could be ones who fought against their god and did what was right."

"So, in the mind of the Druids who put in the spells, I'm as evil as Deirdre?" he asked.

"I'm afraid so."

"Why did Deirdre think I could get in?"

Sonya shrugged. "Maybe she knows a secret I do not."

"Nay. She said me, no' just any Warrior."

"Interesting," Sonya mumbled. "Maybe it has something to do with you betraying her. What did it feel like when the magic touched you?"

"My skin tingled. It was what it felt like when you allowed me to hear the trees."

Sonya smiled then, her eyes tender as she looked at him. "If the magic wasn't painful, then perhaps you don't need me. It recognizes that you may have a god inside you, but you are a good man."

"I'd rather have you with me nonetheless."

She laughed, the sound music to his ears. "I wouldn't dream of allowing you to go alone."

"What do we do?"

"I'm going to touch the markings. My magic will pour inside it. Then, I want you to open the door."

Broc gritted his teeth as Sonya stepped to the markings and placed her hands on them. He could feel her magic swell around her, engulfing him, calling to him. Tempting him.

His body reacted instantly. He had to touch her, any part of her. His hand closed around the end of her braid and held tightly.

Desire and hunger pounded through him, demanding he take Sonya amid the ancient magic, pleading with him to slake the longing which consumed him.

As if she knew what her magic did to him, she turned her amber gaze to him. Time slowed to nothing as the invisible ties that had always bound them wound tighter, pulling him closer to her, closer to the serenity she offered him.

"Broc," she whispered.

He moved to her, unable to stay away from her beguiling eyes and tempting body. His other hand rose to slide around her neck and cup the back of her head.

Her gaze dropped to his mouth, and it was his

undoing. Broc's head lowered as hers rose to his. Their lips met in an explosion of hunger and yearning.

For all the urgency that surged through him, he took his time kissing her. Even with the fierce need to claim her, Broc knew what was happening to them was extraordinary and special.

Her lips were soft beneath his. Supple. Sweet. Enthralling.

A spark of something bright and sharp permeated his body with their kiss. Broc lifted his head and saw the surprise in Sonya's eyes as well. He didn't know what had occurred, couldn't possibly understand.

But something had definitely happened. That something had to do with magic.

"Open the door," Sonya bade him.

Broc reluctantly released her. He gripped the thick boulder and pulled. His muscles strained as he grunted. It was as if magic held the door, refusing to release it. He knew all too well what it felt like to have magic bind something not even his Warrior strength could budge.

A burst of magic flew from Sonya into the markings. The etchings began to glow blue the more magic Sonya used. Broc was about to tug her away, about to leave it all.

"Pull!" Sonya yelled.

He ground his teeth and gave a vicious yank. There was a loud pop as the stone gave way. Broc couldn't believe his eyes. He stopped pulling, but the stone continued to open on its own.

"What did you do?" he asked.

"I'm not sure."

He knew what using that kind of magic could do to her body. Yet, as he looked at her, she didn't appear to be weak. She looked . . . radiant.

"I know," she said, as if reading his mind. "I feel

wonderful. It's almost as if the magic of the tomb gave me strength instead of taking it."

Broc had seen the destructive and healing power of magic, but he had never experienced anything like what had just happened. He couldn't even begin to put into words what had occurred.

"I wish I had a torch," Sonya said when they stood in the doorway.

Broc took her hand. "I will be your eyes."

But as soon as they stepped over the threshold, torches flared to life around the circular tomb one at a time until all were lit.

"God's blood," Broc whispered.

Sonya looked around the burial mound in awe. She shouldn't have been surprised after having her magic strengthened by the magic guarding the tomb, but she was.

In the middle of the crypt, upon a great slab of stone, were the remains of the man. Although the flesh was gone from his bones, he still wore a faded red cloak about his shoulders.

"This is amazing," she said and began to walk around the chamber.

Broc walked the opposite way, his gaze taking in everything. "This burial mound is easily three times the size of the others we've seen."

"There are so many weapons and shields on the walls."

"As well as baskets filled with who knows what."

Sonya and Broc came together at the far end of the tomb and stopped. Before them was a portion of stones that had been smoothed and more of the Gaelic language etched into them.

"What does it say?" Sonya asked.

Broc rubbed his jaw and shook his head. "It speaks about a tablet called Orn."

"What is it?"

"I think it's the artifact. It says the tablet is on the Isle of Eigg, hidden and guarded in a stone circle."

Sonya shifted from one foot to the other. "Does it say anything else?"

"This Tablet of Orn will give us the location to yet another artifact."

Sonya met Broc's gaze. The importance of their find was tremendous. "Deirdre cannot be allowed to know of this."

"She willna," Broc said and used his claws to scratch away the markings.

Sonya twisted her skirts in her hands. "I hope you remember everything."

"I will." He stepped back to look at it. "No one will ever be able to learn what was etched here. We now have what Deirdre sought. We need to leave."

He took her hand and pulled her to the door. They were nearly there when they heard the shriek of a wyrran. Broc slid to a halt.

Sonya's heart leapt into her throat as she stopped beside him. "We can make it to the opening and you can fly us away."

"Nay." Broc turned to her and took her face in his hands. "I will fight the wyrran."

"And Deirdre? Will you fight her as well?"

"Aye."

Sonya didn't like his plan. "And I suppose you want me to run away?"

"I want you to stay here."

"In this tomb?" she said louder than intended. "You must be jesting."

"It's the only way that I know you will be safe. Deirdre willna be able to get to you."

"Nay, I'll be dead."

Broc smiled gently and pulled her into his arms. He kissed the top of her head. "Do you have such little faith in me?"

"I have a tremendous amount of faith in you."

"I vowed I would always keep you safe, even if it meant keeping you safe from me."

She sighed and let the warmth of his bare skin against her cheek fill her. "You have a plan?"

"I have a plan."

"Care to share it with me?"

His chest rumbled. "And leave you nothing with which to occupy your mind?"

"Broc, please," she said as she leaned back to look at him. "I'd rather both of us leave."

"That's no' possible now. Trust me."

The way his dark eyes held hers, as if he needed to hear her words, made her throat burn with emotion. "I do trust you."

He gave her a quick kiss before he was gone.

Sonya barely had time to blink before he closed the door. Locking her in the tomb.

Broc stared at the stone door for one heartbeat, two. Inside was the woman who meant everything to him. Outside was the woman who had taken everything from him once.

He wouldn't allow her to do it a second time.

Broc had known the moment he heard the wyrran that time had run out for them. Under no circumstances could Deirdre know about Sonya.

As much as Broc hated leaving Sonya in the tomb, it was the safest place for her.

And if you cannot get away from Deirdre? You've condemned her to die a horrible death.

He would get away.

There were no thoughts of any other outcome.

Deirdre couldn't gain access to the tomb. Neither could her wyrran. They would feel magic, but it would be the magic of the tomb, not Sonya.

Broc closed his eyes and called forth an image of Sonya in his mind. Her look of complete trust, of utter faith, had rocked him.

Sonya.

She was his heart, his soul. His very breath.

Broc summoned his god and unleashed his fury. Wings sprang from his back, fangs filled his mouth, and claws shot from his fingers.

He tilted his head back and closed his eyes as he thought of every atrocity, every slaughter Deirdre had ever committed or ordered done to the innocents of the land. He thought of the screams of the Druids she had killed, the bellows of pain from the men she had turned into Warriors.

And he thought of his family.

Poraxus growled inside him, eager for a taste of Deirdre's blood, anxious to rip her heart from her chest. He wanted to crush her head beneath his foot, to take her essence and bury it so deep in Hell no one would ever find her.

Broc didn't look at the door of the tomb to his back. He wiped Sonya from his mind, tucking her into a corner of his brain where he had always kept her, a place Deirdre could never touch.

Then he ducked under the archway to clear his wings and locked eyes with Deirdre.

TWENTY-EIGHT

"I knew you would find it," Deirdre said. Her arms were crossed over her chest, her white hair a startling contrast to her black gown.

Broc counted twenty wyrran. He could kill them easily enough. But then again, he'd never battled them with Deirdre near. It could prove interesting.

Above all, he could never take his attention off her.

Deirdre's white brow lifted high on her forehead. "Nothing to say, my dark Warrior?"

"There are many burial mounds in this valley."

Deirdre's smile was malicious and cruel. "Oh, dear Broc, I know you too well. This is the tomb."

"Maybe. Good luck getting inside. The spells are ancient, the magic extremely powerful. You willna be able to get near the tomb."

"That's why I have you," she said as she dropped her arms to her side. "We can do this the easy way."

"Or the difficult way?" he asked with a laugh. "You've already taken everything from me. There's nothing left you can threaten me with."

Her smile hardened. "There's Ramsey."

Broc's lips lifted in a true smile as he thought of his friend. "You can try. You can threaten every Warrior at MacLeod Castle, but each of us has escaped your clutches. You cannot hurt us."

"I can hurt the Druids within."

"Maybe. You've attacked the castle several times already. You've lost each time."

Deirdre's white eyes narrowed as she stepped closer to Broc. Her hair began to twitch at the ends, indicating her anger. "I will no longer be sending my wyrran or any Warriors alone. I will be with them."

"You?" Broc repeated. He wasn't sure what Deirdre was planning, but whatever it was, it couldn't be good.

"Aye, me. The next time MacLeod Castle is attacked, I will be leading my wyrran. You think because you defeated some wyrran, mortals, and a few Warriors that you can defeat me?"

"We did. In your mountain."

Deirdre's face lost any semblance of a smile. "I haven't forgotten all who played a part in that. I wasn't jesting when I said there would be retribution, Broc. You all will suffer mightily at my hands."

"We shall see."

Broc's gut tightened when Deirdre's gaze lowered to the ground. When she lifted her gaze, there was a knowing smile upon her lips, a smile that told Broc she knew he wasn't alone.

"Who is your companion?"

Broc flexed his fingers, his claws eager to sink into wyrran skin. "I am alone."

"Now. What did you do with the woman? I can tell by the tracks left beside yours that it was a female. Tell me where she is."

"I'm alone. Do you want to stand around all day or fight?"

She motioned to the wyrran on her right and they attacked.

Broc knew he chanced being incapacitated again with *drough* blood each time the wyrran cut him, but it was a chance he couldn't avoid. The wyrran were quick and their claws sharp.

He gripped a wyrran by its head and gave a jerk. The sound of a neck breaking was drowned out by the shrieks of the others. Broc snarled as a wyrran jumped on his back and sank its claws in his neck.

Broc reached behind him and took the creature's skinny arms in his hands and pulled out the claws. He continued to pull on the wyrran's arms until they were yanked out of their sockets, then from its body and they dangled from Broc's hands.

The wyrran fell from his back, only to be replaced by another. It became a blur of blood and yellow skin as Broc killed wyrran after wyrran.

Their screeches echoed in his head as his own blood ran down his body to blend with the ground at his feet. He never stopped, never gave up. Poraxus' fury was too great. And Broc had made a vow.

Suddenly something long and white snaked out and wrapped around his throat. Broc hastily cut the strands with is claws. He hated that Deirdre always went for the throat.

Broc ducked more of her hair and spun away. He used his wings to knock three wyrran away from him, and just as he was about to launch himself in the air, something snagged his wrist.

He glanced down to find Deirdre's hair. More of her lethal hair wrapped around his other wrist and his throat.

"Enough!" Deirdre yelled. Her white eyes blazed with anger as she glanced around at the dead wyrran.

Broc began to laugh. "Did you really think the wyrran stood a chance against a Warrior? They never do."

"They took you down before."

"Only because of the *drough* blood."

"Stop killing my wyrran," she said between clenched teeth.

Broc bared his fangs at her. "Stop sending them to attack me and I'll consider it. Then again, I may kill them just because of how ugly they are."

Deirdre screamed and the hair around his neck tightened so he could barely breathe. He tried to get his hands up to cut away her hair again, but the strands were as magical as she was.

"You can cease your fighting. You will not get away from me now," Deirdre said.

Broc's mind raced with possibilities of getting away. He could try to fly. Deirdre wasn't controlling his wings, but she could snap his neck.

"I told you, you would be mine. There is nothing you can do now to escape. By the time I'm done exacting my vengeance, you will do anything I want. You will be mine to control."

Broc didn't bother to argue with her. He'd said it all while chained in her mountain. However, he wasn't about to be taken without a fight. Somehow, someway he would keep himself—and most especially Sonya—from Deirdre.

Sonya has only a few hours in the tomb before she runs out of air.

It would be weeks or months before Deirdre was done with him. Sonya would be long dead by then.

"I can get the artifact," he said.

Deirdre tilted her head to the side and grinned. "What do you plan, Broc?"

"I'll retrieve the artifact from the tomb. For you."

"And why would you do that so willingly?"

Broc knew he had to say something believable. As much as he wanted to keep Sonya away from Deirdre, she might be the only way he could get free long enough to retrieve Fallon and the others.

"Well?" Deirdre said, growing impatient. "I'm curious to hear why you would offer to get the artifact. What could be so important that you would do something like this? For me?"

Broc swallowed. He tried several times to get the words out, but they were stuck in his throat. Telling Deirdre about Sonya went against everything he had done over the past years.

Deirdre's hair squeezed his neck and wrists. "Let me guess. The woman with you?"

"I kidnapped her," Broc lied. He couldn't tell Deirdre the truth. He would find another way to help Sonya.

That piqued Deirdre's interest. "Why would you do that?"

When he didn't answer fast enough she squeezed his neck tighter.

"The tomb," he forced out of lips which could barely move.

As soon as the words left his mouth, the strands eased upon his neck. Broc drew in great gulps of air as he glared at Deirdre.

"Where is this woman?" Deirdre demanded.

"In the tomb."

Deirdre's gaze slid to the burial mound. "In the tomb?"

"I was going in with her when I heard the wyrran. I came out here to fight you."

"This woman is a Druid, then." Deirdre chuckled. "How did you find a Druid, Broc?"

"She's no' a Druid. She's from Glencoe. She led me to the tomb."

Deirdre motioned the remaining wyrran to back away from Broc. "Why don't you take me to this . . . female?"

Broc gave a jerk of his head and her hair released him. He wanted to reach up and rub his neck, but he didn't. She would enjoy it too much.

"Keep your wyrran back," Broc said as he turned to enter the tomb.

"They go where I go."

Broc glanced at her over his shoulder. "I doona thi . . ."

His words trailed off as wyrran began to shriek and fight what looked like six or seven Warriors. Broc halted. All he could do was stare. He had no idea where the Warriors had come from. Or who they were.

Deirdre screamed and rushed out to fight alongside her wyrran. She used her hair along with her magic as she jumped into the fray.

As curious as Broc was to know who these Warriors were, he couldn't waste another moment. He hurried from the tomb and leapt into the air.

He looked down at the first beat of his wings and saw a golden-skinned Warrior standing atop the mountain. And in a blink, the Warrior was gone.

Broc forgot the Warrior and rose into the sky so the clouds would conceal him. He had to fly fast, had to hurry to MacLeod Castle before it was too late for Sonya.

TWENTY-NINE

Sonya stared at the door, her arms wrapped around herself. Thankfully the torches hadn't gone out when Broc shut her inside the burial mound.

A shiver raced over her skin, a reminder of just where she was. She turned and looked at the occupant. Sonya wondered who he was. Had it been his idea to hide the clue about the Tablet of Orn in his tomb? Or had it been decided after his death?

Sonya jumped when she heard the wyrran again. There were many of them by the sounds. They would be attacking Broc again. If he didn't get away from Deirdre, Sonya would die in here. She supposed it was better than dying by Deirdre's hand. At least this way Deirdre would never get her magic.

But she couldn't help but worry how Broc would feel about it. He would blame it on his supposed curse, when in fact the blame lay solely with Deirdre.

With nothing else to do, Sonya began to look for a weapon she could use in case Deirdre was somehow able to open the door. Sonya inspected the spears and swords which hung on the walls.

But it was the sword thay lay in the dead man's hands that grabbed her attention.

Both his hands were wrapped around the pommel

and the sword rested on top of him. Along the blade was beautiful knot work that had been etched into the metal. Mixed with the interlacing plait of knots was more Gaelic writing.

Sonya wished she could read the markings. She held her hand over the sword and felt magic. It was faint, and not nearly as strong as the magic guarding the burial mound, but it was definitely magic.

She longed to grasp the sword, to examine both sides of the blade. Sonya had never cared much for weapons before, but this sword called to her in the same way trees did.

"Amazing," Sonya murmured. She leaned over the corpse when she saw the large garnet stone atop the hilt of the sword.

Garnets were highly prized. The sheer size of the stone, which was as large as a child's fist, must have cost a fortune.

Her gaze then spotted the markings running in a spiral around the pommel. Not only could she not read them, but the bones from the man's fingers and hands blocked her from seeing the rest of the markings.

She itched to move the corpse's fingers and inspect the sword more closely, but Sonya would never desecrate the dead in such a way.

Sonya blew out a breath and began to straighten when something else caught her eye.

It was the barest wink of light off gold, but Sonya saw it nonetheless. She gently, tenderly peeled back the ragged neckline of the man's tunic to better see what was around his neck.

Her lungs locked when she saw the amulet and the double spiral in the gold. The double spiral represented the equinoxes, when day and night were of equal length.

Sonya traced her finger from the middle of one spiral until it curved out and then the other way to the middle of the second spiral.

Somehow she knew the amulet was important to the artifacts, important in the war to defeat Deirdre.

Sonya knew she had to take the amulet and even though she didn't want to disturb the dead, lives were at stake. She lifted the leather strap that held the amulet and cut it with a dagger she had found among the many weapons. She held up the amulet to the light and couldn't stop staring at the oblong shape of the metal and the spirals within.

"If I'm not meant to take this, then I will return it," she told the corpse. "If it is supposed to be used along with one of the artifacts, then I pledge that I will keep it safe until such time. Just as you have."

The torches flickered, and if Sonya didn't know better, she would have thought the spirit of the dead leader had given his consent.

Isla stood in the village near MacLeod Castle and stared into the forest before her. It had been Ramsey who first drew her attention when she found him looking toward the woods. He had stood at the trees and gazed at them for hours until she had to know what he saw.

It wasn't until she neared Ramsey that she noticed the trees were bending the opposite way from the breeze off the sea.

"What is it?" asked a deep voice that always melted her heart.

She waited until Hayden was next to her before she intertwined her fingers with his and nodded to the forest. "Watch."

"They're trees, Isla. They do move with the wind."

She loved her Warrior, but sometimes he didn't always see the things magic could do. "*Look* at them, Hayden. Look at the way they bend, at how they move."

"God's teeth," he murmured after a moment. "Is that what holds Ramsey's attention?"

"I believe so."

"Are they trying to talk to Sonya?"

Isla licked her lips and shrugged. "I think they are trying to tell us something. The only one who can hear the trees, however, is Sonya."

Of a sudden the trees stopped moving.

Hayden cursed and released her hand. "I need to get the others."

Isla didn't take her eyes off the forest. She would bet all the magic inside her that the trees knew where Sonya was, that they were trying to tell those at the castle where to find her.

It took no time at all for the other Warriors to race toward the village.

"What did you discover?" Quinn, the youngest MacLeod, demanded as he skidded to a stop beside her, the first to reach them.

Ramsey turned his head of black hair and locked gazes with Isla. He walked to her, his jaw clenched and lines of worry bracketing his eyes and lips.

"Can you hear them?" Ramsey asked Isla.

She slowly shook her head. "I cannot."

"But you saw? You saw what they did?"

"I did."

Quinn blew out a harsh breath. "Would someone please tell me?"

"Tell all of us," Lucan said as he walked up with Fallon and the other eight Warriors, including Larena.

"It's the trees," Ramsey said, his silver eyes intent.

Isla nodded. "I think they are trying to talk."

"To Sonya?" Quinn asked.

"Nay," Isla said. "To us. I think they are trying to tell us where Sonya and Broc are."

"And if they're in trouble," Ramsey added.

Lucan's brow furrowed in thought, but it was Fallon who said, "They are no' moving now. How long do you think they were trying to talk?"

"About an hour," Isla said.

Ramsey nodded and glanced at the sky.

She knew he was anxious for Broc to return. They were all worried about Broc and Sonya.

Isla looked to the trees, waiting and hoping they would try again. She wasn't surprised when they bent toward them, against the wind just as before.

"Holy Hell," Quinn muttered.

Then the trees swung to the right. They repeated the movements over and over again.

"They're telling you which direction to go in," Isla said. "Go. Now."

The Warriors were readying to leave when a huge shadow flew over them. There was a cry of relief when everyone spotted Broc, but the joy vanished when they caught sight of his empty arms.

Broc circled back when he spotted the Warriors in the village. He had no sooner landed before Ramsey was before him. Ramsey's silver eyes searched his.

"What do you need?" Ramsey asked.

Broc looked at the faces of the Warriors around him and drew in a deep breath. "I had to leave Sonya. Deirdre cannot get to her, but I need to return. Immediately."

"What happened?" Hayden, the tallest of the Warriors, asked in his usual forceful manner.

Broc ran a hand down his face and glanced over his shoulder when he heard footsteps behind him. He should have known the Druids would want to know about Sonya.

He had vowed to bring her home. And he would.

"Broc."

He turned his head when he heard Isla's voice. He could barely look into her ice blue eyes so filled with worry. If they had known about the curse, they wouldn't have let him go after Sonya. Nor should he have.

If she died . . .

"Deirdre was after a second artifact, one which she said I could get to but she could no'," he explained.

"Where is Sonya?" Marcail asked, her turquoise eyes filling with tears.

Broc looked down at his hands and saw the claws and indigo skin of his Warrior form. He had thought as a Warrior he would always be able to protect Sonya, but he had been wrong.

"I found Sonya wounded and about to be attacked by a wolf. There was a storm, and I had no wish to fly with the possibility that she might be hit with lightning. I brought her to a nearby village to heal."

"Sonya was wounded?" Isla asked. "But she's a healer."

"For some reason she believed her magic had left her. She almost didna survive that first night."

Cara, Lucan's wife, put her hand to her throat. "Did her magic leave her?"

"Nay," Broc said. "I always felt it. I was trying to convince her to return with me to MacLeod Castle when I spotted the wyrran. I made the mistake of thinking they had discovered her because of her magic. Instead, they came for me."

Camdyn frowned. "Why you?"

"As I said, Deirdre was after a second artifact. It was locked in a Celtic burial mound that was protected by spells. Neither she nor any of her wyrran could get inside."

Broc looked to the MacLeod brothers who stood

together. "She also told me of her plan to capture all of the Warriors here and turn them to her side by killing us, then reviving us until the evil took over."

Fallon blew out a breath. "We all knew she would be furious."

"There's more," Broc said. "She plans on killing you and Lucan so that only Quinn houses your god. She will turn him as she plans the rest of us, and then together have the child which was prophesied."

There was a moment of silence as everyone took in his words.

"I was captured by Deirdre, and though I told Sonya she should return here, she followed the wyrran back to Cairn Toul," Broc continued.

Larena smiled wryly. "Somehow, that doesn't surprise me."

"Nor me," Reaghan said.

"How did you get free?" Arran asked.

Broc shifted feet, eager to return to Sonya. "Deirdre had used *drough* blood to subdue me and keep me in great pain. My god became . . . resistant . . . to the effects of the blood and grew enraged. I recalled the spell Deirdre used to unlock doors, and I used it to release my shackles."

"Where were you in the mountain?" Isla asked.

Broc turned his gaze to her. "Where she held Phelan."

Isla's eyes dropped to the ground.

"I attacked Deirdre and was about to kill her when Dunmore came down the stairs shouting how he had a Druid who had come to rescue me." Broc paused as he recalled the joy—and terror—of knowing Sonya was inside the mountain. "I beheaded Deirdre and killed Dunmore."

"Thank God," Marcail murmured.

"I found Sonya and we left. I knew Deirdre would go

after the artifact, and since I had gotten her to tell me the details, Sonya and I decided to look for it ourselves."

Ramsey grinned then. "You found it."

"We did," Broc agreed. "It was Sonya's magic which helped me get past the spells upon the tomb. The magic surrounding the tomb seemed to make Sonya's magic stronger. We had just gotten into the tomb when Deirdre arrived. I shut Sonya inside so Deirdre couldna reach her."

Quinn looked at his brothers and rubbed his jaw. "If Deirdre has left her mountain, she is more than determined. We need to be careful."

"How long can Sonya stay in the tomb?" Duncan asked.

Broc shifted his shoulders, his wings ready to stretch out and feel the wind beneath them. "No' long. I want to return for her straightaway."

Galen stepped forward then, his skin turning the dark green of his Warrior. "You will need me."

Broc knew how much it pained Galen to touch anyone. With the simplest touch Galen could see inside someone's mind. The only person he could touch without his power intruding was his woman, Reaghan—the first artifact.

"Come," Galen bade Broc with a smile. "I have control over my power now, and Sonya needs you."

Broc stepped near Galen the same time Fallon did. They would need Fallon's power to jump them from the castle to the tomb in less than a blink. Since Fallon couldn't jump somewhere he had never been, they were using Galen as a conduit.

Fallon gave a nod to Broc and took the black skin of his god.

"Think of the tomb, of exactly where it's at," Galen told Broc.

Broc pictured the outside of the tomb and kept the image in his mind as Galen laid his hand upon his head. In the next instant Broc, Galen, and Fallon were standing outside the tomb.

There was no evidence of wyrran. No sign of Deirdre.

Broc was instantly on guard.

"Broc," Fallon whispered as the three of them backed together.

Broc bent his legs, ready to fight whatever came at him. "I have no idea."

"It appears as though Deirdre is gone," Galen said.

"Doona underestimate her," Broc said. "She wants this artifact. She's already lost Reaghan. She has no intention of losing what she thinks is the second artifact."

Fallon glanced at Broc. "Why are you smiling?"

"I've damaged the one thing Deirdre could have gotten information from in the tomb."

Galen chuckled and shook his head with a wry smile. "Verra smart of you."

"I think Deirdre is gone," Fallon said.

Broc agreed, but he wasn't sure they were alone. He raced into the burial mound and stopped at the door. Fallon and Galen were right behind him. They hissed in a breath as the magic surrounded them.

"Doona fight it," Broc said. "It has the power to kill you where you stand."

A moment later the magic faded from them. Broc pounded on the door. "Sonya! Sonya, can you hear me?"

"Broc?"

He dropped his head to the stone and smiled as his heart rejoiced at hearing her voice. "I'm here. So are Fallon and Galen. We're going to get you out."

Broc gripped the stone and began to pull. When nothing happened, Galen and Fallon soon joined him.

But even their combined Warrior strength could not budge the rock.

"It was Sonya who somehow got it to open before," Broc said as he put his hand over the markings.

Fallon scratched his jaw and eyed the massive stone door. "And she's inside."

Broc leaned close to the door. "Sonya, I need your help to open the door."

Sonya wiped the sweat that beaded her forehead and raised her brows as Broc's voice reached her. How could she open the door? She was on the inside.

Then she recalled that she had used her magic on the markings. She walked to the door and looked for more Gaelic writing, but there was nothing.

Sonya ran her finger over and over the spirals on the amulet. "I just want out of here," she whispered.

There was a loud pop as the stone door began to open. Sonya looked back at the tomb once more before she walked toward the doorway. As soon as she did, the torches went out.

Sonya caught sight of Broc and ran to him. He wrapped his arms wrapped around her as a slight boom sounded, signaling the door had closed again.

"I told you I would return," he said.

Sonya put her lips on his for a short kiss. "I never doubted you."

Phelan didn't know why he helped the indigo Warrior. Maybe it was the fact that he had fought the wyrran and argued with Deirdre. Broc, his name was. Whatever Broc and his Druid had been searching for, Deirdre greatly craved it.

Phelan should have left Glencoe as soon as he sensed the Druid with Broc, and he'd been on his way. But something drew him back. He couldn't name what it was or why it had affected him so. Only that he had to get to Broc.

Now he knew why.

Phelan would never pass up an opportunity to get at Deirdre or her filthy wyrran, even if it meant helping another Druid in the process.

Deirdre had much to atone for in Phelan's eyes; and not even an eternity of torture could make up for what she had done to him.

He smiled as he watched the wyrran fight the Warriors his power created. Phelan had thought Broc would join in and kill the wyrran, but instead he had flown away.

And where was the Druid who had been with Broc? The last Phelan had seen, they had entered the tomb. Which meant the Druid was inside.

Was Broc leaving her there? If so, it was a fitting punishment, a final torture all Druids deserved.

Phelan chuckled at Deirdre's outrage as her precious wyrran were being beaten by Warriors she didn't control. There were times Phelan thoroughly enjoyed his power.

Like now.

If only the rest of his life could give him such enjoyment he might be able to put aside the resentment that filled his soul.

Until then, however, he was going to relish hurting Deirdre.

THIRTY

Broc knew he held Sonya too tight, but he couldn't seem to make his arms loosen their hold. There had been a moment when panic set in and the door wouldn't budge.

Visions raced through his mind of Sonya suffocating painfully, slowly as he stood outside the tomb.

"We should leave," Fallon said.

Broc nodded and buried his face in Sonya's neck.

"Wai—" Sonya said just as Fallon put his hand on Broc's shoulder.

"—t."

Broc lifted his head when they arrived at the bailey of MacLeod Castle. Fallon and Galen moved away as Broc looked down at Sonya.

There was sadness and disappointment in her gaze. "There was something I wanted to show you," she told him.

"Something in the tomb?"

"Aye. There was a sword with the body, a sword with Celtic designs and Gaelic writing."

Broc glanced at Fallon. "We can always return later. I needed to get you away from the burial mound before Deirdre decided to attack again."

He wasn't able to say more as the women surrounded Sonya. Broc stepped back, his gaze never leaving hers.

Soon she was swept into the castle. Sonya turned and looked at Broc once more before the castle doors shut behind her.

Broc tamped down his god as he blinked and focused on the Warriors around him. It was Galen's curious stare which caught his attention.

"What is it?" Broc asked.

Galen lifted a shoulder in a shrug, his blue eyes troubled. "I'm no' sure. I saw . . . something . . . in Sonya's mind when I touched her on our return."

"What did you see?" Broc demanded. His heart lurched as he thought of her thinking of another man.

Galen blew out a long breath. "All I saw was spirals. Two spirals, actually. They were connected."

"The equinox," Ramsey said.

Broc didn't like the feeling that began to fill his chest. "There were many spirals carved all over the tomb, as well as other designs."

Fallon slapped Broc on the shoulder. "Maybe we should ask Sonya. Until the women are finished with her, why doona you rest?"

Broc knew if he went into the castle he'd seek out Sonya. Instead, he took the path around the castle by the kitchen down to the sea to think. Of Sonya, the curse, and his future.

He stood on the shore and watched the waves roll in. The cliffs on either side of him stood like sentries guarding the MacLeod land.

Waves crashed violently against the rocks, sending spray high into the air as the razorbills flew along the swift air currents, their cries drowned out by the roar of the sea.

A sound, barely discernible to his enhanced hearing, reached him. Broc shifted his eyes to the side and caught sight of Ramsey.

"You look troubled," his friend said.

Broc picked up a small rock at his feet and tossed it into the sea. It bounced on the water several times before sinking out of sight. "Have you ever wanted something so desperately that you knew you could never have? And then suddenly, it's yours?"

"I've no' been so fortunate. I do know what it is to long for something you cannot have. If you've wanted this thing and it's now yours, why does that cause a problem?"

"There is a difference in craving something you know you cannot have, and having something you know you cannot keep."

One side of Ramsey's lips lifted in a smile as his silver eyes met Broc's. "You would be wise to let Sonya make her own decisions, my friend."

"What makes you think I speak of Sonya?"

Ramsey snorted. "I doona need magic to sense there is a bond between the two of you. All I have to do is look at you together."

Broc sighed and crossed his arms over his chest. There was a bond between him and Sonya, a bond he had tried to ignore but couldn't.

A bond that had grown stronger, steadier each moment they had been together.

A bond that could kill her thanks to his curse.

Deirdre's gaze scanned the valley. Only two of her wyrran remained, but that wasn't what infuriated her. What had raised her ire was that she hadn't realized until after she had run away from the burial mound that power had been used.

It hadn't been Druid magic. It had been the power of a Warrior.

There was only one Warrior who she knew could

alter a person's perception of their surroundings with such ease.

"Phelan," she murmured.

His power was so great, she and her wyrran had thought they were being attacked by at least a dozen Warriors. Their claws had felt real as they scoured her skin, their roars loud to her ears.

It had been so authentic that most of her wyrran had died because of the wounds they believed had been inflicted upon them.

"Where are you hiding, Phelan? Do you watch me still?"

She knew the gold Warrior loathed her. He had sworn many times through the years that he would kill her. Is that what he had planned? Or had he been helping Broc?

Neither scenario was acceptable to Deirdre. Phelan was a prize she had kept to herself for many decades. Few knew of his existence. Not even Broc had known of the Warrior.

It hadn't taken Deirdre long to determine it had been Isla who freed Phelan. Isla had never forgiven herself for deceiving the boy and taking him away from his family.

Deirdre wasn't sure whom Phelan hated more: her or Isla.

She pushed aside thoughts of Phelan and strode toward the burial mound, the wyrran close at her heels. Deirdre looked to the wyrran on her left. "Open the door of the tomb."

No sooner had the wyrran walked beneath the archway than it screamed and smoke billowed from inside.

"So the spells are as powerful as legend says," Deirdre murmured to herself.

She sank onto the ground and spread the black skirts

of her gown around her. If she wanted in the tomb, she needed to find someone else who could gain her entry.

Deirdre held her hands over the ground and called to her black magic. Words, long unheard, tumbled from her lips. Words of power, words of magic.

Her voice sank into the singsong chant of the ancient dialect. Magic, dark and potent rose up inside her, filling her.

Wind began to howl around her, lifting her long white hair. Thick, black clouds gathered overhead, darkening the skies, but she paid none of it any heed.

Her attention was on her magic. It poured from her hands as flames erupted before her. They shot high into the sky before lowering.

Deirdre smiled into the deep red flames as a face took form.

Broc rubbed his eye and shifted in his seat at one of the long tables in the great hall. He wore a new tunic of bright blue. He had no idea where it had come from, but when he had returned from his swim it, along with new breeches, had been laid on his bed.

He was sure Cara was most likely responsible. Lucan's wife always made sure everyone had whatever clothes they wanted or needed at their disposal.

Broc ran his hands through his wet hair. He glanced at the top of the stairs, waiting to see Sonya. They hadn't spoken of what had transpired between them. There had been no pretty words, no promises of the future.

"She'll come," Ramsey said from beside him.

Broc wanted to see Sonya with a need that bordered on obsessive. At the same time, he feared seeing her. He had enjoyed their time alone together. It had felt right, good.

Now, back at the castle, would they go back to trying

their best not to ignore the passion which tied them together? It was for the best, but Broc wasn't sure he could keep his hands off Sonya after having her for his own.

She was his calm in the storm that was his life.

Broc felt the strength, the sensuous touch of her magic a heartbeat before she came into sight. He lifted his eyes to her and sucked in a breath.

Her long flame curls were free of her braid. They hung in vibrant disarray down to her waist and over her shoulders to her breasts. The pale yellow gown only accentuated her hair and the amber color of her eyes.

Eyes that were locked on him.

Broc slowly rose to his feet as she descended the stairs. She said not a word to anyone as she walked down the opposite side of the table from Broc.

He expected her to stop and sit across from him. Her steps slowed as she neared, but she continued on to the head of the table. Once there, she looked around at the occupants, but her gaze returned to Broc.

He started toward her when she gave a barely discernible shake of her head. Broc didn't like the pain that swept through him. So she wanted to pretend the intimacy they had shared had never happened. Maybe she knew the curse she had been so hasty to disregard was real and she wanted no part of Broc.

Broc looked away from her and sat. If that's what she wanted, that was what he would give her.

For Sonya, he'd cut out his own heart.

THIRTY-ONE

Sonya saw Broc close himself off once again. She wanted to go to him, to tell him . . . she didn't know what to tell him. She hadn't had time to think of all that had happened between them, of everything that had changed.

And the things which hadn't.

The entire time she had been with the other women they had asked her countless questions, questions she had refused to answer. Her mind had been in a whirl since returning to MacLeod Castle.

She and Broc had been trying so hard to get back, but now that they were, Sonya wanted to find the cave again. She wanted the closeness that had developed between her and Broc to grow.

Instead, she feared back at the castle it would be as if she and Broc had never been, as if the love she felt for him had only been a dream.

Sonya took in a deep breath and faced the Druids and Warriors she had called family. She owed them an explanation for leaving.

She looked to Broc for strength, but he refused to meet her gaze.

Sonya gripped the table for support and focused on Fallon, who sat at the other end of the table. "I know everyone has questions, and I will answer them. I left because . . . because sometimes that is the only option a person thinks they have."

"Did someone do something to you?" Cara asked.

Sonya fought not to look at Broc. "As I told Fallon not too long ago, I feared that one day when my healing was needed most, it would abandon me."

Galen's dark blue eyes held a wealth of sadness. "You thought because you couldn't save Reaghan, your healing magic had left."

"I couldn't heal her. She died, Galen."

"But my magic saved me," Reaghan said.

Sonya looked at the couple. Fate had brought Reaghan and Galen together, but it was love which kept them bound. She envied their bond. "All of what you say is true. What you do not know is that Braden was gravely injured just before then. I barely managed to heal him."

"So," Quinn said, "in your mind, your magic had failed."

"Precisely. And then I saw Anice . . ."

Sonya couldn't finish. She hadn't mourned her sister as she should have. Anice had been blood family, but somewhere along their lives a vast chasm had separated them.

Fallon shoved aside his long, brown hair and leaned his elbows on the table. "As you've told us, Sonya, you cannot bring life to the dead. There was nothing you could do for Anice."

"I know," Sonya said. "I shouldn't have left. You are my family now. Thank you for sending Broc to find me."

"We didna send him," Lucan said.

Sonya looked to Broc, but he had his head down, his shoulder length blond hair blocking his face from her. She lowered herself onto the seat and dragged in a ragged breath.

"Where did Broc find you?"

"He said you were injured. What happened?"

"Broc said you followed him to Cairn Toul."

"Cairn Toul? You went in that evil place?"

"Did Deirdre see you?"

"What about this new artifact Deirdre is after?"

The questions came at Sonya at such a rapid succession that she didn't know who asked what. She decided the best place was to start at the beginning.

Everyone grew quiet as she began her tale. She skipped over her time in the tomb, however. The only one who interrupted her was Broc when he filled in his parts of the story.

She was careful to leave out any hints that she and Broc had made love. It was Broc who ended their story with how he flew back to MacLeod Castle for Fallon.

"That's quite an adventure," Larena said. "To have gone into Cairn Toul for Broc took a lot of courage, Sonya."

Sonya shrugged and touched the amulet which hung beneath her gown. "Anyone would have done it."

"Knowing what awaited them in that mountain," Ramsey said with his black brows raised. "I doubt it."

"What happened while you were in the burial chamber?" Broc asked as he slowly raised his head to look at her.

Sonya swallowed hard. "I omitted that part of the story because I believe what I found inside the tomb will aid us."

"How?" Marcail asked.

"It could be in combination with the artifacts or another way."

Fallon gave a small nod. "Tell us what you found."

"As Broc explained, there were weapons everywhere in the tomb. I had begun to look for one to use in case

Deirdre somehow managed to get inside. I saw a sword held by the corpse and wanted a closer look."

"Why?" Arran asked, curious as ever. "It was just a sword."

"So I thought. Embedded atop the pommel was a garnet the size of a child's fist. But that's not what drew my interest. It was the intricate knot work of the Celts along the blade as well as more Gaelic markings."

Broc clasped his hands together on the table. "She mentioned them to me as Fallon jumped us here. We can always return to the burial mound so the markings can be read."

"There was something else," Sonya said. "I saw something around the neck of the body. As soon as I saw it, I knew I was meant to take it."

"Show me," Broc urged.

Sonya pulled out the amulet and lifted the leather strap over her head. She then tossed the amulet to Broc.

He caught it in one hand and looked at it. "Connecting spirals."

Galen, Fallon, and Broc shared a look. The amulet was passed from person to person before it made its way back to Sonya.

She ran her fingers over the spirals as she had done countless times since she first saw it. "The double spirals connected as they represent the equinoxes."

"When the day and the night are of equal length," Isla finished. "The equinoxes have always been potent days for a Druid, *mie* or *drough*, to use their magic."

Broc's head swiveled to her, his dark, sultry eyes studying her intently before he said, "Sonya will be the bearer of this amulet. She found it, and so it should be her right."

There was a loud consensus as everyone agreed.

Sonya slipped the amulet over her head and let the weight of the gold drop between her breasts.

"Broc," Isla called. "You said there were Warriors who attacked Deirdre and her wyrran, making it easy for you to get away from the burial mound. Did you recognize any of the Warriors?"

Broc shook his head. "There were many locked in Deirdre's dungeons, and many more who served her. Although I found it odd that there was one Warrior who stood atop the mound and watched."

"What color was he?" Isla asked as she leaned forward, expectation and hope flaring in her ice blue eyes.

"Gold."

"It was Phelan. He was there!"

Broc flatted his lips and shook his head. "I'm sorry, Isla. I had no idea."

"When we returned to the mound, there was nothing," Galen said. "No evidence of wyrran, Deirdre, or Warriors."

Isla smiled sadly as Hayden put his arm around her shoulders. "Phelan's power is that he can alter any surroundings to whatever he wants. There were no Warriors there, Broc. He only made you think there were."

"And Deirdre," Ramsey added. "She and her wyrran were fighting them."

"Do you think Deirdre captured Phelan again?" Sonya asked.

Broc shook his head. "Nay. For whatever reason, Phelan helped us. We owe him a debt of thanks."

"That we will repay soon," Fallon stated. "Isla has asked us to find him."

Broc grimaced. "I'll find him, but I willna force him to come here. It will be his decision."

"That is all I can ask," Isla said and lowered her ice blue eyes.

A moment later Sonya and the other women rose to begin cooking supper. Broc tried not to watch Sonya, tried not to notice how her hips swayed as she walked, or how the ends of her hair brushed against the sides of her breasts.

He tried and failed.

The attraction Broc had always felt for Sonya had grown during their time alone. What it had grown into he wasn't sure he could say, much less acknowledge. There were too many things standing in their way. His immortality was the largest.

As soon as the women disappeared into the kitchen, Fallon leaned forward. "We need to send someone to the Isle of Eigg to find this Tablet of Orn."

"As curious as I am to find it, I'm no' leaving Marcail," Quinn said.

Lucan tugged on a braid at his temple, and smiled at his younger brother. "We would never ask you to. Marcail needs you, and we need Warriors who will stay behind to protect the Druids."

"I'd like to go," Logan offered.

Broc looked at the youngest of them. Logan had only been a Warrior for one hundred and fifteen years, the one who always had a jest, always knew what to say to make someone smile.

But ever since he had left with Galen to find Reaghan, something had changed. They were all concerned about him. Each Warrior had a past they would rather forget.

Broc knew all too well about trying to outrun your past. It never worked.

When everyone looked at him, Logan rolled his eyes. "I'm hoping to determine who is controlling the damned peregrine that is still keeping watch on us."

Hayden shrugged. "I've seen the falcon less and less over the last few days."

"It's still there," Ramsey said.

Logan slapped his hands on the table, making it shake. "I have to know who is controlling that bird."

"It could be anyone," Broc said. "How do you expect to discover who is commanding it?"

Logan grinned the smile of a man with a plan. "It followed Galen and me when we left. I suspect it will follow whoever leaves again."

"If it wants to keep track of us, why did it no' follow Broc?" Hayden asked.

"It could be Broc was too fast or that it just didna care."

Broc scratched his chin as he realized where Logan was heading. "But you think it will care about you?"

Logan shrugged. "I think it will follow anyone who leaves on foot."

"I'd like to see if Logan's theory is correct," Quinn said. "Since I couldna use my power to communicate with the falcon as I should have, there's obviously magic involved."

Duncan leaned forward. "I'd like to go with Logan."

Every eye turned to Duncan. Broc shifted his gaze to Ian, Duncan's twin. Ian and Duncan shared a silent nod, the bond of twins going deeper than Broc could ever imagine.

"So be it," Fallon said.

"So be what?" Larena asked as she and the other women returned to the great hall with trenchers of food.

Logan took a trencher from Reaghan. "Duncan and I are going to the Isle of Eigg."

Sonya's gaze snapped to Broc's. He saw the need that leapt into her eyes to go with the Warriors. Broc himself had thought to find the tablet when he'd read of its location.

"I would like to go as well," Sonya said.

Broc and Fallon said "Nay" in unison.

Sonya's eyes blazed with anger as she stared at Broc.

"You are too valuable, Sonya," Fallon said into the silence. "We need you and your healing magic here. Besides, you have the amulet to guard now."

Broc sighed and glanced down at his hands. That wasn't the reason he would have used, but Fallon was right. She was too important.

None more so than to Broc.

THIRTY-TWO

Malcolm's eyes snapped open and he looked around from his position sitting against a boulder. He was high atop a mountain with only the rocks and grass around him.

Yet, he had heard his name.

He reached his left hand down beside him and grasped his sword. No fire blazed to hinder his eye-sight, yet he knew there was something around him, something that stopped him from seeing what was right there.

"Are you afraid, Malcolm?"

The female voice, stronger now, came at him from all sides. He didn't move, didn't give in to the urge to jump to his feet and search for the woman.

"I can see that you are," she said. "Yet, you do not run from me."

"Show yourself," he demanded.

There was a stir in the air and suddenly a woman appeared. Malcolm rose to his feet. She wore a black cloak with the hood pulled over her head, shrouding her.

Her hands lifted to push the hood back enough so he could glimpse her face. Malcolm could only stare in mute silence at her beauty.

Not too long ago he would have charmed her, wooed her until she was in his bed. Now, with his scars and useless right arm, he didn't even bother to try.

He had always appreciated stunning things, so he let his gaze linger on her oval face. She had high cheekbones and a delicate bone structure. Her lips were a little on the thin side, but her mouth was wide, her eyes expressive. He just wished he could see the color of her eyes and hair.

"Who are you?" he asked.

Her head cocked to the side. "You don't know me?"

"Should I?"

"Oh, aye, you should." She let the hood fall away to show her white hair. "After all, it was me who ordered your death."

Malcolm snarled and said, "Deirdre."

"You don't have to say my name as if the very sound makes you ill."

"It does."

"Ah, but you were just admiring me a moment ago."

"A mistake I regret."

He watched her carefully. How could he have thought she was lovely? He should have sensed the evil within her. Not that he could have done anything. Deirdre had found him. But why?

"You once were a fine Warrior for your clan, weren't you?" Deirdre asked.

A thread of foreboding rose up in him. "As you can see, I'm no' much of one now. Thanks to you."

"I can change that. I can take away the scars and heal your arm so that you may use it again."

"Why would you do such a thing?"

"I need you, Malcolm."

He snorted and shook his head. As much as he would like to be the man he once was, he would not sell his soul to Deirdre. "There is nothing you can say or do that will make me do as you ask."

"What if I vow to leave Larena alone? That when I

attack MacLeod Castle, she will not be harmed or taken?"

Malcolm thought of his cousin, of all she had lost and the happiness she had found with Fallon.

"I could make you do what I want," Deirdre said.

"Why do you no', then?"

She smiled then. "Having you willingly come to me will make things so much better. Think of Larena. You heard what the Warriors said about my mountain. Do you want her subjected to what I would put her through? Torture and rape?"

Malcolm shook his head. He would do anything to keep Larena safe. She was his family. "What do you need me to do?" he finally asked.

"First, I will release your god."

Malcolm staggered backward, his mind refusing to believe what he had just heard. "What?"

"Aye. You will be my first Warrior, Malcolm. You will lead my armies and do all that I ask. Because the first time you don't, I will kill Larena."

Malcolm swallowed, his heart shriveling in his chest. He had fallen into Deirdre's trap, had done exactly as she had wanted. He should have been stronger and withstood her.

But he would leave her now.

He began to turn away when Deirdre started to chant. Her face was lifted to the sky, her arms out to her sides. Malcolm grimaced as he felt something push against his body. It was vile and rough as it sought entry through his skin.

The more words Deirdre spoke, the more difficult it was for Malcolm to remain standing. His legs gave way and he fell to his knees, a bellow ripping from his throat as he felt his bones popping in and out of place all over his body.

Deirdre's voice rose higher, the words coming quicker, but Malcolm could barely hear them. The soul-shredding pain that tore through him left him deaf to anything else.

Muscles tore, bones broke all through his body. The pain was unlike anything he had ever felt, it was so powerful and agonizing. His body was no longer his own. He could actually feel something inside him, a presence that roared and growled its frustration.

But worst of all was the sudden and overwhelming need Malcolm had to feel blood on his hands, to take someone's life. To watch that life drain away.

Malcolm squeezed his eyes shut as more images of death and blood filled his mind. There was a new voice in his head, a deep, vile voice that demanded Malcolm coat the earth in blood.

After what seemed like an eternity, the pain faded away. Malcolm fell back on his haunches and let his chin drop to his chest.

"I have to say, Malcolm, you are a truly stunning Warrior."

He lifted his face at Deirdre's words before he glanced down at his hands. His skin had changed to maroon, so dark at first glance he thought the color was black.

Inside his mind, he could hear a voice full of rage. It was telling Malcolm his name, who he was. Malcolm clenched his fists as the truth of his god, Daal, the devourer, could not be denied.

He was a Warrior.

Malcolm threw back his head and unleashed the power he felt growing inside him. Lightning forked above and around him.

Deirdre clapped, a pleased smile upon her lips. "So, lightning is your power. Interesting. And your god?"

"Does it matter?"

She shrugged. "Keep your secret for now, but you will tell me, Malcolm. Now, rise. There is much we need to do."

Malcolm knew the other Warriors could control when their gods were visible or not, but they'd had centuries to gain command over their gods. He didn't want to wait that long. Nor did he think he had the time.

He shut out Daal and concentrated on pushing him down, imagining the maroon color leaving his skin and the claws disappearing.

After several tries Malcolm realized Daal was too powerful to be ruled. For now. But Malcolm would not give in to his god.

He might not have joined in the conversations at MacLeod Castle, but he had listened. If he was going to win against his god, he had to stay strong and not allow the rage that now filled him to rule his life. He needed to not feel anything, to have nothing bother him. He needed to be soulless.

"Malcolm," Deirdre called.

He rose to his feet and numbly followed her. It was only then that he realized he could move his right arm as he had before the attack.

THIRTY-THREE

Sonya sat on the edge of her bed in her chamber long after the others had found their own beds. She couldn't sleep, couldn't think of anything other than Broc.

They had shared just a few nights together, but those few nights had altered her entire existence. It seemed wrong not to have Broc with her, not to know he was near.

She wondered where he was in the castle. And, God help her, she wondered if he thought of her, of their time together.

Sonya knew she shouldn't dwell on such things, but she couldn't help it. As soon as she saw Broc that first time she had known he would mean something to her.

And to have spent the best—and most frightening—moments of her life with him might have to sustain her the rest of her years.

Nothing had been said between them about a future. No promises, no possibilities.

They had taken those few treasured moments and made the most of them. She didn't regret any of it. But she did regret that they could be over.

You won't know until you ask him.

Did she dare? *Could* she dare?

She and Broc had never shied away from each other

at the castle. In fact, Sonya had found herself searching for him and only him over the last weeks.

But even then she had been careful to keep herself apart from him. She had feared, even then, of getting too close to him, of opening herself up to the possibilities of . . . anything.

The threat of dying made her put those silly fears aside. And look what it had given her. The very thing she had dreamed of. Broc.

She now knew he had cared for Anice, but he hadn't been in love with her. It didn't mean he felt anything more for her, only that he felt the pull of attraction between them.

Sonya could stand the silence of her chamber no more. She rose and walked from her room. When she had first come to the castle, it had felt massive, as if she would never learn her way about the long corridors and many stairways. Now, it was diminished after such an adventure with Broc.

She walked into the great hall to find it empty. It used to be that Malcolm could be found there when he wasn't roaming the edges of the cliffs.

Malcolm was gone now. Would she ever see him again? The likelihood was slim, but she hoped that one day he might return.

Sonya left the castle and stepped into the bailey. The moon was high and the stars numerous. A few clouds dotted the sky, illuminated by the moonlight.

Her eyes had always looked upward. Whether it was to the sun or the moon, the sky had mesmerized her. Was it because her fate had been connected to Broc's all along?

A shadow moved and pushed from the castle wall. Logan's form took shape as he neared her. "Cannot sleep?"

Sonya licked her lips as she shook her head. "I want to visit the trees. Isla told me what happened, about how they helped. I would like to thank them."

"You know it isna safe."

"Then come with me if you must, but I am going to see the trees."

She didn't have to ask permission. If Broc had been near, she was sure he would argue that he should accompany her, but he wasn't near. He hadn't been near her since they returned.

Maybe that's why she wanted to see the trees. Oh, she did want to thank them, but maybe deep down she knew it would force Broc's hand.

If he came, it meant he cared enough to forget about the stupid curse.

If he didn't, it meant . . . well, it meant she at least had her memories.

Sonya squared her shoulders and walked to the huge wooden gate. As she approached, another shadow moved. She sighed and stopped short of rolling her eyes.

"I'm not running away," she said to whoever it was.

Ramsey's silver gaze met hers as he opened the door within the gate. "I know."

"I'm going to the trees."

He smiled and took her hand to help her through. "I know."

Sonya turned once she was through the gate and looked at Ramsey. "You aren't going to try and stop me?"

"Should I? You said you were no' running away."

"And you aren't going to tell me it would be safer to wait?"

Ramsey shook his head. "You'll be safe."

She thought over his words as she walked to the village. Some of the Warriors had taken up residence in the cottages. Fallon wanted all the Druids within the castle, and she understood his reasoning.

Deirdre and the wyrran had attacked the castle several times and destroyed the village twice. It was better to have the Druids where Deirdre couldn't reach them as easily.

Sonya arrived at the back of the village and halted. There was a barrier created by Isla's magic around the castle and village. To others outside the magical barrier, it appeared as if the land were bare, keeping the inhabitants safe from unwanted visitors.

It didn't stop Deirdre. It did give the wyrran pause, and if other Warriors didn't know about it, they wouldn't proceed through.

Before, Broc had always been adamant about going with Sonya out of the barrier when she wanted to commune with the trees. She found it odd that no one was stopping her this time.

It could be that everyone knew there were no wyrran hidden in the forest. Sonya had been gone for several days. Many things could have changed during that time.

She put her hand out and felt the slight resistance to the shield. The feel of Isla's powerful magic enveloped Sonya as she stepped through the invisible field.

Sonya let out a long sigh as she exited the barrier. The whispers of the trees surrounded her, wrapped her in their emotions.

She hurried to the first tree and laid her hand upon the rough bark. "How I've missed you."

In answer, the trees swayed, their words mixing together as they all spoke at once.

Sonya laughed and walked deeper into the forest. This is what she had missed most when she thought her magic gone. This is what she had been craving since she realized her magic had returned. This is where her magic was the strongest, where she could find peace and restore her inner balance. Where she heard the music of her ancestors.

She closed her eyes as the trees swayed around her, welcoming her. They bent low to lovingly brush her with their limbs. She spread her arms out to her side and her head dropped back as she released her magic to merge with the trees.

Their words, whispered and gentle as leaves falling, reached her.

"*. . . missed you, Sonnnnnnnyaaaaaa . . .*"

"*. . . tried to tell the otherssss where to find you . . .*"

"*. . . feared for you . . .*"

"*. . . don't leave us again . . .*"

A tear fell down her cheek as the weight of their worry for her settled around her.

"I'm sorry," she told them. "My magic left me, or I thought it had."

"*. . . stay with ussssss . . .*"

"*. . . we neeeeed you . . .*"

Long ago, when Druids had walked freely upon the land, there had been many who could speak to the trees. Through the years the number had diminished, and as far as the trees told Sonya, she was the last.

The trees needed her as much as she needed them. But what would happen once she was dead? Would there be another who could take her place?

Or would the special, spectacular words of the trees fade into the past?

Broc stood on a small outcropping halfway down the cliffs, watching the sea. He had wanted to be alone and as far away from Sonya as he could get, lest he be tempted to go to her.

He had taken one look at his bed and known he couldn't sleep there. Not alone. Not without Sonya.

Broc blew out a breath and went down on his haunches. He leaned back against the cliff, the hard, jagged rock digging into his spine. There had been many kinds of pain he had experienced over the centuries, but the one in his chest far exceeded the others.

At least at MacLeod Castle he didn't need to worry for Sonya's safety. Even though he wasn't near her, he could feel her magic. It had always been strong, but since the burial mound, it had grown more intense. Brilliant. Compelling.

No sooner had the thought gone through Broc's mind than the link he felt with Sonya's magic was gone, as if it were snapped in half.

Broc stood and unleashed his god as he jumped into the air. His wings took him up and over the cliffs. Broc soared around the castle, using his power to search for Sonya.

And just as he thought, she wasn't there.

It took less than a heartbeat for his power to tell him she was outside Isla's barrier in the trees. He let out a breath he hadn't known he was holding, his heart once again easing from its frantic beating.

Broc flew out of the shield and over the tops of the forest. He dropped to the ground behind Sonya and simply watched.

The trees swayed from side to side in a gentle rocking motion. Broc remembered when Sonya had allowed him to see the trees through her magic, had permitted him to hear their whispers. He hadn't understood their words, but he had heard them.

Broc weaved through the trees as he walked around Sonya until he stood in front of her. He couldn't take his eyes from her, couldn't stop the pounding of his heart in his chest. Her magic engulfed him. Surrounded. Overwhelmed.

And he yearned for more.

Her magic was sensual and seductive, tempting and beguiling. She charmed him, lured him, captivated him.

Made him hunger. Crave. Yearn.

For her. All for her. Her touch, her kisses, and her beautiful body.

Sonya's long curls lifted on the breeze created by the trees and her skirts swirled about her legs. But it was the pure, glorious smile upon her face that took his breath away.

Her head lifted, and she opened her eyes. Her gaze of amber flecks mixed with gold watched him. Curiosity and anticipation flashed in her depths.

Broc's skin tingled with the feel of her magic. His gaze dropped to her mouth. He wanted to taste her again, to feel her tongue against his as he plundered her mouth.

He took a step toward her before he realized what he was doing. But once he had begun moving, he couldn't stop. He closed the distance between them until their bodies were breaths apart.

"Broc," she whispered, and searched his face.

There was so much that needed to be said, so many things he should tell her. But the only thing he wanted to do was take her in his arms and show her how much he needed her, how much he longed for her.

He jerked her against his chest and claimed her mouth. She opened for him, her tongue colliding against his in a frenzy that sent his already heated blood to boiling.

Need, wicked and crushing, surged through him. There was no turning away, no tearing his lips from hers. However wrong it was for them to be together, he had to have her.

Broc deepened the kiss. The passion, the fervor, of Sonya's response sent him reeling. She was irresistible and all too enticing.

He reached between them and covered her breast with his hand. Her fingers dug into his neck as she arched against him, a low moan mixing with their ragged breaths.

The desire raging in him swelled each time he held her, touched her. Kissed her. It grew more difficult to keep his distance, and he found he didn't want to.

He wanted Sonya as his own.

He knew he didn't deserve her, shouldn't crave to have her. But he did. God help him, he did. He was ready to forget the curse, forget everything as long as he could have her.

Broc ended the kiss and cupped Sonya's face to make her look at him. "I want you."

THIRTY-FOUR

Sonya looked into Broc's dark brown eyes and smiled. "Take me. I'm yours."

It seemed to be all the answer he needed. He jerked at her skirts as she reached to unfasten his breeches. Their fingers tangled, causing them to laugh and share another hot, lingering kiss.

The trees had told Sonya Broc was there long before she opened her eyes to find him in front of her. Even if the trees hadn't told her, she would have known.

Her body knew when Broc was near. She might not have the power of a god, but when it came to Broc, she was attuned to him in a way she couldn't deny or explain.

"I love your hair," he said as he pulled her gown over her head and tossed it aside.

"My hair is a curse."

He shook his head and jerked off his boots. "It's beautiful. Just as you are."

They removed the rest of their clothing and fell together on the ground in a tangle of arms and legs. Sonya sighed as Broc's weight moved atop her. She ran her hands over his back and the muscles that bunched and moved beneath her fingers.

His mouth kissed down her throat and across her chest before his lips closed around a nipple. Sonya plunged her hands into his blond locks and cried out. He alternated between suckling the hard peak and swirling his tongue around it.

Sonya ground against him, seeking his arousal. She needed his hard, hot length inside her, needed to feel him thrust and fill her, to join their souls.

Her sex throbbed as her desire rose higher. Broc's mouth and hands were everywhere, teasing her, tempting her. Their lips clashed with another scorching kiss.

Sonya burned for Broc. For his hands. His mouth. His body.

She pushed against his shoulder and rolled him onto his back as she straddled his hips. Sonya reached for his rod, but just before her hand closed around him, Broc had her on her back, pinned beneath him.

And then he was inside her.

Sonya cried out and wrapped her legs around his waist. He slid inside her deeper, stretching her. She rotated her hips, needing to feel the friction.

Broc buried his head in the crook of her neck and gripped her hip with one hand. He moaned long and low, the sound full of passion and need.

He leaned up and kissed her as he began to thrust his hips. Each stroke of his tongue matched that of his cock. It sent her spiraling all too quickly, her orgasm building fast.

Sonya tried to pull back, to delay that glorious moment, but Broc wouldn't let her. He demanded she give all of herself. Since she could never deny him, she rose up to meet him each time he plunged within her.

His tempo quickened until he rose up on his hands. He thrust fast and hard, driving deeper each time. All Sonya could do was hold on to him as he took her to the edge of pleasure before she tipped over the side.

The climax was swift and powerful as it swept her

up in its bliss, threw her into the stars, their light blinding her as her body clutched around him.

Dimly she heard Broc shout her name, felt him thrust deep enough to touch her womb once, twice, three times before a shudder ran through him. Sonya pulled him down to her and wrapped her arms around him. She held him as his seed poured inside her.

Tightening the bond between them.

Deirdre reached MacLeod Castle just as dawn broke the sky. Though she couldn't see through the shield of Isla's magic, Deirdre knew the castle. She had gazed at the gray stone of the castle many times, a castle she had watched burn.

That day so many centuries ago had been one of celebration. She'd had the three MacLeod brothers. Everything she had ever wanted would soon be hers. Or so she had thought.

Ever since the brothers had escaped, she had been trying to lure them to her side. When that hadn't worked, she decided she would force them. That hadn't worked, either.

Not even holding Quinn in Cairn Toul had been to her advantage as she had thought it would be. She had been overconfident. And it had cost her all she had amassed through the centuries.

She was starting over, and though it irked her, she had learned her lesson.

Her wyrran were loyal. They had proven effective in finding and bringing Druids to her. They had even captured several men who had housed gods.

But when it came to battling those at MacLeod Castle, the duty was best left to her.

She could walk into the castle now and kill everyone. But what fun would that be? She wanted them to suffer, wanted them to realize it was futile to fight her. She wanted to see all hope stripped from them piece by piece.

Her new plan was already in motion. She had thought to begin with Broc, but just as she had assumed, there was another who could gain access to the burial mound and the second artifact. Her new army of Warriors would begin with Malcolm. She had plans for every Warrior in the castle.

No one would escape her wrath this time.

Deirdre lifted the hood of her cloak over her head and moved toward the lovers who lay in naked splendor amid the forest.

It seemed that each of the Warriors who came to MacLeod Castle found themselves a Druid. In order to lure these powerful Druids, Deirdre merely had to turn their Warriors. It wouldn't prove too difficult. They were men, after all.

Animals scattered from her path and birds that had awoken with the new day quieted as she neared. Men never paid attention to animals. If they did, they would know she was coming and prepare.

Deirdre halted ten paces from Broc and his flame-haired lover. Deirdre could sense her *mie* magic. Was she the healer Deirdre had heard about?

A moment later the *mie's* eyes flew open and she sat up. "Who are you?"

Deirdre smiled and glanced at a still slumbering Broc. Her face was hidden by her hood, so the Druid didn't realize the predatory gaze that was locked on her. "I'm here to deliver a warning."

"What kind of warning?" The Druid put her hand on a tree to help her rise. Her long hair fell over her shoulders to cover her breasts.

"No one is safe with the MacLeods."

"No one is safe anywhere as long as Deirdre is alive."

Deirdre cocked her head to the side. "No truer words have been spoken. Heed my warning, Druid. Everyone has been marked." Then she turned and walked away.

"Wait. Who are you?"

Deirdre chuckled as she continued on. Aye, this plan was going to be truly wonderful to watch unfold. Not to mention the glee she would feel as each of the Warriors and Druids succumbed to her.

And they would succumb.

Sonya stared after the cloaked and hooded woman as she faded into the trees. The warning echoed in her mind, growing louder and louder each time. She forgot her nakedness and ran after the woman. Sonya wanted to know who the woman was, but she also wanted to know how everyone was marked.

"Sonya!"

She slowed when she heard Broc's shout. No matter where she looked, she couldn't find a trace of the woman.

"What is it?" Broc asked as he came to a halt beside her.

Sonya took his hand to help stop her own from shaking. "There was a woman. She said everyone at the castle was marked."

Broc's gaze narrowed as it slid around the forest. "Where is she? Who was she?"

"I don't know. I woke up and she was there."

"Did you see her face?"

Sonya shook her head. The trees began to sway, their whispers growing incessant. She rested a hand on one and listened.

". . . Deirdre! Deirdre! Deeeeeeeirdre! . . ."

". . . not safe. She was here . . ."

". . . they're all marked. Sonyaaaaa is marked . . ."

Sonya shivered as she turned to Broc. "The trees say it was Deirdre."

"Shite," Broc said, and pulled her behind him as he ran to their clothes.

They dressed hurriedly. Sonya had just grabbed her stockings and shoes when Broc's arms went around her. In her next breath they were flying to the castle.

As soon as they approached, Broc began to shout for the others.

Sonya's gaze was on the forest. Deirdre had been there. Within strides of her. Why hadn't Deirdre taken her or tried to kill her? Why had she delivered the warning? Why hadn't she tried to attack the castle? Or taken Broc again?

Broc's arms tightened around her as he landed them in the bailey. "I should have sensed her," he whispered. "She could have taken you."

"I don't blame you." Sonya stepped out of his arms so she could see his face. "If she had wanted to take me, she could have."

Broc opened his mouth to say something when the MacLeods came rushing into the bailey. Hayden jumped from somewhere atop the castle and landed beside them.

"What happened?" Fallon asked.

Broc looked at the gate and then down at Sonya. His heart still pounded, the acrid taste of fear filling his mouth. "I think we need to wake everyone."

"Aye," Sonya said. Her hand still trembled within his.

Broc didn't release her as they followed the others into the castle. When Sonya took a seat at the table, she pulled him down beside her.

But Broc couldn't sit. He paced the great hall as everyone came in.

"Broc? Sonya? Someone please tell me what has happened," Fallon said.

Broc ran a hand down his face and tried to tamp his god down, but the fury and fear were too great. His wings flapped, the force of them sending a current of air around the others and blowing hair into their faces.

He growled and focused on calming himself. Once he had control of his god and his emotions, he looked at Sonya, who sat watching him with worried, filled eyes.

"There was a woman in the forest," Sonya said. "She . . . she was cloaked with her hood over her face. I never saw her."

Broc cursed and leaned his hands against the wall. He pushed his claws into the stones as he thought of how close Sonya had been to Deirdre. Deirdre had to have known Sonya was a Druid.

Why had Deirdre not taken her? Just what plans did she have?

There was a slight pause before Lucan said, "I gather by Broc's anger this woman said something to you."

"Aye," Sonya said. "She said everyone at the castle was marked."

Broc dragged his claws out of the stone and whirled around. "God's blood! It was Deirdre! She was here!" he shouted.

Marcail's face lost all color. Quinn and Hayden rose from their seats and headed toward the door. Duncan, Ian, and Arran were right on their heels.

"Hold!" Fallon shouted and jumped to his feet.

Hayden shook his head as his skin turned the red of his god and small red horns protruded from the top of his head. "I'm going to find her."

"She's gone," Broc said.

Sonya glanced at Broc. "He's right. The trees waited

to tell me who she was until she had left. I think they feared what I might do if I knew."

"None of this makes sense," Camdyn, another Warrior, said. "She had already captured Broc a few days ago. We all know how desperately she wants Druids. Why no' take one or both?"

"A damned fine question," Broc mumbled.

Sonya wrapped her arms around her middle. "It was as if she was gloating, as if she wanted us to know we were marked."

Ramsey blew out a breath. "Deirdre doesna do anything without a plan. There was only one reason for her to tell us she has marked us."

"Fear," Ian answered.

"Aye," Ramsey said with a nod. "She wants us looking over our shoulders, wants us to be extra careful."

Reaghan rubbed her hands together as if seeking warmth. "Do you think she has managed to capture some of the Warriors who escaped? Like Phelan?"

"Or Charon," Arran added.

Sonya watched Broc walk to her and tuck a strand of her hair behind her ear. She hated the worry she saw in his dark depths.

"The only thing I know is that we have to be vigilant. She didna take me or Sonya today. There is a reason for that, even if we doona know it yet," Broc said.

Fallon rose to his feet and looked at each Warrior and Druid. "Nothing has changed. Deirdre is still out there."

But everything had changed for Sonya. She loved Broc. And he had nearly been taken from her again.

THIRTY-FIVE

Sonya quickly plaited her hair and walked into the kitchen. She needed something to do with her hands, something to take her mind off the fact Deirdre had come to see her.

She felt a gentle touch on her shoulder, and then Cara said, "It will be all right."

"She's right," Reaghan said with a firm nod.

Marcail sat on a stool and put her hand on her stomach and her unborn child. "I wish I had your optimism, Cara."

Isla handed Marcail a bowl and a spoon. "Stir that for me, please."

There was a pause before Marcail did as Isla asked.

Isla moved to stand beside Sonya. "Deirdre marked all of us the moment our men stormed her mountain."

"Aye," Larena said with a soft sigh. "As soon as we heard she hadn't died, we all knew her retaliation would be swift."

Marcail dropped the spoon and wiped at her eyes. "What does it mean, though? 'Marked'?"

"I think it means she has something in store for each of us," Sonya said. "She didn't say as much, but it was implied."

"Did you see her?" Reaghan asked.

Sonya shook her head. "I saw nothing other than her

cloak. She held it together in front of her, and the hood was pulled up in such a way that her face was obscured."

"Why the ruse?" Larena asked.

Marcail snorted. "Precisely. Why not show Sonya who she was?"

"I suppose it has something to do with her plan," Isla said.

Cara rolled her eyes. "Whatever that might be."

The subject was quickly changed. Sonya paid no attention to anyone. Her mind still went over every word Deirdre had spoken to her again and again. There had to be something she was missing, something that would help them.

"We're very happy for you," Isla said as she began to knead the dough.

Sonya glanced up. "Happy?"

"For you and Broc."

"Oh." Sonya shrugged and continued to clean the fish they would have for their noon meal.

"Sonya," Isla said. "There is no need to deny your feelings for him any longer."

She smiled then. "I'm not."

"Is he?"

"Nay. We just haven't had a chance to . . ."

"Talk," Isla finished. "I can understand that dilemma. Hayden and I had the same problem."

Sonya turned to her. "I knew our chances of returning weren't good. I didn't want to die without knowing him."

"No one can blame you for that. We've all seen the way you look at him and he looks at you. You both needed to come together. If you care for him, fight to keep him."

"Listen to her," Cara said.

Marcail nodded, her many small braids atop the crown

of her head moving with her. "These Warriors are fierce in battle but can be very stubborn. Especially when it comes to the women they care about."

"Our mortality," Cara added.

Sonya wiped her chin with the back of her hand. "He's not said as much, but I believe the fact that I'm not immortal bothers him."

"Nay," Isla said. "It is his immortality which troubles him. He will have to endure long after you are gone."

Reaghan grinned and nudged Marcail's arm. "Make it so Broc has no choice but to see you as his, Sonya. Once he has claimed you, there will be no turning back for a Warrior."

The women erupted in laughter.

Sonya smiled, but she wasn't convinced. It was going to take much more than that. It was going to take persuading him his "curse" couldn't hurt her.

Broc stood with Ramsey and Quinn atop the battlements. He had tried to convince Fallon to allow him to look for Deirdre, but Fallon had said it didn't matter where Deirdre was, that they needed Broc at the castle.

"I agree with Fallon," Ramsey said. "I think Deirdre is gone."

Broc stared at the forest. "I'd like to find out for myself."

"If she had wanted in the castle, she could have gotten in," Quinn pointed out.

Ramsey put a hand against the sawtooth battlement wall. "For whatever reason, Deirdre left you and Sonya alone. Rejoice in that."

Magic, strong and pure, sizzled around Broc. He recognized the feel of Sonya's magic and turned toward it. She walked from the kitchen to Cara's garden.

Her hair was pulled away from her face and was once

more in a braid. The thick plait slid over her shoulder to hang in front of her as she bent over to tend to a plant.

"We've all been waiting for you to claim her," Quinn said.

Broc frowned and glanced at the youngest MacLeod. "Was my attraction so obvious?"

"Aye," Ramsey said. "As was hers for you."

"She's mortal."

Quinn smiled wryly as he faced Broc. "So is Marcail. Lucan faces the same obstacle with Cara."

"And Galen and Hayden have yet to know if Reaghan and Isla are still immortal," Ramsey added.

"What I'm trying to say," Quinn said, "is that if you love her, then it shouldna matter."

Love. Did Broc dare to admit it, did he dare to dream of sharing a life with Sonya? Did he dare to subject her to the curse or, worse, test it to see if it was gone?

He knew he wanted her beside him, wanted to share her smiles, her laughter, and whatever else came their way.

But would it be enough when he watched the life fade from her eyes?

"I'll admit I'm holding out hope that somehow our gods are bound again," Quinn said into the silence.

Broc turned his head to Quinn. "And if they are no'? You will accept that you will live on as Marcail and your unborn child willna?"

Quinn's head jerked with a nod. "I love her more than anything. Whatever time I have with her I will cherish and enjoy every moment of. I doona want to lose her, but I would rather spend a few years with her than never know the love between us."

Broc thought over Quinn's words as he continued to watch Sonya. Maybe Quinn had the right of it. Whatever time Broc might have with Sonya was better than no time at all.

Sonya's head suddenly lifted and their gazes clashed. It was time to talk to her, time to speak of what was between them. And if there was a future for them.

He jumped from the battlements and landed softly, on bent knees in the bailey. Broc's long strides took him around the kitchen to the garden. But Sonya wasn't there. He caught sight of her walking toward the village.

Broc inwardly smiled when Sonya looked over her shoulder at him. He didn't waste another moment following her. Broc didn't need to use his power to find Sonya, all he had to do was follow the trail of her magic.

It led him through the village and inside one of the newly completed cottages. He pushed open the door. Sonya stood facing the hearth, her face in profile to him.

He stepped over the threshold and softly closed the door behind him. Words ran through his head, words he wanted to say to Sonya, but he didn't know where to begin.

She exhaled and turned to face him. The corners of her lips were tilted in a soft smile. "I'm glad you followed me."

"I couldna stay away if I wanted." The truth of his words slammed into him like an arrow. And suddenly the curse didn't matter.

Nothing mattered as long as he had Sonya. He took a step toward her, his hands itching to touch her smooth skin. "There is much I need to say."

Her amber gaze dropped from his. "And much I would speak of as well."

"I know I'm no' the best of men," Broc began. He moved closer a step. "I doona have a title or the land that was once mine. The only thing I have is coin and . . . myself."

His heart pounded loudly in his chest. He had never mastered the art of flattery, had never learned how to charm women. All Broc knew to do was speak the truth. A truth that came straight from his heart.

He didn't expect Sonya to accept his offer. There was so much more that awaited her if she took a mortal. But, as he stared at her, Broc knew he would give Deirdre his soul if only Sonya would be his.

"I care not for your coin, land, or title," Sonya said. She lifted her head and searched his eyes. "Those things do not make the man I have watched risk his life countless times, the man I know will always be there for me."

Broc took another step, bringing him even closer. "Is it enough? Will knowing I will be there for you without fail be enough?"

"Is it enough for you?"

"I fear forever might no' be enough." He took the last step which brought him to her.

Sonya inhaled deeply. "It wasn't until I saw you standing outside Marcail and Quinn's chamber that I knew you would change my life. I had no idea then that you already had. When you are near I want to be with you. When you are gone, all I can think of is you."

"Sonya . . ."

She raised her hand to quiet him. "Everything I had hoped for died when I saw Anice in your arms. Your grief made me believe you were in love with her."

"I wasna."

"I know that now. When I knew there might be a chance Deirdre would find me, I decided I wouldn't live my life watching anymore. I wanted to know what it felt like to be in your arms. To feel you."

Broc swallowed hard. "And afterward?"

"I knew whatever had pulled me to you before would

never let go. I told you once I was yours. I meant it then. And I mean it now. I love you."

He touched her cheek, then slid his hand around to the nape of her neck. The words he had never thought to utter filled him. "I love you."

The smile on Sonya's face was radiant, making her amber eyes flash. She rose up on tiptoe and wound her arms around his neck. "I fear I'm dreaming."

"You've said the words. You are mine now. I willna let you go. Ever."

"Just what I wanted to hear," she said before she kissed him.

Broc nibbled her lips before he slanted his mouth over hers and swept his tongue inside. Passion and fire exploded within him.

Everything in his life had changed, just as it had when Deirdre had first taken him all those years ago. But this time Broc embraced the love Sonya offered and looked ahead with a smile.

"There's one more thing I would ask of you," he said between kisses.

Sonya laughed breathlessly as she leaned her head back so he could kiss her neck. She had everything she could ever want, and she had never been so deliriously happy. "Anything."

"Be my wife."

She stilled and looked into his dark, beautiful depths. "I . . ."

"I know I'm immortal, and there may be a chance the spell to bind my god will never be found. There's also the chance the curse will come to you. It is for that reason I contemplated staying away from you. But I cannot. You have my heart. You have always had my heart. Immortal or mortal, I am nothing without you."

Sonya blinked away the tears which suddenly filled

her eyes. "And I am nothing without you, my dark Warrior. Aye, I will marry you."

He smiled as his look turned wicked. Broc guided her backward until her legs bumped against the bed. "When?"

"Wh . . . whenever," she said with a gasp as he ripped her gown down the middle and cupped her breast.

"Tonight. I want you to be mine tonight."

Sonya smiled as he laid her on the bed. She was already his. Now and forever.

THIRTY-SIX

Broc sat at the table in the great hall with Sonya pressed against him. She was officially his, and had been for two days now. The wedding had been hasty, the ceremony quick, but they were joined.

Thankfully, Cara had convinced the priest not to venture too far from the castle or Broc would have had to find one himself.

For the last few hours they had been discussing their next move. Larena wanted Malcolm found, and Isla wanted Broc to search for Phelan.

Logan stood at the door even now waiting for Fallon to give him the nod to travel to the Isle of Eigg and search for the Tablet of Orn.

Camdyn, Lucan, and Arran were arguing in favor of drawing Deirdre to the castle to try to learn what she had planned.

"If she didna tell Sonya before, she willna tell you now," Broc said. "Deirdre has her mind set on her newest plan. Nothing will dissuade her from it."

"Not even the knowledge of the Tablet of Orn?" Marcail asked. "Maybe we could tempt her with that."

Fallon shook his head. "I doona want her to know of it. If she hadn't told Broc of her search for the burial mound, we wouldna know of the Tablet."

"She said there was an artifact there," Ian pointed out as he rubbed his jaw.

Duncan, his twin, nodded. "She did. There is a difference between an artifact and a clue."

"Maybe the artifact was the amulet I took," Sonya said.

Broc frowned. The twins were right. Had they left the artifact behind? "We have no idea what the artifacts are. We only know of Reaghan because we were told she was the artifact. There were so many things in the tomb that any of them could have been the artifact."

"There's no doubt there is magic in the amulet," Reaghan said. "It could be the artifact."

"Yet, Sonya had been drawn to the sword," Hayden added.

Broc ground his teeth together. He looked at Sonya and said, "We have to go back to the burial mound."

"Aye," Fallon said. "I'd feel better if we searched to make sure the amulet was the only artifact. We can always bring the sword with us just in case."

Logan pushed away from the door. "We can no longer hold off, Fallon. I need to go to the Isle of Eigg."

Fallon gave a nod. "You and Duncan be careful. Return as soon as you can."

Duncan clasped hands with his twin before he went to stand beside Logan. "I will say the same to you. Deirdre may be setting a trap at the tomb."

"I doona think so," Broc said. "Deirdre doesna know what the artifact is."

"Regardless, you'll need to be careful," Galen said.

They said their farewells to Logan and Duncan as the two Warriors set off on their quest. Broc took Sonya's hand in his and brought it to his lips.

"I'm not afraid," she said.

He chuckled. "I know."

"The sooner we go, the sooner we return," Fallon said.

Sonya winked at Broc. "Then let's go."

Malcolm stood beside Deirdre as he stared at the burial mound. He glanced down at his right arm, still unused to seeing it without the scars or being able to use it.

"Get inside the tomb," Deirdre told him. "Find me the artifact."

"How will I know what it is?"

Deirdre's white eyes burned brilliant. "You will feel its power."

Malcolm paused only a moment as he thought of Larena and everyone at MacLeod Castle. But any remorse he had he pushed aside.

He walked to the archway of the burial mound. The magic flowed freely over and around him. It pulsed with an odd cadence he found both intriguing and fearful.

Nothing stopped him as he moved beneath the archway to the huge stone door. He couldn't read the Gaelic symbols, but Deirdre had told him what they meant. She had also told him he was the only one who could get inside the tomb.

The magic grew stronger the closer he moved to the stone door, its touch running deeper, almost as if it were learning him.

Malcolm gripped the stone and tried to pull open the door. Not even his considerable new strength could budge it. He tried three more times before he leaned a hand against the doorway.

Magic hissed along his palm before the markings began to glow blue. And the door opened.

Malcolm stepped over the threshold and the torches

flared to life. He looked around at the tomb. So many weapons. Then he spotted the sword atop the corpse. He felt its power, felt its attraction.

There was only the briefest hesitation before he took the sword. As soon as he touched it, the markings glowed the same blue as those outside the door for just a moment.

Malcolm walked from the mound and didn't look back. He had gotten what Deirdre wanted. She ruled him now.

And he feared she always would.

Broc stared in shocked silence at the open tomb. Sonya pushed passed him and entered the mound. He heard her gasp, but he didn't need to see inside to know something was missing.

Someone had gotten into the mound. But who?

"I thought you said you were the only one who could enter," Fallon said.

Broc shrugged. "Deirdre must have found someone else."

"But who?"

Broc had a suspicion, but he wasn't ready to blame Malcolm yet.

Sonya walked out of the tomb and shook her head. "The sword is gone."

"This doesna make sense," Fallon ground out as he ran a hand through his hair.

Sonya sighed. "Deirdre said Broc was the only one who could open the tomb."

"Yet, you helped me," he said.

She scrunched her face. "Did I? Or was it you all along?"

Broc didn't have an answer.

"What now?" Fallon asked.

Sonya straightened her shoulders and lifted her chin. "We find the sword, of course."

"Nay," Broc said. "We find the Warrior who did this. We find Malcolm."

Phelan found himself in the precarious position of being curious about what was in the tomb and why everyone wanted inside. He'd stayed after using his power on Deirdre to find Broc and two other Warriors return for the Druid.

He'd seen Broc and Sonya's reunion. So the Warrior hadn't left her to die. He'd left her in the tomb for protection against Deirdre.

What Phelan didn't understand was why the Warriors didn't see how evil the Druid was. Didn't they realize all Druids were evil? Or was Sonya different?

Phelan might have spent over a century in Cairn Toul, but even he could remember what it felt like to have his mother's loving eyes look down upon him. It was definitely love he saw between Broc and Sonya, and joy on the other two Warriors' faces.

But they had left too quickly for Phelan to approach them. Then, it wasn't long before Deirdre returned. With a newly made Warrior.

The maroon Warrior looked irritated, and there was hate blazing in his eyes. A look Phelan knew all too well since he had directed it at Deirdre himself many times.

Somehow the maroon Warrior got inside the tomb and emerged with a sword. Deirdre quickly took them away from the tomb.

And just as Phelan had expected, Broc and Sonya returned with other Warriors. They had come for the sword, but they were too late.

Phelan debated on approaching them. He heard the

name MacLeod and remembered Isla telling him if he ever needed anything to find the MacLeods. Was one of them down there now?

And if he was, did Phelan dare to talk to him?

Phelan decided it wasn't time to meet any of the MacLeods. He still had exploring to do. He'd missed his Scotland, and he wanted to see all of her.

Not to mention, there was the pretty tavern maid he'd seen three days before. He thought he might return. For her.

With one last look at Broc, Sonya, and the other Warriors, Phelan turned his back on the burial mound and the MacLeods.

THIRTY-SEVEN

Mallaig, West Coast of Scotland

There was something about a marketplace that always made Logan think of his family. He usually kept memories of his parents and younger brother pushed far back in a corner of his mind, but once he had reached the mainland port of Mallaig, those memories had bombarded him.

He hadn't tried to rid himself of them. In fact, he had allowed himself a few moments to remember a happier time, a time when life had been pleasant. A time when he had been a good son.

A time before he had betrayed his family.

"You're quiet," Duncan said from beside him as he surveyed the port town from the docks to the houses that lined the coast.

Logan shrugged and let his eyes continue to wander the teeming market. "Maybe I'm thinking."

Duncan snorted. "You who makes jests and tease everyone mercilessly? I think no'."

It was true. Logan had created a different side of himself, one that always wore a smile and made jests to hide the truth. It had worked effectively. Everyone thought he was something he wasn't.

And if he had any say in it, no one would know the truth.

Logan turned to Duncan and regarded his friend. "I have no' asked since we left MacLeod Castle, but why did you come? Why leave your twin?"

"I wanted to do something in this quest of ours. No' that I doona enjoy protecting the castle and the Druids within, but I'm a Warrior. The god inside me wants to fight. And so do I."

Duncan didn't need to say more. Logan understood everything he didn't convey into words. The only way to understand what it was to be a Warrior and contend with the constant fury and evil of the god inside them was to be a Warrior.

"And you?" Duncan asked. "Why did you leave the castle again?"

"As soon as Sonya mentioned the Isle of Eigg, there was an overwhelming need for me to reach the isle. I cannot explain it, but the closer I've gotten to Eigg, the more it feels as if this is where I'm supposed to be."

Duncan let out a long breath. "I've seen much in the way of magic throughout my two hundred years as a Warrior. I've seen the good magic of the *mies* and the evil of the *droughs*."

"You think it's magic pulling me here?"

"What else?"

Logan wasn't sure what to think anymore. Memories he had hidden away for more than a century were returning, with no way for him to shove them away.

He didn't know what was in store for him in the coming days, but whatever it was, he knew it would alter the course of his future. He didn't care what it was as long as he could continue to fight against Deirdre.

The oath he had made to put an end to her rode him

tirelessly. He hadn't felt as if he were doing enough, which is why he was anxious to find the next artifact, the Tablet of Orn, which would lead them to the place where Deirdre's twin, Laria, slept.

"The isle is protected," Duncan murmured, his brown eyes narrowed in concentration.

Logan felt it. The magic was solid. Resilient. Stalwart. "There must be many Druids who make Eigg their home."

"Aye. Many. Do you think they'll allow us on their isle willingly?"

Logan grimaced as he recalled how the Druids at Loch Awe had reacted after learning he and Galen were Warriors. The magic of those Druids had waned. That of the Druids on Eigg had not. They wouldn't easily be fooled.

"No' if they fear Warriors. We'll have to convince them we are no' working with Deirdre."

Duncan nodded, but before he could utter a word, the feeling of magic—*drough* magic—engulfed them.

"Deirdre," they replied in unison as they unleashed their gods.

They spun around, ready to attack, to find Deirdre and a dozen yellow-skinned wyrran. Logan started toward the wyrran. It was Duncan's growl that had him looking over his shoulder.

Two Warriors had taken hold of Duncan, and while they couldn't subdue him, it was Deirdre's black magic added to the mix that kept Duncan immobile.

Logan cursed and bared his fangs at the two Warriors.

Deirdre's soft laugh as she approached made Logan's skin crawl. "Surprised? Wait until you see the next surprise I have in store for you."

Logan met Duncan's gaze. They were strong, but

with Deirdre's magic, she could hold them indefinitely. Somehow Logan had to get them out of there before Deirdre did something irreversible.

Out of the corner of his eye, Logan spotted movement. He shifted his gaze and his breath caught in his lungs. He couldn't believe his eyes when he recognized Malcolm. Shock soon turned to bewilderment as Malcolm's skin changed into deep burgundy, wine-red-tipped claws shot from his fingers, and the same burgundy color filled his eyes.

In an instant Logan knew what Deirdre was about. He let out a roar when Malcolm moved to Duncan. Deep inside Logan, his god, Athleus, bellowed for blood, demanded death. And Logan was about to give it to him.

Before Logan could reach Malcolm, something halted him, as if he had run into an invisible wall. He tried to move his arms and legs, but it was useless. Deirdre's laughter caught on the breeze and echoed in the air as her black magic surrounded and incapacitated him.

"There's no use struggling," Deirdre told him as she approached. "Just as Duncan can't. Besides, you know how powerful I am."

Logan's gaze shifted to Duncan. His friend's lips were peeled back in a snarl, his fangs gleaming in the sunshine. Malcolm said not a word as he stood before Duncan and waited.

"You might have nearly destroyed me, Logan, but I have returned stronger than ever," Deirdre said.

"Next time we'll make certain you stay dead."

Deirdre threw back her head and cackled. Her white hair began to swirl around her, a warning that she was gathering her magic.

Her eerie white eyes locked on Logan. "You were one of my best. You who came to me seeking to unbind the god inside you."

Logan's chest clenched as Duncan's gaze narrowed and he let loose a low, angry snarl.

"Ah, so none at MacLeod Castle know what you've done," Deirdre chuckled, glee shining in her eyes. "How very . . . interesting."

"What do you want?" Logan demanded.

The smile which pulled at Deirdre's lips spoke volumes. "Why, I want everything. And I'm going to get it."

With a slight nod of her head, Malcolm drew back his claws and severed Duncan's head from his body. Rage threatened to devour Logan. Athleus was ready to take over, ready to erase all that Logan was.

Logan roared his fury and fought against Deirdre's magic while he struggled to keep control of his god. He hadn't saved Duncan, hadn't even come close to helping his friend.

And now Duncan was gone.

Logan thought of Ian, Duncan's twin, of Arran and Quinn and the other Warriors. It was up to Logan to deliver the devastating news.

If he managed to get away.

"It's time for your punishment," Deirdre said as calmly as if she were speaking of the weather. "Afterward, you will be brought to Cairn Toul. You came to me to be a Warrior. Therefore, you are mine."

Suddenly, Deirdre's magic was gone and Logan was swarmed by the wyrran and three Warriors. He widened his stance, ready for whoever came first.

Instead, they rushed him at once. The pain was blinding, but nothing could overshadow the wrath which governed him. His god demanded death to avenge Duncan, and Logan wouldn't deny him.

Claws raked over his body from both the Warriors and the wyrran. He was thrown onto the ground as they continued to claw viciously at him.

But Logan fought back. He might have been outnumbered, but he landed quite a few slashes of his own. It would be more than just his blood shed that day.

As quickly as his wounds healed, more were inflicted. He was losing blood too fast. His strength began to wane, but still he refused to give up. Deirdre would not take him. He would not return to Cairn Toul and the evil which grew there.

Of a sudden, his attackers retreated. Logan lay upon the ground, his chest rising and falling rapidly as he blinked the blood and sweat from his eyes. He knew the next moments could be his last, and though he hadn't fulfilled his vow, anything was better than being Deirdre's prisoner.

"You always were a great Warrior," Deirdre said as she stood over him. Her hair scraped the ground and caressed his arms and chest. "When I'm through, you will willingly join my new Warriors, led by none other than Malcolm. You should never have allowed him to leave MacLeod Castle."

Logan rose up on his elbows and glared at Deirdre. How had he ever thought her beautiful? He had been naïve the first time he had seen her, but not even that should have stopped him from seeing—and sensing—the evil that she was.

"I will never be yours," he vowed.

"You were once. You will be again."

"Never."

"We shall see."

Logan gritted his teeth as he felt her magic once more. All Druids had magic, but the *droughs* gave their souls to the devil in order to use the more powerful black magic.

There was nothing Logan could do against the magnitude of her magic, no matter how hard he tried. And try he did. To no avail.

This was it, then, he thought. His end. He wasn't afraid to die, and in some ways he welcomed it. But he hadn't achieved his promise.

And then suddenly the sickening feel of even more *drough* magic surrounded him. Deirdre looked up, her white eyes wild with . . . was it fear?

A small smile pulled at Logan's lips.

It was all the time Logan needed to gain his feet and attack the wyrran. The diminutive creatures might have viciously long claws on their hands and feet and mouths full of teeth, but they were no match for a Warrior.

Logan killed five before the Warriors realized what he had done. That was the difference between a newly made Warrior and one who'd had a century to learn his god.

He ducked a massive swing from the orange Warrior's arm, only to sink his claws in his opponent's belly. The Warrior gave a grunt as blood spilled down his front. Logan kicked him in the chest, sending him sprawling backward.

Logan turned and braced himself for the next attack, only to find Malcolm standing before him. "What have you done?"

Malcolm blinked slowly. "I had no choice."

"There is always a choice." Logan didn't give him a chance to respond as he called forth the power of his god. He could feel the sea behind him, feel the way it gathered and answered his call. With just a thought, the water rose up in a massive column shaped like an arm. The arm descended and a hand appeared.

Just before the hand could lift Deirdre away, the air shimmered around her as the black magic increased. Logan took a step back, trying to get away. He watched as Deirdre, her wyrran, and her Warriors were surrounded by the shimmer.

Deirdre's face lifted to the sky as she let out an angry shriek.

And then they were gone.

Logan blinked and released the water. There was only a hint of black magic that hung in the air, and it was receding quickly.

Somehow Deirdre had vanished. Logan didn't know how, and didn't really care. She was gone, and that was all that mattered.

He let out a sigh. Then he turned and looked at the body of Duncan. Ian would never forgive Logan, but Logan would never forgive himself for what had happened. It was another sin he would shoulder until the end of his days.

He dropped to his knees beside Duncan, his jaw clenched tightly against a flood of emotion. It should have been him lying on the ground, not Duncan.

It took a moment for Logan to feel the *mie* magic surrounding him. He jerked his head around and looked over his shoulder to find a group of six Druids—two men and four women—watching him.

One of the younger women with long, dark hair approached him. "We felt Deirdre. I'm sorry we didn't arrive in time to help save your friend."

"Brenna," barked one of the men who stood off to the side, his black eyes narrowed with disgust on Logan. He held a staff in his hands, obviously a leader among the Druids.

Logan gained his feet and turned to face the Druids. "You know what I am?"

The leader gave a single nod of his head. "You are no' welcome here, Warrior. We've been watching you for some time. My daughter thinks your intentions are good. But I know the true nature of your kind."

Logan clenched his jaw. His emotions were too raw,

too exposed for him to dole out his usual charm. It took everything he had not to show the Druids exactly what the true nature of a Warrior was.

But he latched on to something the leader said. "You've been watching us?"

At that moment the call of a peregrine sounded above him moments before the magnificent bird flew over the Druids.

"Ah. I see," Logan mumbled. "You've been spying."

"Watching," Brenna said in earnest. "I've seen you battle the wyrran and save Druids. I've seen you battle Deirdre. With my magic I'm able to see through the eyes of an animal. The falcon allowed me to use her so I could learn more about you and the other Warriors at MacLeod Castle."

Even though Logan now had the answer to the falcon, it didn't appease him. Nothing would until he returned Duncan's body to Ian.

Logan squeezed his eyes closed. When he opened them, he turned to the leader. "Listen to your daughter. She speaks the truth. We are waging a war against Deirdre."

"And no' doing a verra good job of it," he responded.

"Who are you?" Logan demanded.

"Kerwyn, leader of the Druids of Eigg."

Logan raised a brow, not at all impressed. "No' all Warriors are the same. The sooner you believe that, the sooner we can win this war. Consider that the longer Druids such as yours hold out, the more of you die."

He turned and looked at Duncan's body and thought of his brethren at MacLeod Castle. There was no doubt Ian already knew the link between him and Duncan was gone. Logan had wasted enough time. He needed to get back to the castle.

"Why did you come here?" Brenna asked softly behind him.

Logan turned his head to the side. "That no longer matters at this time. I'll return soon, though."

"You willna be welcomed," Kerwyn declared. "Consider yourself warned, Warrior. We'll take action the next time you set foot near our isle."

Logan raked a hand through his hair before he gathered Duncan in his arms, the Druids forgotten. His friend and fellow Warrior deserved a proper burial, surrounded by friends and family.

Logan would return Duncan to MacLeod Castle and Ian.

A twinge of worry settled in Logan's gut. With Duncan gone, Ian would suffer the full force of their god.

Logan's stretched his legs into a run. He had to run faster than he ever had before. Time was of the essence.

THIRTY-EIGHT

Ian had been sitting with the others in the great hall as they readied for supper. He had been laughing at something Arran and Camdyn were arguing over when it happened.

It was as though a blade of ice sliced him in half. The link that had always bound him and Duncan was severed. Vanished. Disappeared.

There was only one thing that could do that—death. The grief that ripped through Ian was crushing. He tried to rise from the table, but only managed to trip in his haste.

He bellowed in rage and grief as his fangs filled his mouth. He couldn't wrap his head around Duncan being gone, couldn't fathom his twin no longer being with him.

Ian could hear the others around him, their voices and concern, as they tried to understand what was going on.

But Ian was lost.

While he roared in anguish, his body seized. His muscles refused to move, while his fangs and claws grew longer. Farmire, the god of battle, raged inside him.

Fury the like Ian had never felt swallowed him. He wanted death and blood. But more than anything, he wanted revenge for his brother.

Whoever had killed him would suffer.

And Ian would start with the one who was supposed to have watched his brother's back—Logan.

Arran looked from Ian to Quinn as everyone struggled to keep Ian on the ground. He fought them mercilessly, his roars deafening.

"What is happening to him?" Lucan demanded.

Arran sighed as Quinn gave a small nod of his head. "It must have something to do with Duncan."

"Not just something," Marcail said. "I saw Duncan react similarly when Ian was being tortured in Cairn Toul."

"This is different," Quinn said. "This is . . ."

"What I imagine I resembled when my god was unbound," Ramsey finished.

The Warriors shared a look, the unspoken realization sweeping the hall. Duncan was dead.

"Who?" Fallon asked as he put his full weight on Ian's shoulders to keep him down.

Broc grunted. "You know who. Deirdre. She told me she was going to kill Lucan and Fallon so the god you three share would then only be yours."

"Holy Hell," Quinn mumbled.

Hayden, the largest of the Warriors, was practically sitting on top of Ian. "Isla!" he called to his wife. "Use your magic!"

As one, the Druids of MacLeod Castle stepped forward and focused their magic on Ian. In a matter of moments he was unconscious.

Galen rose to his feet and wiped his brow with the back of his hand. "What do we do with him now? When he wakes, it'll be the same."

"Aye," Ramsey said. "He's suffering at the loss of his brother, but more than that, his god is trying to take over. Ian's rage might very well allow it."

"Shite," Fallon said as he rose to his feet and punched the wall, his fist going through the stone. "This isna what we need right now."

Lucan let out a weary breath. "If Duncan is dead, do we assume Logan is as well?"

"I'm no' sure," Quinn answered. "Deirdre could have taken him."

"Taken or dead. Either way, it has set us back," Camdyn said.

Arran ran a hand down his face. Ian, Duncan, and Quinn had been his closest friends while they'd been held by Deirdre. To know that one of them was gone forever was inconceivable.

Quinn clapped Arran on the shoulder. "Duncan will be avenged."

"I have no doubt." Those at MacLeod Castle were a family, a very close family. What you did to one, you did to all. "I fear that we'll lose Ian as well. What if he cannot control the addition of Duncan's portion of their god?"

"He will. I know it." Quinn looked at the now still form of Ian. "If anyone can, it's Ian. He's had two centuries learning his god. Duncan's half should be easy enough to control once Ian gets past his grief."

The hall grew quiet as each of them realized the next few weeks and months were going to be the hardest to watch as Ian struggled.

The door to the castle was thrown open and Logan stepped inside, a body hanging over his shoulder. He was covered in blood. "Where is Ian? I've brought Duncan's body home."

"So he is dead," Fallon said softly.

Logan nodded. "It was Deirdre. She had three Warriors with her, one of which was Malcolm."

Larena sucked in a shaky breath and turned to Fallon as his arms wrapped around her. "Nay. Not Malcolm."

Logan knew Larena and her cousin had been close, but everyone needed to know what had happened. "Malcolm struck the killing blow, Larena."

No sooner had the words left his mouth than the air began to shimmer around Ian.

"Get back," Logan called. "Everyone get back."

"What is it?" Broc demanded as he tugged Sonya away from Ian. "The magic feels . . . wrong."

Logan shrugged. "I doona know, but I saw it surround Deirdre, the wyrran, and the Warriors. And then they were gone."

The hall was gripped in silence as they all watched the shimmer cloak Ian. Then, in a blink, he, too, was gone.

"It's Deirdre," Lucan said.

"Nay," Isla said as she took in a steadying breath. "That magic was . . . different. It takes a very powerful Druid to cast a spell over a distance."

Logan nodded. "She's right. Deirdre was furious when she felt it. And she fought against it."

"Something more powerful than Deirdre?" Ramsey said thoughtfully. "This doesna bode well."

Broc swallowed as he watched the Druids surround the spot where Ian had just been. So much had happened. With Deirdre they knew what to expect, knew what she was about. She might surprise them on occasion, but at least they could guess what her next move might be.

If there was someone else they had to fight, they first had to discover who it was. And why they were all of a sudden making an appearance.

The magic of the spell turned sour. A sign of black magic. Sonya turned to Broc, her face pale. Isla clutched her chest, and Reaghan put her hand on the wall to steady herself.

"What is going on?" Broc asked through clenched teeth.

Hayden went to Isla. "I'd also like to know. I feel Isla's fear."

Reaghan waited until Galen put an arm around her before she said, "Very potent black magic. The spell is vastly complicated."

"It's a spell I have heard about but never knew anyone who dared to use it," Isla explained.

"What is it?" Quinn demanded.

Sonya lifted her face to Broc. "It's a spell that pulls someone through time."

It was as if all the air had been sucked out of the castle. For a heartbeat Broc couldn't breathe. "How? Why?"

Arran shifted his feet, his hands clenching and unclenching at his side. "Find Deirdre, Broc. You're the only one who can tell us if she really has been moved through time."

Broc kissed the top of Sonya's head and released his god. Indigo colored his skin as his wings sprouted from his back. He thought of Deirdre, and for once he didn't find her immediately.

Sweat beaded his skin as his god's power surged through him, seeking Deirdre throughout all time. Broc's muscles locked, his body shaking with the effort it took him. But then he found her.

Her thread was faint, but that wasn't what made his stomach turn. It was the knowledge that she had indeed been pulled through time.

He turned his attention next to Ian. It took him even longer than it had to find Deirdre, and by the time he did, his legs could barely hold him up.

Broc opened his eyes and looked at each individual in the castle. "Deirdre is four centuries into the future. And so is Ian, though he isna with her."

Marcail's knees buckled. Quinn helped her into a seat, his hand held protectively over her swelling stomach.

"She's no longer a threat then since she isn't here," Cara said.

Ramsey shook his head slowly. "If only that were true. In the future, everything could change. We've no idea who pulled Deirdre forward, or why."

"We doona know why Ian was taken either," Logan said. "I do know it was the same magic. That isna all that happened in Mallaig. I found the falcon, or rather who was controlling it. It's a group of Druids of Eigg. The one who was able to see through the peregrine's eyes to watch us was named Brenna. They felt Deirdre's magic and came to battle her."

"Except she was taken," Camdyn said.

Logan nodded. "The Druids on Eigg were watching us to see what we would do. They doona trust us, that was made clear by their leader Kerwyn. I doona think it matters, though. The only recourse we have now is to follow Ian and Deirdre."

Lucan blew out a harsh breath. "Maybe no' all of us."

Logan nodded. "That was my thought as well."

"I know the spell," Isla said into the stillness that had once more descended. "And with the combined magic of the Druids here, we might be able to make it work."

Reaghan licked her lips. "Together we can do it."

"Though," Isla said as she looked around her, "there's no guarantee that whoever goes will land together."

Logan stepped forward. "It doesna matter. I'm going to look for Ian as well as the Tablet of Orn. Doesna matter what century Deirdre is in. She still needs to die."

"Include me," Camdyn said as he stepped forward.

Broc looked to Ramsey and saw his friend push away from the wall.

"Me as well," Ramsey said.

Arran's body was rigid as he moved beside the other three. "Deirdre needs to pay for killing Duncan. And Ian will need someone he trusts in his present state."

Broc looked around the hall at the other Warriors and their women. To the four stepping through time, it would be just a matter of heartbeats before they would see the castle again.

To everyone else, it would be centuries.

Ramsey turned to Isla. "You can strengthen the shield around the castle to hold off time for those inside."

Isla frowned as her eyes took on a faraway look. "Because we will need all of us to awaken Laria."

Ramsey nodded. "Precisely."

Fallon rubbed the back of his neck as he looked at the four Warriors who would travel through time. "Be careful. We doona know what Deirdre is about."

"Which is why we need to get there soon," Logan said.

Sonya pulled out of Broc's arms to go with the other Druids who were now circling the four Warriors.

He couldn't help but wonder if he would ever see them again as the castle began to hum with magic. The Druids' chanting grew louder the stronger their magic became.

Broc wished he would have spoken to Ramsey one

last time. His gaze met Ramsey's silver one. Ramsey gave him a ghost of a smile, and then he and the others were surrounded by shimmering air.

Then they were gone.

"Godspeed, my brothers," Broc murmured.

EPILOGUE

Scotland
Present Day

Declan Wallace smiled and clasped his hands in front of him. All his work, all the research into the spells had paid off.

The great and feared Deirdre now stood before him. Her white eyes glared daggers at him.

"Who are you?" she demanded.

Declan shrugged and let his eyes take in her slim figure and the black gown that only made her white hair and eyes more beautiful. "Someone who has gone to a great deal to bring you to me."

Her eyes narrowed as her magic built. "What have you done?"

"There's no need to attempt to use your magic on me. It willna work. And I brought you here because, together, the world awaits us."

He saw the ends of her hair twitch along the floor. He knew she would try to use her magic. Any good *drough* would. But he wasn't just any *drough*.

He was the one who would conquer the world.

And master Deirdre.

Read on for a sneak peek at the first book in Donna Grant's exciting new Dark Warrior series

MIDNIGHT'S MASTER

Coming in June 2012
From St. Martin's Paperbacks

As Logan listened to Hamish speak of Mallaig and its trials, Logan found himself thinking of his childhood and his family.

He usually kept memories of his parents and younger brother pushed far in a corner of his mind, but once he had reached the mainland port of Mallaig those memories had bombarded him.

He hadn't tried to rid himself of them. In fact, he allowed himself a few moments to remember a happier time, a time when life had been pleasant. A time when he had been a good son.

A time before he had betrayed his family.

Memories he had hidden away for over a century were returning with a force too strong for him to shove away easily.

He didn't know what was in store for him in the coming days, but whatever it was he knew it would alter the course of his future. He didn't care what it was as long as he could continue to fight against Deirdre.

The oath he had made to put an end to her rode him tirelessly. He hadn't felt as if he were doing enough, which was why he had stepped forward to find the next artifact, the Tablet of Orn. The tablet would lead them to the place where Deirdre's twin, Laria, slept.

Laria was the only one who could kill Deirdre.

Logan took a deep breath, Hamish's words barely registering. The deluge of conversations, haggling, and laughter assaulted him at every angle along the dock.

In the distance Logan spotted a market. A person could find any number of items at a market. Fruits, vegetables, cloth, baskets, ribbons, and even weapons. It was a visual spectacle he hadn't realized he'd missed until then.

The sights, the sounds, the smells. It was all just as he recalled. The only thing missing was his mother examining a piece of cloth they couldn't afford while his younger brother begged for a coin to buy a sweetmeat.

An ache, bone deep and crushing, began in his chest. He couldn't breathe, couldn't move. Could do nothing to hold back the tide of memories.

If he gave in, if he allowed the memories to take him, he would never return. They were as demanding and insistent as his god, Athleus.

He fisted his hands, thankful when his claws plunged deep into his palms and blood dripped between his fingers.

It was that pain, though momentary, which allowed him to get the upper hand to his recollections and shove them back into the a deep, dark corner of his mind.

When he opened his eyes he glanced down at his skin to confirm it hadn't turned the silver of his god. Only then did he raise his gaze.

"Mallaig has survived," Hamish said, his voice low and full of pain.

Logan could understand the old man. "We all survive. There is no other choice."

Hamish lifted his gaze and gave a single nod. "Aye, lad. Ye've the right of it. What have ye survived being one so young?"

"Naught you'd believe, old man," Logan said with a smile he knew didn't quite reach his eyes.

He turned his head to look around him and stiffened as his gaze collided with a woman's. But not just any woman. She was stunning.

Dazzling.

Mesmerizing.

For a moment he couldn't form a coherent thought as he drank in her extraordinary beauty. She stood still as stone, her wide, expressive violet eyes trained on him.

Her black hair hung thick and straight just past her shoulders where the ends lifted and swirled around her in the breeze coming from the sea. Her skin was unblemished, the color of cream, which beckoned to be touched. He longed to stroke it, to see if it was as soft and smooth as he imagined it would be.

His blood began to pound through his body. His balls tightened, eager to know the taste of her lips and the feel of her curves against his. He grew hard just thinking about holding her, of skimming his hands along her body.

Logan had always enjoyed women, but never in all his years had one affected him as this one did. She intrigued him. In a way that made him wonder if he should approach her or run the other way.

She was bundled against the weather with a hat of some kind that covered her head in various shades of pink stripes. She was of average height, but there was nothing common about her. She was a siren, an irresistible enchantress.

And he was smitten. Besotted. Infatuated.

He had to know her, but more than that, he had to taste her. Touch her.

Claim her.

Logan rose, intending to discover her name and every secret she had when he felt it glide over his body. Magic. It was soft, almost hesitant, but it was magic.

A delicious, succulent feel of magic that he had never experienced before.